CROW CREEK CROSSING

"Mister, you ain't got the brains God gave a prairie dog. Either that or you figure you've lived long enough." When Cole still made no sign of moving, Black Hat nodded toward a wide-shouldered brute of a man. "If you don't get your sorry ass outta that chair right now, ol' Skinner there is gonna break your back for you."

Cole glanced at the grinning half-wit, who appeared eager to do the job, and knew that he had little choice. It was obvious that he was likely to take a licking if he didn't act quickly and decisively. "That would be a mistake," he warned, and in one swift move, grabbed for the Henry rifle propped against the chair, cranking a cartridge into the chamber as he brought it up to level on Black Hat. He had no desire to kill anyone, but he had no intention of taking a whipping.

His quick response caught them by surprise, but there was no concern evident in any of the faces staring at him. "Well, ain't you the feisty one?" Black Hat said. "You fixin' to have a gunfight against six of us? That don't seem too smart to me."

"I expect that's so," Cole replied. "But I don't figure to have a gunfight with all of you, so I'm settin' my sights on just one. I reckon that will be you, Mr. Bigmouth, and I'm damn sure I'm gonna get you."

CROW CREEK
CROSSING

Charles G. West

A SIGNET BOOK

SIGNET
Published by the Penguin Group
Penguin Group (USA) LLC, 375 Hudson Street,
New York, New York 10014

USA | Canada | UK | Ireland | Australia | New Zealand | India | South Africa | China
penguin.com
A Penguin Random House Company

First published by Signet, an imprint of New American Library,
a division of Penguin Group (USA) LLC

First Printing, July 2014

 REGISTERED TRADEMARK—MARCA REGISTRADA

ISBN 978-0-451-46820-8

Printed in the United States of America
10 9 8 7 6 5 4 3 2 1

For Ronda

Chapter I

Cole Bonner stood at the top of a low ridge, looking back over a treeless sea of grass, watching the progress of the covered farm wagon a mile and a half behind him. Halfway down the ridge, Joe, his dark Morgan gelding, lingered, casually munching the short grass left by a dryer-than-normal summer. Cole watched the wagon for a few moments more before shifting his gaze back toward his horse.

One of the best trades I ever made, he thought, even though he had given up two horses in exchange for the powerful Morgan.

But Joe had proven his worth on the trek across Nebraska that had begun almost two months before, one day after Ann Sumner said *I do* and became Mrs. Cole Bonner. He smiled when he thought about Ann's reaction when he had told her of the three most important decisions he had made in his entire life—the trade for Joe, the purchase of his Henry rifle, and marrying her. She demanded to know why marrying her was listed third, fully aware that he said it only to tease her, a practice he seemed to find delight in.

Ann had wondered why he had chosen to name his horse Joe, and his response had been "It's as good a name as any, and Joe seems to like it all right." The truth of the matter was that he couldn't think of any clever name that would apply to the horse, so he'd settled on the first one that came to him.

Certain now that the folks in the wagon could see him atop the ridge, he waved his hat back and forth over his head, a signal he used to tell them he had found water, or a campsite if it was nearing the end of a day's travel. From that distance, he could see John Cochran driving the wagon, his wife, Mabel, seated beside him. Ann, with John and Mabel's three kids, was walking beside the wagon.

Cole's gaze naturally lingered on his bride. It was a vision that never failed to remind him of what a lucky man he was. She could have had any young bachelor in Lancaster, but she'd picked him. The thought always amazed him, for he had certainly never shown any indication of having serious plans for providing for a family. He had seldom had any thoughts beyond what he might be doing the next day, which was almost always the same thing as the day before: working for Henry Blacksmith. Blacksmith owned one of the biggest cattle ranches near Lancaster, Nebraska.

Well, he thought, *I reckon I've got a future to think about now, working for myself.*

He took his time walking back down the ridge to his horse. It would still be a few minutes before the wagon caught up to him, and as he climbed up into the saddle, he continued his reverie of the solid future he now saw before him.

"I'll be an old family man," he announced to Joe. "Maybe have a dozen young'uns."

He grinned mischievously when he thought of the pleasure he would have in the process. Sometimes he would admit to himself that without Ann's influence, he probably never would have agreed to set out for Wyoming Territory to build a farm. Truth be told, Ann had never really given him any choice in the matter of what they were going to do. She had a future all planned, and he just found himself fortunate to have been picked to share it with her. He had never told her of the dream he had carried in his mind since he was a young boy. That dream was to ride beyond the flat plains of Nebraska and Wyoming and experience the Rocky Mountains for himself, to ride the high country where God rested His clouds. A simple life with Ann was worth sacrificing the dream, and he vowed that he would never mention the craving to her.

John Cochran had bought his parcel of land on Chugwater Creek, sight unseen, but he trusted the advice of his friend Walter Hodge, who claimed to be doing well in that valley. John's plan was to grow wheat and raise cattle to sell to the military. Ann was set on going with her sister and her husband, with plans to find her and Cole's homestead, hopefully close to theirs. When he thought about it now, Cole shook his head, realizing that he had allowed himself to be totally dominated by his new wife. But deep down, he knew he didn't really care where he went, or what he did when he got there, as long as he was with her. He couldn't explain what being in love was, but whatever it was, he knew for damn sure that he had a hell of a dose of it.

John had already guaranteed that he could make a

first-rate farmer out of him, in spite of Cole's protests that it might be more of a challenge than John anticipated.

"Hell, I can't raise dust without a horse under me to kick it up," he had joked.

He knew, however, that he could do anything another man could do, and he was anxious to show Ann that he could provide for her as well as any man. And he certainly couldn't think of a nicer couple to team up with than Ann's sister and John. Mabel had wholeheartedly welcomed him to the family, and her children were already calling him Uncle Cole.

It's going to be a good thing, he told himself, and nudged Joe with his heels.

"Looks like another railroad camp on the other side of this ridge," Cole called out to John as the wagon approached. Eight-year-old Skeeter, John and Mabel's youngest, ran ahead of the wagon to reach his uncle first. Cole reached down and lifted the boy up to seat him behind the saddle.

"Good," John replied. "That means there oughta be good water. I think everybody's about ready to quit for the day. We can't be much more'n fifty miles or so from Crow Creek Crossin'."

John's friend had told him that Crow Creek Crossing was the place where he should leave the railroad's path and head due north. He had been told that the Union Pacific should reach that point possibly by the time his little party arrived. Even if the railroad hadn't, there was already a sizable tent city growing there on the banks of Crow Creek, so he would know it to be the place he was looking for.

Cole took a moment to smile at his wife before

turning Joe to lead the wagon alongside the railroad tracks past the ridge.

"Get up, Joe!" Skeeter sang out as the big horse moved in response to Cole's gentle press of his heels. The boy's older brother and sister ran along behind them, eager to see the night's campsite.

As had been the case before, the railroad crews had been none too tidy in the condition they left their campsites. So Cole led his party a little farther up the stream to camp where a couple of cottonwoods stood close to the bank.

"This all right with you?" he asked the small boy hugging his back. Skeeter said that it was. When John pulled the wagon up beside him, Cole said, "This looks like as good a spot as any. Skeeter said it was all right."

Mabel chuckled in response. "If Skeeter says it's all right, then I guess we'll settle right here." She turned to her other two children. "Elliot, you and Lucy know what to do."

They responded dutifully, having gone through the routine every night during the past two months. Cole lowered Skeeter to the ground, then dismounted. After helping John with his horses, he pulled his saddle off Joe and hobbled the Morgan to graze with them beside the stream, about fifty yards from the wagon. With help from Elliot and Lucy, Mabel and Ann soon had a fire going and supper started.

The two men walked together to check on the condition of the horses, leaving the women and children to prepare the meal.

"It's gettin' pretty late into August," John said. "I sure hope to hell we can find this piece of land I bought and get us some shelter built before the bad weather hits."

"Like you said," Cole replied, "Crow Creek Crossin' can't be much more'n fifty miles from here. We oughta be able to make that in plenty of time."

"Maybe so," John said, "but according to the directions I got from Walter Hodge, my place on the Chugwater is thirty-five or forty miles north of Crow Creek. We've been makin' good time so far. And thank the Lord we ain't seen no sign of Injuns."

Cole nodded. "I reckon they've been stayin' away from the railroad crews and the army patrols."

They had discussed the possibility of Indian trouble before but weren't overly concerned about it. Troops had been sent along to protect the railroad workers, and they were trailing pretty close behind the track-laying crews.

"I'd like it better if there were some thicker stands of trees beside some of these streams," John commented. "Make it a little harder to see our camp."

"I know what you mean," Cole replied, then laughed. "Hell, I thought Lancaster was short of trees. Looks like, from what we've seen since we left, there ain't more'n a handful of trees between here and Wyomin'. Reckon we'll be able to find enough timber to build a couple of houses by the time we reach Chugwater Creek?"

John cocked his head, concerned. "Walter said it ain't all like this. I reckon we'll see, won't we?"

"I reckon."

Ann stepped up to greet him with a kiss on his cheek when he walked back to the fire.

"We'll have supper ready in a little while," she told him, and gave his hand a little squeeze. He glanced down to meet an impish grin from ten-year-old Lucy.

It seemed that every time Ann made any fond gesture toward him, it was always caught by one of the three kids, and it never failed to make him blush. Aware of his embarrassment, Ann smiled and said, "Pay her no mind. She just likes to see you squirm."

Overhearing Ann's comment, Mabel remembered when she and John were newlyweds. Ann wasn't much older than Skeeter at the time, and she recalled that her sister had done her share of giggling whenever she caught the two of them stealing a kiss or an intimate embrace.

"Go fill the bucket with water, Lucy," Mabel said.

She felt some compassion for Cole and Ann. Spending your honeymoon with a family of five on a wagon afforded little private time together. She was happy for Ann. Cole Bonner was a good man, and his adoration for her sister was written all over his face. She and John had talked about the fortunate pairing of the two young people and looked forward to working together to forge a comfortable living in the Chugwater valley. Her thoughts were interrupted then when John suddenly spoke.

"Wait, Lucy," he ordered calmly, his voice low but cautioning. "Get in the wagon. Mabel, you and Ann get Elliot and Skeeter and get in the wagon."

Mabel hesitated. "What is it, John?"

"Just get the kids in the wagon," John replied firmly, his voice still calm but dead serious. She quickly obeyed his order.

"Where?" Cole asked, alert to the caution in John's tone, his voice soft as well. He eased his Henry rifle out of the saddle scabbard and cranked a cartridge into the chamber.

"I think we've got some company sneakin' up

behind that mound of scrubby bushes on the other side of the stream." With no show of haste, he reached into the wagon boot and pulled a Spencer cavalry carbine from under the seat.

Cole looked toward the mound but saw nothing. He trusted John's word just the same and didn't doubt for a second that there was someone threatening their camp. Assuming they were Indians, he said, "They're probably after the horses. You stay here behind the wagon, and I'll get over to the edge of the stream to keep them away from the horses."

"You be careful," John warned. It was a risky move. There was very little cover on the grassy expanse where the horses were hobbled.

"Cole, be careful," Ann pleaded, having heard the conversation between the two men as she huddled with the children in the bed of the wagon.

"I will," Cole replied hurriedly as he left the cover of the wagon and made his way quickly toward the three horses grazing unsuspectingly near the stream.

He dropped to one knee when he heard the thud of an arrow against the trunk of one of the large cottonwoods they had pulled the wagon under. Using the tree for cover, he scanned the mound of berry bushes John had pointed out.

After a few seconds passed, he saw what he searched for when the bushes parted enough for him to see a bow. A few moments later, another arrow embedded itself in the tree, close to the first one. It was plain to see that the raiders were intent upon keeping him from getting to the horses. He rolled over to the other side of the tree and fired three quick shots into the bushes where he had spotted the bow.

Then, without waiting to see if he had hit anything, he sprang to his feet and ran for the horses, looking for someplace to use for cover when he got there. His series of rifle shots having caught their attention, all three horses held their heads up and stared at the man running toward them, but they did not attempt to bolt.

His only choice for protection from the arrows that came whistling around him as he ran was a low dirt hump, which he reached safely because of a blistering volley of shots from John that forced the Indians to hug the ground behind their mound of berry bushes. Everything was quiet for a few minutes, and then John called out, "Cole, you all right?"

Cole yelled back, "Yeah. I don't think they've got anything but bows, but I'm afraid they're gonna hit the horses. If you can keep 'em pinned down, maybe I can crawl back and take the hobbles off the horses and get 'em the hell outta range of their bows." It seemed obvious that the horses were what the raiders were after, but if they couldn't steal them, Cole was afraid they'd try to shoot them just to leave the party on foot.

"All right," John shouted. "If you can bring 'em back here behind the wagon, we could guard 'em. They must not be able to shoot those arrows this far. At least there ain't been any come close to the wagon yet. You just holler when, and I'll lay a blanket of fire on that berry patch."

"All right," Cole yelled back. "I'll tell you when."

He immediately started pushing himself back from the hump, still hugging the ground, pulling his rifle behind him. Evidently the Indians could not see him, for he managed to slide back to the Morgan's feet and began untying the hobbles before an arrow suddenly thudded into the ground inches from his leg.

"When!" he shouted, and John opened fire immediately. No longer concerned with any efforts to stay out of sight, Cole didn't waste any time removing the hobbles from the other horses. He jumped on Joe's back, grabbed the lead ropes of John's horses, and headed back to the wagon at a gallop. He reached the wagon with no arrows fired from the berry patch, slid off his horse, and tied all three up to it.

John took his eyes off the mound for only a second to glance at Cole. "Now let's see what they're gonna do," he said. "Looks like we got us a standoff." Then he stole another glance toward the fire they had built. "I wish to hell they'da waited till after supper."

"John, what are we gonna do?" Mabel called from within the wagon. "Are they still out there?"

"I don't see much we can do," her husband answered. "Just wait 'em out, I reckon. As long as we've got the upper hand on weapons, there ain't much they *can* do without gettin' shot. They mighta already gone, decided it not worth the risk. We can't see a blame thing on the other side of those bushes."

Everything John said was true, but Cole didn't care much for hiding behind the wagon all night, not knowing if there were Indians still planning to jump them sometime during the dark hours ahead. As John said, there was a strong possibility that the raiders had conceded the contest since they were overwhelmingly outgunned. But Cole wanted to know that they were indeed gone. So he studied the lay of the land between the wagon and the low mound on the other side of the stream, planning the best route to take him safely to the rear of their position. When he was satisfied that it was to work around behind them, there was nothing left but to wait for darkness to cover him.

The wait was not long, for as soon as the sun dropped below the western horizon, it was as if someone had blown out a lantern. Within minutes, darkness enveloped the two big cottonwoods.

"Cole, I'm not sure this is a good idea," Ann protested when he told John what he was going to do.

"Those Indians might be long gone," Cole told her. "And if they are, there ain't no sense in us stayin' holed up behind this wagon. If they're not gone, then maybe I can encourage them to leave with a few rounds from my rifle. I'd like to know how many we're dealin' with, anyway." He turned to John then. "Keep a sharp eye. I'll let you know if they're gone so you don't shoot me when you see me comin' back." He was off then, disappearing into the darkness.

Passing the campfire that was already dying out, having been left unattended since the discovery of the Indian raiders, Cole crossed the stream and made a long arc on his way to get behind the mound that had protected their attackers. With the absence of a moon, his range of vision was restricted to no more than a couple of dozen yards, so he made his way cautiously.

When he came upon a draw that led up between two ridges, he estimated that he was now directly behind the raiders' position at the mound. He had started to close the distance between himself and the mound when he was momentarily stopped by the whinny of a horse behind him. Dropping to his knee at once, he prepared to defend himself, but there was no one there. He realized then that the Indians must have left their horses farther back up the draw.

That answers the question of whether or not they've gone, he thought.

He got to his feet again, knowing he had to exercise even more caution now that he was sure they still had designs on the wagon party of white people.

The top half of a full moon appeared low on the horizon as he stepped carefully toward a stand of scrubby trees between him and the bush-covered mound by the water's edge.

When that thing gets a little higher in the sky, this whole prairie will be lit up, he thought.

It made him hurry his steps a little until he reached the stand of trees. With his rifle up in a ready position before him, he stepped between the trees, coming face-to-face with a young Cheyenne warrior intent upon working his way behind the wagon.

There was a moment's hesitation by the two adversaries, both taken by surprise. They regained their composure and reacted almost at the same time. With no time to notch an arrow, the warrior drew his knife and launched himself to attack. Blessed with reflexes equal to, or even quicker than, his assailant's, Cole stepped to one side, capturing the brave's wrist in his hand to deftly throw him flat on his back.

Quick as a great cat, Cole had his rifle trained on the Indian's chest, poised for the kill—but he failed to pull the trigger. Able to see the Cheyenne clearly now, he discovered that he was little more than a boy. It occurred to him that it was the reason he had been able to throw him to the ground so easily. Undecided then, he took a step back while still holding the rifle on the helpless boy, finding it difficult to kill one so young.

Thinking he was doomed to die, the Cheyenne boy could do nothing but lie there with eyes wide with fear as Cole brought the Henry rifle to his shoulder and aimed it directly at his head. He could not, however, bring himself to take the boy's life. He took another step back and ordered, "Get up! Get outta here!" He motioned toward the draw where the Indian ponies were tied. "Get goin'!"

Hearing the white man's commands, the boy's two companions, also boys, ran toward the confrontation. Cole turned to face them and threw two quick shots near them in warning. He waved them on with his rifle.

"Get on those ponies and get outta here," he ordered.

Their ambitious attempt to steal horses thwarted, they did as they were told, going by the white man's motions and the tone of his voice, for they knew very little English. Finally realizing that their lives were to be spared, all three hurried up the dark draw.

Wondering how he was going to explain to John why he let them get away when he clearly had the jump on them, he turned to go back to the wagon. He had taken no more than two steps when he felt the solid blow of an arrow in his back. The impact caused him to stumble, but he quickly recovered and cranked three shots into the darkened draw. He had no way of telling if he had hit one of them or not, hearing only the tattoo of horses' hooves on the hard floor of the draw.

Cursing himself for a softhearted fool, he tried in vain to reach for the arrow shaft in his back. It felt as if it was embedded pretty deeply, and he could feel the back of his shirt slowly becoming wet with blood, but the pain was bearable.

Maybe it ain't too serious, he thought hopefully, as he hurried back to the wagon. "It's me, John," he called out when he got back to the stream. "I'm comin' in."

"Come on, then," John replied. He walked a few steps from the front of the wagon to wait for him. "We heard the shootin'," he said when Cole came up from the stream. "What happened?"

"They're gone," Cole said. "It was just some young boys tryin' to steal horses."

"Did you hit any of 'em?" John pressed, eager to hear what had happened.

"No, I don't think so. Like I said, they were just boys."

"Well, I hope they found out what it'll cost 'em to come after our horses," John allowed. "At least they didn't cause no harm."

"That ain't exactly right," Cole said, grimacing with the discomfort he was beginning to feel." He turned then to show John the arrow embedded in his back.

"My Lord in heaven!" John exclaimed. "You got shot!"

"I got careless," Cole admitted.

"Mabel! Ann!" John blurted. "We need some help. Cole's been shot!"

Already climbing out of the back of the wagon, Ann almost fell the rest of the way when John yelled. Horrified when she saw the arrow shaft sticking out of Cole's back, she ran to him. "Cole, honey," she cried in distress, "what happened?"

"I got careless," he repeated, thinking it fairly obvious what had happened.

Her tone became scolding then. "What are you doing walking around with that thing sticking out of you? Sit down so we can take care of you." Wringing her hands as she watched him sit down on the ground, she looked to Mabel for help.

Having just climbed down from the wagon herself, Mabel was as stunned as her sister had been. With her children now crowding around to gape at the arrow protruding from their uncle's back, she recovered her calm and salvaged her role of authority.

"Elliot," she directed, "go get that fire started again. Lucy, you can get that bucket of water now." She hesitated then to ask Cole, "You did say those Indians were gone?" When he replied that he was pretty sure they had, she continued to issue instructions. "I've never had to doctor anything like this before, but I know we'd best get that thing out of your back. From the way you're moving around with it, I'd say it hasn't hit anything critical inside you." She turned to Ann. "Let's see if we can get his shirt off of him."

"Be careful, if you don't mind," Cole said. "I ain't got but two good shirts. Try not to make the hole any bigger than it already is."

"Cole, honey," she said, her brow furrowed with concern, "how can you worry about that old shirt? You've been wounded!"

"We'll save the shirt," Mabel stated flatly. "I can't guarantee the patient, though." She was amazed by the casual manner in which Cole regarded his wound. "Is that arrow paining you?"

"Yeah, some," he answered. "I'd sure like to get it outta me."

"Well, let's get to work," Mabel said. "Let's see if

we can get that shirt off. Ann, why don't you see if you can work the hole up over that arrow while I pull it over his head?"

With eyes getting bigger by the second, Skeeter crowded in to watch. "Can I touch it?" he asked Cole.

"I'd rather you didn't," Cole told him. "It's a mite tender right now."

"Get out from under me," Mabel scolded the boy. "Stand over there by your pa." Scrunching up his nose in protest, he nevertheless minded his mother.

With everyone out of the way, they began the work of removing the arrow from Cole's back. As it turned out, the arrow had not had enough force to puncture any vital organs inside his body, but it did embed itself firmly in his muscular back, luckily up near the shoulder. It required some cutting with Mabel's sharpest knife to remove the arrowhead, which left a sizable gash in his back. When the operation was completed, Mabel splashed the wound generously with some whiskey from John's one bottle of rye. "Maybe that'll kill whatever they mighta put on the arrowhead," she said. That was the only time the patient winced during the entire surgery.

Fascinated by the whole procedure, Skeeter asked if he could have the arrowhead. "Why, I was gonna give that to your mama," Cole teased. "But I reckon you can have it if she don't want it." The precocious youngster looked at once to his mother hopefully.

"I reckon I can do without it," Mabel told him, laughing. Serious again, she advised Ann to try to keep the wound clean and keep an eye on it to make sure it was healing all right. "Maybe we'll find a doctor in one of the railroad camps when we catch up with them. There's no telling what kind of poison those savages dip their arrows in."

The wound was slow in healing. In fact, Ann was concerned that it might be infected as Mabel had warned. Cole was less concerned, thinking that he would heal, just as he always did with any other wound. Even though it caused him some pain, he didn't let it slow him down as they continued on, following the progress of the Union Pacific. The pain, however, was more of a discomfort than a crippling inconvenience. They saw no more of the horse thieves, Cole having been accurate in his guess that they wanted no more of the repeating rifles the white men carried. He was reluctant to tell John how he came to get shot by the Cheyenne boys, but eventually John pried the story out of him.

"You shoulda shot that one when you had him on the ground," he said, "and any of the other two you had a shot at."

"They were just young boys, tryin' to impress their folks by stealin' our horses," Cole said in defense. "I just got careless."

That was as much as he was willing to confess. He knew John's feelings about Indians—that the only good one was a dead one. But Cole didn't have it in him to shoot a helpless boy, and the one he had under his sights looked to be no more than thirteen or fourteen years old. Cole had never killed a person before, and he didn't want to start with a killing that seemed more like murder. He hoped that John would let the incident rest.

"He'll learn some harder ways," John told Mabel

when talking about her young brother-in-law privately. "He's damn sure strong enough, and he don't seem to fear nothin'. He's just too softhearted, but that'll change out here where somebody will run you into the ground if you don't take a hard line."

Mabel did not agree with her husband's assessment. "He's just a decent man," she said. "He'll do fine out here, and I know he'll take good care of Ann. The rest will come in time."

Chapter 2

Catching up with the construction crews, they came to the end of the tracks some forty miles short of Crow Creek Crossing. The crew worked from sunup to dusk, and when they had finished for the day, there were plenty of opportunities for them to part with their pay. In fact, there was a temporary town of tents and board shacks in place that could be easily dismantled and carted to the next location. Since there were no women in the "town on wheels," however—except for those tents advertising prostitutes—John and Cole deemed it unwise to camp too close, though they were keen to enjoy the feeling of protection afforded by the large crew of workers.

"I'da thought the army woulda sent a detachment of cavalry to guard the crews," John commented, seeing no soldiers in sight.

"There're plenty of men with guns," Mabel said as she looked down the temporary street of saloons, shops, and bordellos with no shortage of idle loafers.

"I guess the Indians aren't anxious to pick a fight with all these armed men hanging around."

There was a dentist in a tent next to the saloon, and Ann encouraged Cole to have him examine the wound in his back. But Cole declined, insisting that it was healing fine, although it gave him some pain.

"All right," Ann replied, "but if that wound isn't a whole lot better by the time we reach Crow Creek, we're going to find a doctor."

"Whatever you say, dearest," Cole teased. Though he felt certain there would not be one at Crow Creek, since they would arrive there long before the railroad reached that point.

Although anxious to get on to their destination, since the summer was in its latter days, John gave in to the children's curiosity to see the building of the railroad. He delayed their departure the next morning long enough to let them watch the grading of a new section and the laying of the rails.

While watching the work, John and Cole engaged in conversation with Stephen Manning, a foreman of one of the crews, and asked him when he expected to be at Crow Creek. Manning told them that at their present rate they would be there no sooner than two months or more, depending upon whether or not the weather continued to be in their favor.

"I was told there was already a town of sorts there," John said, concerned now that his little party of pilgrims might not find the right place to turn toward the Chugwater Valley.

"You won't have any trouble findin' Crow Creek Crossin', I would think," Manning told him. "Accordin' to what the surveyors tell us, there is a sizable settlement there already. I suspect we might find ourselves winterin' in that spot before we push on into the mountains west of the crossin'."

The foreman's words served to ease John's concerns, and he allowed the children a few more minutes to watch the construction. "I'm headin' back to the wagon," Cole told him. His thoughts were for the two women waiting in the wagon. There were too many single men around, who had been starved for female companionship, to leave a pretty young wife alone for too long. There was also the possible opportunity to spend some time with Ann without the constant chaperoning of Skeeter. "I need to see about Joe," he offered lamely as he turned to leave.

"I'll go with you, Uncle Cole," Skeeter announced immediately.

Damn, Cole swore to himself, then had to laugh at the youngster's persistence.

Elliot, mature beyond his twelve years, caught his brother by the sleeve. "You stay here with us. Uncle Cole don't need you houndin' his every step."

Cole smiled broadly as he continued walking. *I've got to remember to do something special for that boy*, he thought. *Now, if I could send Mabel off on some chore for a few minutes . . .* The thought extended an already wide smile.

By the time they rolled into Crow Creek Crossing, they found a city in the early stages of birth. Though the places of business were still mostly housed in tents, permanent buildings of lumber were already under construction. Back on the Fourth of July, while Cole and his new family were still plodding across Nebraska, General Grenville Dodge, the Union Pacific's superintendent of construction, had arrived with engineers, surveyors, railroad representatives, land agents, and military officers. Dodge and his crew had remained in Crow Creek Crossing for two weeks, platting a site two miles long and two miles wide. The site had been in Dodge's mind for some time as the division point in the railroad across the vast prairie land. It was generally downhill from that point five hundred miles east to Council Bluffs, Iowa. To the west, the railroad started a serious climb up Sherman Hill and the mountains beyond. In addition, the new arrivals found that there was no longer a Crow Creek Crossing, because the name of the town had been changed to Cheyenne, an attempt to appease the raiding Cheyenne Indians that hunted up and down Crow Creek.

Since stores of general merchandise were readily available in the fledgling city, they took advantage of the opportunity to add to their stores of basic supplies before changing their course due north, following Walter Hodge's instructions.

"Accordin' to Walter's directions," John said, "we need to head straight north, and we oughta strike Lodgepole Creek after about twenty miles or so. When we get to Lodgepole, he says to turn more to the northwest, and we oughta strike Chugwater Creek after maybe fifteen miles." He looked up from his notes and looked at Cole. "That's about as close as he could get us to his place. Dependin' on where we strike the Chugwater, he'll be either upstream or down. We'll just have to search him out from there, but he's on that creek somewhere."

"Maybe if we start out early in the mornin', we could make that twenty miles to Lodgepole in a day," Cole suggested.

"We oughta," John agreed.

"Let me take a look at that wound," Ann interrupted. Cole submitted to her examination, and she had to admit that it looked pretty well into healing. Only then did she approve of continuing their journey, however. "All right," she said, "we can start in the morning." So after restocking their supplies, they camped north of the town to wait for morning.

As they had speculated, the trip to Lodgepole was accomplished in a day's time, and they made camp that night on the bank of that creek. A shorter day the following afternoon found them at the Chugwater. Upon striking the Chugwater, there was a noticeable air of excitement over the whole party, a sense that they were moments away from their new home.

However, there was also an uncertain feeling on the part of the adults. For the first time since leaving Lancaster, both Cole and John questioned their decision to follow Walter Hodge to Wyoming. The reason was quite simple. Setting out with a vision of fertile farmland awaiting them, they were now struck with a land that seemed almost desertlike in its appearance. Flat and arid, it looked as if it would present quite a challenge to any man who sought to farm it.

"I reckon we'd best find Walter Hodge's farm," John said. And that was to be a matter of sheer guesswork when it came to deciding in which direction to start their search. "I expect the thing to do is to decide this the way a scientist would," he joked, in an effort to lighten the tentative mood that was beginning to descend upon them. He then looked in the canvas money bag he kept under the wagon seat for a twenty-dollar gold piece. "Now, it's important to have a qualified person flip it. I reckon that would be you, Skeeter."

He handed the coin to his youngest. "Heads it's upstream, tails it's downstream. You ready, Skeeter?"

The precocious youngster nodded enthusiastically, feeling the importance of his appointment as the direction-determining official. With a solemn expression on his freckled face, he flipped the coin high in the air and yelled, "Heads!"

"I knew he'd say heads," Lucy remarked impatiently. "He didn't say call it, Skeeter. It doesn't matter what you call." The coin landed with tails up, however, so they set out downstream.

They continued in that direction until darkness forced them to make camp. After no sign of Walter's farm, or any farm, the decision to be made was whether to keep going in that direction or to assume they were going the wrong way. Everyone was impatient to reach their new home, and there was a tendency to fear that they had somehow failed to follow Walter Hodge's instructions correctly. "We might be miles and miles away from where we were supposed to strike the Chugwater," Mabel fretted. "Are you sure that was Lodgepole Creek we camped at last night? Maybe it was some other nameless creek, and that's the reason we're so far from where we're supposed to be."

Obviously irritated by his wife's accusations, John replied sharply, "Yes, that was Lodgepole Creek. Wasn't it, Cole?"

"I think it was," Cole replied.

"We did just like Walter told me to do. Hell, did you think we were gonna hit it right on the nose?"

"Well, you don't have to get up on your high horse about it," Mabel snapped back.

Cole couldn't suppress a grin as he made a suggestion. "I expect we're not too far from where we're supposed to be. I think we just got a bad toss of the coin. We shoulda gone upstream. Skeeter tried to tell us to go upstream when he called heads. If we start out in the mornin', we'll get back to where we first struck the creek in a couple of hours, and we'll have the rest of the day to find your friend's place."

"What if we don't find it upstream?" Ann asked.

"We will," Cole insisted. "But if we don't, we'll give Skeeter a good lickin' for leadin' us wrong." He grabbed the youngster then and turned him over his knee, pretending he was going to spank him. "Like tryin' to hold on to a greased otter," he said when he finally let the giggling boy worm his way free. Grinning, Cole looked up to find Ann's admiring gaze on him. He knew what she was thinking, picturing him as a father to their child, who might be coming along in seven or eight months, if she could believe the symptoms she was beginning to feel. At that moment, he felt secure in the belief that his life was on the right path, and it occurred to him that it wouldn't hurt to say a little prayer of thanks when he had a private moment.

Cole's prediction turned out to be accurate, for they sighted a log cabin by the creek early on the following afternoon. It could be none other than Walter Hodge's cabin. Of that, John was certain. On the other side of the cabin, a barn stood in the early stages of completion. As they approached the cabin, a wiry man with a full mane of snow-white hair and beard came out of the barn. He paused when he caught sight of the wagon with a mounted rider beside it coming up the creek. He immediately broke out a grin and called to the house, "Frances, they're here!" He was joined moments later by a pleasantly plump woman, drying her hands on her apron.

It was a joyous reception. Both the Cochrans and the Hodges were glad to be reunited, and the Bonners were welcomed to the party as well.

"As soon as you folks get rested up and have a little somethin' to eat, we'll go take a look at your land," Walter said. "Your piece joins mine, and you've gotten here at a good time. I've just finished with the plantin' of my winter wheat, so I'll be able to help you get a cabin built before heavy weather sets in. Cole here looks like a stud horse, and my boy, Sammy, will be back from Crow Creek Crossin' with a wagonload of supplies tonight. You might have even seen him when you were there and didn't know it was Sammy. Hell, the four of us oughta be able to build a whole town before winter hits."

"I reckon," John said. "And Elliot's a pretty good worker, too. I'm ready to get started. Tell you the truth, though, I ain't especially hungry right now. I'd just as soon go on and take a look at my land. How 'bout you, Cole?"

"Suits me," Cole replied. So the three men left the women and children to eat and visit while they rode out to view John's land.

Although it was not the paradise that Mabel and Ann had pictured, it was decent land, they decided, land that hardworking men could make a living on, acres of pasture and land for crops next to the creek. With no delay, they began building a cabin, and by the time the Union Pacific reached the city of Cheyenne that November, they were settled in the cabin and had started work on a barn.

Cole and Ann had already picked out a site for their home, and when weather permitted, Cole prepared to go into Cheyenne to file on it. A government land office had been built in the rapidly growing town, and as soon as Cole found out about it, he was anxious to make the land legally his and Ann's. She was already starting to show a little, and they were both anxious to have their own place.

It was the middle of December when he gave Ann a parting kiss and stepped up into the saddle. "Don't go wandering into any of those saloons with their prostitutes," she lectured.

"Well, I don't know," he teased. "I might need a little drink after that long, cold ride."

"Is that so?" she said. "If you're cold, you go to the diner and get a cup of coffee. That'll warm you up better than anything you'll find in a saloon."

He laughed and gave her arm a little squeeze. Had she been able to see into his thoughts, she would have known that she had nothing to fear. In the few short months since they had married, she had become his whole world, and nothing interested him outside that world. She stepped away from his stirrup and softly whispered, "Hurry home."

"I will," he replied, then turned Joe's head toward Cheyenne, planning to be back in two days at the most, for he had very little business in town other than registering his claim.

He arrived in Cheyenne after a long day in the saddle to find scant resemblance to the little settlement called Crow Creek Crossing. The town had swollen in population like a wound that had festered with infection. He went to the stables, where he and John had bought some extra grain for the horses back in August, to ask where the land office was, since he didn't see it when he rode the length of the street. The proprietor told him the office was located on a side street, but that it was most likely closed for the day.

"Where did all these people come from?" Cole asked, for the street was crowded with men, many of whom were loud and boisterous.

"Railroad men and the riffraff that comes with 'em," Leon Bloodworth, the proprietor, said. He went on to explain, "When they started layin' the tracks west of here, up Sherman Hill, the bad weather pretty much shut 'em down for the winter. So the railroad told 'em to go home and come back in the spring. Well, a lot of them boys' homes are too far away to get there and back in time to claim their jobs, so they just moved into town. And the town can't handle 'em. The saloons and the whorehouses go all night long to take whatever money the railroad men have left. The sheriff can't keep the peace. One of 'em shoots another one of 'em damn near every night. It got so bad the God-fearin' men of this town had to take matters in their own hands and form a vigilance committee. So what you see tonight ain't as bad as it was."

"It still looks pretty wild to me," Cole remarked, "but I'll take your word for it. I'd like to stable my horse for the night. I've got no reason to visit a saloon, but I would like to buy a little supper before I turn in. And if the charge ain't too much, I'll just bunk in with my horse."

"I won't charge you no extra, since you and your partner bought grain from me before. And if you're lookin' for a quiet place to take supper, there ain't none. But your best chance is the hotel dinin' room. Maggie Whitehouse tries to run a respectable place, and the food's fair to middlin'."

"Much obliged," Cole said. "I'll give Maggie a try."

He walked past two saloons on his way to the hotel. It appeared that both were doing a booming business, although it was still early in the evening. Ann's word of warning came to mind, causing him to smile to himself, and he thought if he was going to spend the price of a couple of drinks of whiskey, he'd most likely spend it on some trinket or doodad for her instead. This would be the first night they would be apart since their marriage, and he had to admit he missed her. *I'd better not ever let her know what kind of hold she's got on me,* he thought, although he suspected she already knew.

Inside the hotel, he headed for a door with a sign over it, identifying it as the dining room. It led to a large room with one long table with benches in the center and smaller tables with four chairs each lined up along the walls. The room was crowded. Only a few of the smaller tables were unoccupied, and all but one of them had dirty dishes on them. There were a couple of empty spaces at the long table, but there was not much room between the battling elbows on each side of them. So he seated himself at the one clean table against the wall, propped his Henry rifle against one of the empty chairs, and waited. After a short time, a young woman, looking bored and weary, stopped before the table. It occurred to him that, in spite of the expression she wore, she looked strong and able. Her hair, raven black, was pulled back from an honest and not unattractive face. It was plain to see that she had no concern for dolling up for the benefit of her customers.

"Stew?" she asked.

"What's the special tonight?" he asked.

"Stew," she repeated with a look of undisguised impatience.

"What kinda stew is it?" he asked.

"Cowboy stew," she replied, her expression approaching painful. "Look, mister, you wanna eat or not?"

"I'll take it," he said, anticipating an invitation to leave if he didn't. "With a cup of coffee," he added. She turned toward the kitchen without another word.

Back in a short time, she placed a large bowl of stew before him and a plate with bread beside it. "I'll be back with your coffee in a minute or two," she said. "Got a new pot just comin' to a boil."

"Much obliged," he said to her back as she hurried away again. He turned his attention to the bowl of food before him, tore off a chunk of bread and dipped it in the stew, then bit off a mouthful to test. It tasted a lot better than it looked, so he set into it with a will. He couldn't identify all the ingredients, but it was some kind of beef stew, which he had already suspected, since she called it "cowboy stew." By the time she brought his coffee, he had eaten half of the bowl.

"You musta been hungry," she commented upon seeing the progress he had made.

"I sure was," he responded. "That's pretty good stew."

"Just pretty good?" she asked, teasing him. Then went to work clearing the dirty dishes from the table next to his. "Maggie thinks it's damn good," she tossed at him as she filled her arms with dishes.

"I won't argue with that," he said. "Tell Maggie she's right. It's damn good."

"I'll tell her," she said, already on her way back to the kitchen.

He reassessed his impression of his waitress. He had first thought she was grumpy. He decided now that the poor girl was just tired. Looking around him at the crowded room, he thought the reason was obvious. She needed help. His stew finished, he took a few tentative sips of the steaming-hot coffee. It was still a bit too hot, so he took a chunk of the bread left on the plate and dipped it in the coffee and ate the soggy mouthful.

He didn't pay much attention to the trio of men when they ambled into the dining room a few minutes later, except to note that they probably weren't railroad workers. Most likely, he wouldn't even have noticed that, but they sat down at the table next to his, which the waitress had not finished cleaning. He glanced up to meet the eye of one of the men, who favored him with a smile that more closely resembled a sneer. Cole gave a polite nod, and it was answered with a cold, unblinking stare. *Friendly cuss*, Cole thought, and returned his concentration to his coffee cup.

It didn't register in his mind right away, but several diners got up abruptly from their tables and left the dining room. The waitress came from the kitchen then and, seeing the three men at the table, hesitated for a few moments before coming over to finish clearing it. When she did, she made it a point to first ask

Cole if he wanted more coffee. When he said he did, one of the men spoke. "Never mind his coffee, Mary Lou. You'd better see about gettin' us somethin' to eat first. We've been settin' here a helluva long time."

"Humph." She uttered a little snort, as if wondering how he knew her name. "You just walked in," she said. "You ain't been here two minutes." Pointedly turning to Cole again, she said, "Soon as I wipe this table off, I'll get you some more coffee."

"'Preciate it," Cole said. He took another look at the men at the table. All three wore long raincoats, and the one doing the talking wore a black flat-crowned hat with a band that looked like a silver belt. It seemed to Cole that the waitress was accustomed to dealing with the likes of the three leering men, so he saw no need to stick his nose in it. He concentrated on draining the last gulp of coffee from his cup while the young woman started wiping the table with a damp rag. The door opened then and three more men walked in to stand looking around the room.

"Tom," one of the men at the table called out. "Over here."

It occurred to Cole then that he might find himself in a spot he'd rather not be in, especially when a couple more patrons suddenly got up and hurried out the door. *Not a good sign,* he told himself. *They must know something that I don't.* But he was not inclined to get up and leave before he was ready. *I'll just mind my own business and let the six of them mind theirs,* he thought.

The man called Tom and his two friends walked over to join the three seated at the table, openly surveying the waitress's behind as she finished cleaning the table. "Thought you'da already et by now," Tom said.

"Well, we ain't yet," the man wearing the black hat replied. Then he suddenly grabbed the waitress's wrist. "'Cause Mary Lou ain't brought no food yet."

Cole felt the blood getting hot in his brain, and the muscles in his forearms tensed. It did not go unnoticed by the defiant young woman. Well acquainted with the kind of men she was dealing with, and with no wish to cause Cole to become involved, she jerked her hand free, causing the man to laugh. "Don't you worry yourself, mister," she whispered aside to Cole. "I can take care of myself."

"That's right, mister." The antagonist sneered, having overheard. "Ol' Mary Lou can take care of herself. You don't need to worry none on her account. You're leavin' now, anyway." He shifted his eye to his friend again. "Tom, we need more room. Why don't you pull that table over next to ours and we'll make it one big table?" There was no doubt he was referring to Cole's table.

"You can use one of the other tables," Mary Lou said.

"I want that one," he said, his tone no longer civil.

The whole dining room went suddenly silent, and all eyes shifted to focus upon the lone young man, who now knew there was no peaceful option available to him except to slink cowardly out of the saloon. And that just wasn't his style—never had been, no matter the odds. But six to one didn't promise much success for him in a fistfight, and a couple of the men, grinning at him in anticipation of his reaction, were pretty stout-looking fellows, eager for a tussle. Cole looked up from his cup and smiled when he spoke. "You gentlemen are welcome to this table right after I have another cup of coffee." He turned to Mary Lou then. "I'd appreciate that coffee whenever you get a chance."

Glaring at him in total disbelief, Black Hat remarked, "Mister, you ain't got the brains God gave a prairie dog. Either that or you figure you've lived long enough." When Cole still made no sign of moving, Black Hat nodded toward a wide-shouldered brute of a man. "If you don't get your sorry ass outta that chair right now, ol' Skinner there is gonna break your back for you."

Cole glanced at the grinning half-wit, who appeared eager to do the job, and knew that he had little choice. It was obvious that he was likely to take a licking if he didn't act quickly and decisively. "That would be a mistake," he warned, and in one swift move, grabbed for the Henry rifle propped against the chair, cranking a cartridge into the chamber as he brought it up to level on Black Hat. He had no desire to kill anyone, but he had no intention of taking a whipping.

His quick response caught them by surprise, but there was no concern evident in any of the faces staring at him. "Well, ain't you the feisty one?" Black Hat said. "You fixin' to have a gunfight against six of us? That don't seem too smart to me."

"I expect that's so," Cole replied. "But I don't figure to have a gunfight with all of you, so I'm settin' my sights on just one. I reckon that will be you, Mr. Big-mouth, and I'm damn sure I'm gonna get you."

"He's bluffin', Slade," the man called Tom said. Two more of the patrons took a quick gulp of their coffees and headed for the door. The rest of the room was frozen in a deadly silence.

"Hold on a minute, Tom," Slade cautioned. "You ain't the one lookin' down the barrel of that damn rifle. Don't nobody make a move."

Wondering why Mary Lou had not been back to the kitchen with more dirty dishes, Maggie White-house finally got curious enough to go out to the dining room to see for herself. "Mary Lou," she called out as she went through the door, "what in tarnation is goin' on here?" Her question was unnecessary, for she saw the apparent confrontation between Cole and the six men. "Not in my dining room!" she exclaimed. "You can just take yourselves outside and do your fightin' in the street like the mad dogs you are."

Both sides of the standoff ignored the annoyed woman's demand. With six pairs of eyes fixed on Cole's rifle, trigger fingers were beginning to itch as the seconds dragged slowly by. "Take it easy, boys," Slade cautioned again, lest one of his gang decide to make a play and cause him to get gut-shot in the process. "The lady's right. This ain't no fittin' way to act in her dinin' room, so we'll just let it go this time."

Somewhat relieved, Maggie was still worried that the trouble wasn't over as long as the man holding the rifle remained. It was obvious to her that he wasn't the real cause of the confrontation, but she suspected it was going to be difficult to order the six ruffians to leave. It might be easier to feed them and let them go on their way with full stomachs. So she decided to appeal to their lone adversary. Leaning close over his shoulder, she said softly, "Mister, it looks like you've already finished your supper. I'd appreciate it a whole lot if you would leave before trouble starts up again. If you will, your supper's on the house."

"All right," Cole said, fully understanding her problem. "I'll go." He rose to his feet with a cautious eye on the men watching him. Mary Lou gave him a nod of thanks as he backed slowly past her on his way to the door. Like a pack of hungry wolves, Slade Corbett's gang of troublemakers watched him closely as he withdrew, restrained by the rifle held ready to fire. Tense with the anxiety of permitting him to simply walk out unharmed, one of the men saw an opportunity to act when Cole took one hand off his rifle to open the door. His .44 failed to clear his holster before Cole, reacting without consciously thinking about it, swung his rifle around and cut him down. The shot set off an instant explosion of gunfire, aimed at Cole, but not quick enough to hit him as he ducked out the door. The only casualty, other than the man Cole shot, was Mary Lou, who had been unfortunate enough to have walked toward the door after Cole.

"Get that son of a bitch," Slade yelled, and charged toward the door. He was immediately discouraged from going farther when a couple of rifle slugs ripped off some chunks of the doorframe and sent them flying. Maggie's screaming caused him to look at the wounded girl lying on the floor, and he decided it best to get out of there before the law came. He was thinking of the strong possibility that some of the patrons who had left the dining room at the first sign of trouble might have already alerted the sheriff. "Let's get the hell outta here," he ordered then. "Out the back door!"

"What about Frank?" Tom Larsen exclaimed, pointing to the man Cole had shot.

"What about him?" Slade replied curtly. "He's dead. Leave him. I ain't stickin' around to have a chat with the sheriff and his damn vigilantes about a man dumb enough to think he can draw his pistol faster than a man can pull a trigger." Slade was not averse to standing his ground against the sheriff and his two deputies, but he was well aware of the vigilance committee that had taken matters into their own hands before. Known as the "Gunnysack Gang," they had held more than a dozen hangings already since the town had been overrun with felons.

The five men ran through the kitchen and out the back door to the alley behind the hotel. The problem now was to get to their horses, which they had left at the hitching rail in front of the saloon next to the hotel. They had to count on the excitement in the dining room to divert attention from the saloon. "We've got to leave this damn town," Slade told them, "and I mean right now."

"I wish we coulda et first," the slow-witted Skinner complained.

In front of the hotel, Cole backed cautiously away when it appeared he had stopped anyone trying to come out the front door. He had killed a man, something he had never done before, but in the heat of the moment, he had not had the time to consider the right or wrong of his actions. His thoughts now tended to lean more toward removing himself from the scene, so he started toward the stables and his horse. "Hold on there, mister." He heard a voice behind him and turned to see a man holding a shotgun on him. He wore a badge on his coat. "I think we need to have a little talk with you." He waited a moment for a deputy to catch up to him. "Jake, relieve this fellow of his weapon and take him up to the jail. We'll hear what he has to say after we take care of his friends."

"They're no friends of mine," Cole said.

"Glad to hear it, son," the sheriff replied. "We'll hear your story directly."

With Cole on his way to jail, the sheriff and his

other deputy began a cautious approach toward the hotel. Reaching the door, and seeing no sign of an ambush, the sheriff suspected the outlaws must have gone out the back, so he instructed the deputy to go around to the alley. "And watch yourself," he cautioned. He went in then to find Maggie Whitehouse trying to comfort Mary Lou, who had taken a bullet in her shoulder.

Seeing the sheriff, Maggie blurted, "They ran out the back!"

He hesitated momentarily when he spotted the body lying on the floor. "He's dead," Maggie said. The sheriff nodded briefly and ran through the kitchen to the back door. Stepping out into the alley, he heard a volley of what sounded like three or four shots fired at the same time. With his shotgun held ready before him, he hurried around the building to find his deputy lying on the ground, dying from four bullet wounds in his stomach and chest, and the sound of horses galloping out the north side of town.

Chapter 3

With no recourse to protest his arrest, Cole was forced to spend the night in Cheyenne's jail. There was no one to hear his claim of self-defense, except an old man named Pete Little, whose job it was to sit in the sheriff's office while a posse went after Slade Corbett and his friends. The posse had been hastily recruited soon after the shootings, made up of merchants and their hired help. And they had left that night while the outlaws' trail was still fresh, but after several hours, they gave up the chase, deciding that it was too dark to follow the tracks. It would be safe to say that a majority of the posse was not especially eager to catch up with the fugitives, not relishing the idea of a fight with the five gunmen. It was early morning when the posse returned to town, weary and hungry. Pete brought Cole a plate of food for breakfast, which he appreciated, but neither the sheriff nor his remaining deputy came back to the office until almost noon.

According to Pete, they were catching up on the sleep they had lost the night before.

"Well, young feller," the sheriff began upon returning to the office, "I don't reckon we'll schedule you for a hangin' after all. I talked to Maggie and Mary Lou, as well as some of the folks who saw the start of the trouble last night. They all said you never started it, and one feller who's a foreman or somethin' with the Union Pacific said he ran into you back down the line a ways. Said you was just a homesteader travelin' through here to settle up by the Chugwater. He didn't think you was the kind to start trouble. Anyway, it wasn't you that shot Mary Lou. You did shoot that other feller, though, but they said he tried to shoot you first. So it looks like you ain't gonna enjoy any more of our hospitality. I'm sorry to say they got away. They're a mean bunch. We didn't know they was Slade Corbett's gang of murderers till Maggie heard a couple of 'em call him by name. Anyway, you're free to go."

"Is the girl Mary Lou gonna be all right?" Cole asked as he waited for the sheriff to unlock the cell door.

"Yeah, she'll be fine—took a slug in the shoulder— might not be carryin' too many trays for a spell, but she'll be all right." He handed Cole his rifle. "Maggie said you was like greased lightning with this Henry. I ain't gonna be gettin' no paper on you anytime soon, am I?"

"No, sir," Cole answered. "Last night was the first time I've ever used that rifle on a man. I can't say as I feel too good about takin' a man's life, even one like that. I don't intend for it to happen again. I've got a new wife and a piece of ground up on the Chugwater that I'm fixin' to go file on at the land office right now. I don't figure to have any time for any mischief."

"Good for you, boy. Say, what is your name, anyway?"

"Cole Bonner."

"Well, pleased to meet you." He held out his hand. "My name's Jim Thompson. Welcome to Cheyenne. We're looking for new families like yours."

"Thank you, Mr. Thompson. I think we're gonna do just fine out here," Cole said. "My wife and I came out here with her sister and her husband and their three kids. I expect you'll see them in town at some time or another."

He walked away from the sheriff's office feeling very contented with his introduction to the law of Cheyenne. He had a feeling that he and Ann had made the right choice in coming to Wyoming Territory with John and Mabel, in spite of the confrontation that caused him to kill a man. It still troubled his mind, but if he had taken time to consider his actions, he would have been the one lying dead on the dining room floor.

When he left the land office, his land registered, he had one more call to make before going to pick up Joe at the stable. He thought it the decent thing to do to stop by the hotel and inquire about Mary Lou's condition. Maggie saw him when he came in the door, and she went to meet him. "How's Mary Lou doin'?" he asked.

"See for yourself," Maggie answered, as Mary Lou came from the kitchen just then, carrying a tray of food with one hand. The other was bandaged and supported in a sling. "Doc Marion fixed her up last night, and she showed up for work this morning, sassy as ever."

"I'm sorry she got hit because of me, but I'm glad she's gonna make it all right," Cole said. He stood there for a few minutes, watching Mary Lou as she bent low to set the tray down on a table with her one good arm before arranging the dishes for a man and his wife.

When she was finished, she walked over to join Cole and Maggie. "I see Jim let you outta jail," she said in greeting. "Pete Little said you was spendin' the night there."

"Yep," Cole replied. "I reckon it was better'n sleepin' in the stable like I had planned to do. They wouldn'ta served me breakfast at the stables." They laughed at his remark. "I just wanted to tell you I'm real sorry you got shot," he went on.

"I appreciate your concern," Mary Lou said, "but I'm gonna be just fine. In a couple of days, I'll be servin' hash with both hands again. To tell you the truth, I'm mighty glad to see you didn't get yourself hurt. That's a mean bunch of cutthroats we were dealin' with. If I'da known they was Slade Corbett's gang of outlaws, I wouldn't have been so sassy-mouthed with 'em myself." She smiled warmly at him then. "I could tell by the look on your face that you didn't like the way they were treating me, and it looked to me like you were thinking about doing something about it. So, thank you for that."

Cole shrugged, slightly embarrassed. "I ended up gettin' you shot instead."

Mary Lou laughed. "It's the thought that counts," she said. "It didn't look to me like anybody else in the place was gonna offer to help." When she saw that he wasn't sure what to say, she saved him. "You gonna eat with us now?"

"Ah, no, ma'am," he quickly replied. "I'd best be gettin' along toward home. I've already stayed in town longer than I expected to. My wife will think I've forgotten the way home."

"Well, don't forget us next time you're in Cheyenne," Maggie said.

"No, ma'am, I won't," Cole said, touched his finger to his hat brim respectfully, then turned and headed toward the door.

"Say howdy to your wife for us," Mary Lou called out after him. "Tell her she's a lucky woman."

"I will," Cole replied. "Don't know if she'll believe that last part, though."

He was almost out the door when a man sitting with two others at a table near the door spoke to him. "Glad to see you're walkin' around free this mornin'." Surprised, Cole paused to reply. The man looked familiar, but he wasn't sure why. "Stephen Manning with the railroad," the man reminded him. "We met at one of our line camps east of here."

"Of course," Cole said. "I couldn't place you at first."

"Looks like you didn't waste any time lettin' folks in Cheyenne know you're here," Manning said with a wide smile.

"It wasn't exactly the way I wanted it," Cole said. Eager to get on his way, he nodded politely to the two men sitting with Manning. "I expect I'd best be gettin' along." Then remembering something the sheriff had told him that morning, he said, "The sheriff said you vouched for me last night. Said you told him I didn't start the trouble. I'm much obliged."

"Glad I was able to tell him what I saw," Manning said.

Cole gave him a firm nod and said, "I 'preciate it." He walked out the door then and headed for the stables.

"Heard you got tangled up with a bad bunch last night," Leon Bloodworth said when Cole walked into the stables to pay for his horse's board and stall.

"Reckon so," Cole replied, realizing that everyone in town knew about it by then.

"Well, friend, I think it's a damn lucky thing you're still walkin' around today, and that's a fact. There ain't a meaner collection of rattlesnakes in the whole territory than that gang of killers. And what I heard was you pulled a bluff on all six of 'em!" He slapped his hand against his leg. "Whooee, I bet you was sweatin' aplenty."

"I was," Cole said matter-of-factly. "How much do I owe you?" He had heard enough about the confrontation in the dining room, and he was eager now to get back up on the Chugwater. Ann would soon be worrying about him.

He wasted no time saddling Joe and was quickly aboard and guiding the big Morgan on the north road out of town. Joe seemed glad to see him and took to the road cheerfully, seeming to want to shake the dust of Cheyenne as much as his master.

Cole had planned to make the ride back home in one day, but he hadn't counted on spending the morning in jail. And by the time he was able to get away, it was well into the afternoon. So he resigned himself to riding half the distance, then stopping overnight before getting home early the next day. It was only natural that he should have thoughts about the possibility of some attempt by Slade Corbett to seek revenge for the killing of one of his men. But it hardly seemed likely in view of the fact that they had killed one of the sheriff's deputies and shot Mary Lou. Common sense told him that the outlaws seemed to have a great deal of respect for Sheriff Jim Thompson. They would most likely be on the run to leave this territory as far behind and as soon as possible. So his only concern was to get home to Ann as quickly as he could.

Smiley Dodd rode up the bank of the creek, where his four friends lay about a campfire, waiting for his report. "Any of that coffee left?" he asked as he dismounted and hurried up to the fire.

"Well?" Slade Corbett pressed, ignoring the question.

"There ain't but one man on the place that I could see," Smiley said as he picked up the coffeepot and swished it around. "Two women—one of 'em pretty young—three young'uns, girl and two boys, looked no more'n ten or eleven for the oldest." He paused to swish the pot around again. "I swear," he complained, "there ain't no coffee left in this damn pot. Why the hell didn't one of you pull the damn thing offa the fire?"

"We save that for you," Jose Sanchez mocked. "We know how you like to do it."

"Go to hell, you damn Sonora cockroach," Smiley responded sharply, in no mood for Sanchez's sneering sarcasm.

"Maybe I send you to hell," Sanchez said, and drew the long skinning knife from its sheath, then held it up before his eyes as if aiming it at Smiley. "Maybe I scalp you first, like them damn Injuns. Then I carve you up."

"Yeah? And maybe you'll get a bullet in that sick brain of yours," Smiley retorted. Sanchez liked to taunt all of them, but he seemed especially partial to Smiley, possibly because the rotund and balding miscreant always responded predictably. Skinner was too dim-witted to realize he was being baited. Tom Larsen, like Slade, would most likely shoot him if his taunting irritated him. So he picked Smiley for most of his amusement.

"I've a good mind to shoot both of you," Slade said, finally tiring of Sanchez amusing himself by baiting Smiley. "You sure about what you saw, Smiley? There ain't but one man in that barn they're workin' on? 'Cause if we ride down there and somebody starts shootin' from inside that barn, I swear, I'll personally make sure you get hit."

"There ain't nobody else," Smiley insisted. "I rode all around that place. If there was somebody workin' inside that barn, I'da seen him."

"All right, then," Slade ordered. "We ain't doin' no good just settin' around this fire. Let's get goin' and welcome these homesteaders to the territory."

"Somebody's comin'," young Elliot Cochran announced.

"Where, son?" John paused, giving his axe a rest.

"Yonder, by the bank," Elliot said, and pointed toward the trees lining the creek upstream. Everyone stopped to look.

"I see 'em," John said when he spotted the five riders breaking free of the trees along the creek.

"Who do you suppose they are?" Mabel asked, shading her eyes with her hand while she gazed at them.

"Why, I don't rightly know," her husband replied. "But you and Ann best go in the house till we find out. Take Skeeter and Lucy with you. Elliot, look inside the barn door and bring me my carbine." They all did as they were told. When Elliot brought the cavalry rifle and handed it to his father, he took a firm stand beside him. "You'd best run on in the house with your brother and sister," John told him.

"I'll stand by you, Pa," Elliot insisted.

It was too late to argue with the boy. The five riders were already approaching the cleared yard before the barn, so John remained standing in front of the barn, his son beside him.

"Afternoon," Slade called out when they drew up before him. "Looks like you folks have done a lotta work on the place."

"Afternoon," John returned. "There's a lot left to do. Where are you fellers headin'?"

"Nowhere in particular," Slade said, then very deliberately reached inside his coat and pulled the Colt revolver from its holster.

Although he was standing there, holding his Spencer carbine by his side, John was too surprised to act before the .44 slug slammed into his chest. Elliot screamed in shocked horror as his father dropped to the ground. He turned to run but got no farther than a few yards before a bullet from Tom Larsen's pistol struck him in the back.

"Now," Slade calmly said to Smiley, "if what you said is a fact, then there ain't nobody in that house but two women and two young'uns, right?"

"That's right," Smiley assured him. "There ain't nobody else around."

Always eager to use his knife, Sanchez stepped down and knelt beside John Cochran. "I take his scalp. Anybody comes along after we leave will go looking for Injuns." He pressed the point of his skinning knife against John's hairline, causing the dying man to make a feeble effort to resist. "Hey," Sanchez announced, "he ain't dead yet." The discovery seemed to please him. "I finish him off after I scalp him." He took pleasure in knowing the man would experience the pain of having his scalp lifted before he was mercifully killed. "I get the boy next."

Unwilling to wait while Sanchez enjoyed himself, the other four rode on toward the house, where the two horrified women sought to protect the children and themselves. Paralyzed by the shocking scene just witnessed, Mabel could not think until Ann screamed, "Get the shotgun!" Only then did Mabel seem to remember the weapon by the fireplace, and she went at once to retrieve it.

"Take the children into your bedroom!" she told Ann as she opened the breech to make sure the gun was loaded. Then she took a stand facing the front door and cocked the hammers. There was nothing else she could do, so she waited, tears streaming down her face at the thought of her husband and firstborn lying dead on the ground. In the bedroom, used now by Ann and Cole, her sister huddled in the corner with Lucy and Skeeter close up under her arms.

Slade wasn't sure what might be waiting for them inside the cabin, but he was damn sure they were going in. With guns drawn, the five outlaws dismounted and cautiously approached the house. Slade didn't hear any sounds coming from inside, but he could picture the terrified women and children trying to find someplace to hide. Stepping up to the stoop that served as a front porch, he slowly lifted the latch, but it was bolted on the inside. He took a step back then and motioned to Skinner.

"Bust it open," he directed. The oversized brute grinned, eager to exhibit his bullish strength. He stepped forward and sized up the door, pressing one giant palm against it to get an idea of the thickness. Satisfied, he backed away a couple of steps, lowered his shoulder, and charged the door. The massive blow splintered the doorframe and the door swung open to bang against the inside wall. The simpleminded giant had a wide, self-satisfied grin on his face when he was met with a full load of buckshot from both barrels at a range of no more than six feet. The force of the shot was enough to send him staggering backward out the door to collapse in the front yard. His companions reacted instantly, pumping half a dozen shots into the defiant woman, killing her before she dropped to the floor.

"Hot damn!" Smiley blurted facetiously. "Reckon she's dead?"

Not particularly grieved by the loss of Skinner, Tom Larsen remarked caustically, "That big half-wit finally made himself useful." Seeing no one else in the front room, he looked at Slade. "Looks like the place is ours. The rest of 'em is hid in here somewhere. Let's root 'em out."

"I want to see the young woman," Sanchez said. "I hope she don't have no shotgun."

"I expect we'll find her and the young'uns in there," Slade said, and they all turned toward the closed bedroom door.

* * *

Cole looked up at a gray sky as he neared the center of the valley. It had not snowed in the last two days, but it looked as if it might soon.

Not before I get home, anyway, he thought.

If he remembered correctly, the knoll he had just left behind was about four miles from the cabin he and John had built. When he got to the creek, he would be on his land. The thought made him eager to get started on his own cabin, the house where hopefully a son would be born sometime in the summer. The thought of his wife caused him to nudge Joe with his heels, asking for a little faster pace.

Spotting a wisp of smoke in the distance, he knew that now he couldn't be more than two miles from John and Mabel's place. John had said that he might burn out some of those brambles and sage if it didn't snow. He wanted to clear off enough brush for a garden, hoping to plant it in the spring. But when the wind shifted toward him, there appeared to be a little more smoke than he had first seen, and he suddenly had a cold feeling in his gut. He had no explanation for it, but something told him that the smoke was an indication that something was wrong. He nudged Joe into a lope.

As he rode along the bank of the creek, the first sign he saw that told him his feeling of alarm might be justified was the remains of a fairly recent campfire. He saw tracks of several horses close by, which increased his concern. As he approached the last stand of trees that blocked his view of the cabin, he kicked the Morgan into a full gallop, no longer able to contain his apprehension. And when he left the cover of the trees, he cried out involuntarily when he found the smoking ruins of the cabin. The barn was still standing, but his last desperate hope was shattered when he saw the bodies of John and Elliot lying where they had been shot down. He was almost overcome with revulsion when he saw that they had been scalped.

Indians! They had been attacked by Indians!

Indians had been known to take white women captive in the past. This thought was all he had left to hope for. Leaving the bodies, he ran toward the house, only to have the last of his hopes disappear when he found Skinner's body lying flat on his back before the front door, his pants legs singed from being so close to the burning house. His neck, face, and upper chest looked to have been torn apart by a shotgun blast at close range. Still, there was enough left to recognize him as the huge man whom Cole had been threatened with in the hotel dining room. He was easy to identify. The man called Slade had called him Skinner.

So this was not the work of an Indian war party, after all. *The gang of murderers has come back to destroy my life,* he thought. But how could they have known this was his place? He turned and looked at the pile of burned timbers with only two partial walls still standing. His heart pounded with the dreadful scene he might find if he entered the ruins, but he knew that he had to go in. He had to know for sure.

Suffering a reluctance that he had never known before, Cole went into the smoky ruins of what was left of John Cochran's dream, stepping over charred timbers and debris as he made his way into the front room. The first body was in the middle of the floor, burned beyond recognition, and he sobbed as he knelt beside it. Judging by the size, he knew that it had been Mabel, since Ann was much smaller.

After a moment, he rose to his feet and forced himself to go into what had been his and Ann's bedroom. There he found her. The sight of the fragile body, which was, like Mabel's, burned beyond recognition, was too much for him to stand. He sank to his knees helplessly, his heart beating as if about to burst from his chest, and great sobs of despair choked his throat so that he could barely breathe. Unlike with Mabel's body, there was not a shred of clothing evident, making it impossible not to imagine the torture she must have suffered before her death. He dropped from his knees, no longer able to remain in that position, to sit beside the charred body of his wife, amid the ruins of his life. For without her, there was no life. Drowning in total despair, he sat there beside her for over an hour, lost, with no reason to go on.

He sat inside the burned house until the afternoon began to drain away into evening. A snort from the big Morgan gelding reminded him that there were still responsibilities to take care of, and he realized that his horse wanted water but would not move as long as his reins were on the ground. Drained of tears and grief, Cole strained to pull himself together.

"I've got graves to dig," he announced to his grieving soul, and he got to his feet.

The bodies of Lucy and Skeeter were in the corner of the room, both heads shattered by gunshots at close range. He had to pause and take a deep breath when he thought about the precocious little rascal who used to dog his every step. He quickly told himself to keep his mind on the chore to be done and went at once to the barn, where he knew he would find a shovel. In the barn, he also found the carcasses of John's two horses. The murderers had evidently thought the pair not worth their trouble.

It was well after dark when he finished digging the one large grave. He had thought about digging Ann's grave apart from the others, but he changed his mind when he decided it would be better for her to be with her family, and not alone. When he finished filling the grave, he said a few words over the dead. For the most part, it was an apology to them all, especially to his beloved Ann, for not being there to protect them. He would forever feel guilt over their deaths.

Although he had not eaten since early that morning, he had no desire for food, not even coffee, but he felt a weariness that seemed to drain his very soul, so he lay down next to the grave to sleep, reluctant to leave Ann's body.

When he woke up, he found that a light snow had fallen during the short night. He sat up and looked around him at the darkened ruins and the unfinished barn, looking cold and dead. He knew that he needed to leave this place. His grief was turning more and more toward bitterness, and his sadness from the night before, when he just wanted to crawl into a hole and die, was replaced by a desire for revenge. He swore on the grave that he would not rest until all who had participated in the murder of his wife and family had died by his hand.

His mind, so severely dulled by the grief and despair that had taken it over, began to function logically again. There remained four men to be dealt with, four debts to be paid. He was certain of the number, remembering that there had been six men who baited him in the hotel dining room. He had killed one during the brief shoot-out, and another was now lying dead on the ground near the house. He commanded his brain to remember the other faces, especially Slade Corbett with the silver hatband. He didn't know the names of the other three, except the tall, serious-looking man they had called Tom. He would remember the other two by their faces. One was a pudgy man with a shaggy beard, and the other looked to be Mexican.

With something to drive him on now, he scouted around the house and barn, looking for the tracks that would tell him which way they headed when they had left. They had apparently not worried about being followed, for after a short scout around the clearing, he found the unmistakable tracks of six horses that the light snow had not been able to cover up. They led to the north, following the Chugwater. Once he was certain there was a trail to follow, he returned to the ruins of the cabin to search among the ashes for anything he could use. There was nothing of value left. The murderers had taken everything, so he was left with nothing except his horse, his weapons, and the clothes he wore. He was not without some money, however, provided the outlaws had not found the canvas bag he had buried in a corner of the back stall in John's barn. It contained three hundred dollars, his total fortune, left to him when his father passed away four years before. It was intended to be used to build a cabin and buy seed to plant. Now it would be used to hunt four men.

Crow Creek Crossing, he thought, and wished to hell he had never heard of it. It would remain in his brain forever with the end of the pleasant life of Cole Bonner with his dreams of family and prosperity.

As he prepared to leave, he suddenly paused. So caught up in his grief, he had given no thought toward Walter Hodge and his family. Surely someone would have seen the smoke coming from this direction, and possibly heard the gunshots. Their house was no more than two miles away. Why had they not responded? The sobering thought struck him then that perhaps Walter and his family had suffered the same fate as his. Though the tracks he found leaving the scene of the massacre led in the opposite direction from Walter's place.

Still, he had to make certain, so he turned Joe and headed toward Walter's farm.

Chapter 4

To his relief, he spotted Walter Hodge driving a horse and wagon from his wheat field, heading toward his barn. Seeing the lone rider approaching from the south, Walter's son, Sammy, signaled his father. Walter pulled his horse to a stop and turned to follow Sammy's outstretched arm. Both father and son watched intently until the rider came close enough to identify.

"Hey-yo, Cole," Walter sang out when Cole was near enough to hear his greeting. There was no indication that Cole had heard, for he did not acknowledge but continued to approach them. Close enough now to see the grim expression on their young neighbor's face, Walter was pressed to ask, "What's wrong?"

Having already learned what he had come to confirm, Cole was not interested in wasting time before returning to pick up the trail left by the killers. So he quickly told Walter what had happened. Walter and

Sammy were both horrified to hear of the murders and professed to have been totally unaware of the tragedy that had taken place. They claimed there had been no hint of smoke, saying that it probably had been after dark when the cabin was burned, and the wind had evidently been blowing in the opposite direction.

"And you heard no gunshots?" Cole asked.

"No," Walter said, shaking his head in disbelief. "Maybe for the same reason we didn't smell any smoke." He kept shaking his head sadly. "Frances will be devastated. I'm so sorry for your loss," he added. "I'll get Frances and we'll get over to your place right away."

"Ain't no use," Cole stated grimly. "Ain't nothin' left but the barn. I buried everybody."

"You must be about spent," Walter said. "Come on up to the house and let us get you something to eat or a drink of likker, maybe."

"No, thanks," Cole said. "I just came over to make sure you folks were all right and let you know what happened. I've got to get back while there's still some daylight left."

"What are you gonna do?" Walter asked. His immediate concern was his family and if they were in danger.

"The same thing you'd do, I reckon. I'll be goin' after them." Sensing Walter's concern, he told him that he suspected that he was targeted because he had killed one of the gang. And the tracks he had found indicated that the killers had headed on, following the Chugwater. "Just the same, it wouldn't hurt to keep a sharp eye out for any strangers."

Then he turned his horse abruptly and started

back at a lope, leaving Walter and his son to stare after him, still staggered by the unthinkable tragedy.

"You be careful," Walter called after him. Cole did not acknowledge him. "I didn't like the look in that man's eye," he said to Sammy. "He's liable to be ridin' into his own death. Damn, that's sorrowful news. We best go tell your mother."

He didn't express it to his son, but the incident was certainly tragic enough to make him question his family's safety. He had counted on John Cochran and Cole Bonner to be there in time of need or danger. Now he was the lone man again.

It was not a difficult trail to follow since the four outlaws continued along the banks of Chugwater Creek. But with little knowledge of the country he was traveling, Cole could not speculate where they might be heading. With a mountain range to the west of him, he guessed that he was not too far from Fort Laramie. And if they stayed on their present course, they would probably strike the Platte River some distance west of the fort. It made little difference to him where they were heading, whether or not it was Fort Laramie or hell itself—he would follow them there and deliver his sentence of death.

As he rode doggedly on, stopping only when it was necessary to rest his horse, he felt empty inside, as if his soul had been torn out of him. There were no thoughts of a future beyond killing the men who had destroyed his life and taken the only thing he truly valued from him. And with nothing to detract from the monotony of the ground he trod upon, it was difficult to discourage thoughts of his beloved Ann. Every memory of their brief time together only served to increase his pain. So he was glad, when near the end of the day, he was suddenly distracted by a movement in the middle of the creek ahead of him.

At once alert, he pulled his rifle from its scabbard and squinted in an attempt to identify it. When about forty yards from the bend in the creek where he had first seen movement, half a dozen antelope came up from the edge of the water, moving in a single line. With his rifle already out and ready to shoot, it was an easy shot, and he brought the lead antelope down. There was no time for a second shot, even had he wanted one, before the swift animals bolted away. Only then did he realize that he had not eaten anything since leaving his wife's grave. The thought reminded him that he had to continue to take care of himself while searching for his wife's murderers. And that he could not go without food.

"I reckon this is where we'll camp for the night," he announced to Joe. The big Morgan appeared glad to hear it.

With no coffee, and no pot to boil it in, not even a cup, he had to settle for drinking water from the creek, same as Joe. He was fortunate to have the skinning knife he always carried, and a flint and steel in his saddlebags with which to build a fire. He went about the business of skinning and butchering the antelope, telling himself that it was important to keep his strength up. Thinking of the three hundred dollars he had, he decided he would have to spend some of it to better equip and supply himself the first chance he got.

That opportunity came two days later when he approached a small settlement on the Laramie River.

* * *

It appeared to be the start-up of what might become a sizable town, with a short row of log buildings and tents already in place. Looking down the street, Cole saw a saloon, a general store, a stable, a blacksmith, and a barber, plus a couple of other buildings that had no signs to identify them. He figured any information regarding the four men he trailed would most likely be obtained at the saloon, but he decided to visit the general store first, because along with his other supplies, he needed to buy cartridges for his rifle.

"Howdy," Mort Johnson greeted him when he walked into the store. Cole only nodded in reply. The owner of the store looked the stranger over thoroughly before asking, "What can I help you with?"

"I'll be needin' some things," Cole said as he eyed a small coffeepot on a shelf behind the counter. "A box of .44 cartridges to start," he began, then called off the basic food supplies he needed, which consisted primarily of coffee beans, salt, and dried beans. "How much for that coffeepot?"

"That's a dandy, ain't it?" Mort replied. "Just the right size for a feller travelin' alone." He paused to glance out the open door and saw Joe tied to the hitching rail. "I reckon you ain't got no family with you." Cole didn't say whether he did or not, so Mort went on. "What brings you to Johnstown? I don't recall seein' you come through before."

"Is that the name of the town?" Cole replied.

"Yup," Mort said, always eager for a chance to talk about it. "It was named after me. My name's Mort Johnson, and I've run this here tradin' post for twelve years. Wasn't nobody here but me until four years ago when folks started movin' in. I guess they thought it was a good place to settle, since the Injuns hadn't bothered me." He chuckled proudly. "They named the town after me, but they shortened it from Johnsontown to Johnstown."

"How much for the coffeepot?" Cole repeated.

"Dollar and a half," Mort answered. "You never said whether you was passin' through or stayin'."

"Passin' through," Cole said. He listed a couple more items that he needed, one of which was a blanket to make a bedroll. After he paid for his purchases, he said, "I'm looking for four men who musta come through here ahead of me, maybe a day or two ago."

Mort frowned before asking, "They friends of yours?"

"Nope," Cole replied. "I'm just lookin' for 'em."

"You ain't by any chance a lawman, are you?"

"No," Cole said. "I'm just lookin' for 'em—thought maybe you mighta seen 'em."

Still with a deep frown on his face, Mort said, "I've seen 'em all right. Night before last they shot Cotton Smith, the bartender in the saloon. We don't hold still for that kind of trouble in Johnstown. We're a respectable town, and to make sure it stays respectable, we have a vigilance committee to see that outlaws and murderers don't hang around here." He paused and laughed when he realized what he had just said. "I reckon I shoulda said we got a committee to see that outlaws and murders *do* hang around here."

Tense now with the realization that he might be catching up with Slade Corbett and his men, Cole ignored Mort's attempt at humor and pressed for more information. "So they got away from your vigilance committee?"

"Yeah, all except one, and he's locked up in jail,

waitin' for a detail of soldiers to come get him and take him over to Fort Laramie for trial."

Cole immediately felt the muscles in his arms tensing.

One of them is here!

His expression remained stoic, however, never revealing the storm raging inside him. "If he shot the bartender, why didn't you just go ahead and hang him?" he asked.

"Tell you the truth, we was of a mind to, but he ain't the one who shot Cotton. It was the mean-lookin' son of a bitch with the silver hatband that pulled the trigger."

"Slade Corbett," Cole muttered softly to himself.

"Is that his name?" Mort asked. "I ain't ever seen a meaner snake than that feller. The one we caught said his name's Smiley Dodd. We were lucky to get him. Buck Wiley, the blacksmith, got ahold of his coattail when they jumped on their horses—pulled him right outta the saddle and landed him on his ass. The other three got away, though, and I don't reckon they'll come back to Johnstown. And the army will take care of Mr. Smiley Dodd."

"What do you think the army will do with him?" Cole wanted to know, not at all pleased with the notion of handing him over to be tried. The army might not know how vile a murderer this man was.

"I ain't got no idea," Mort replied. "Throw him in jail for a while, I guess, because he didn't really do anything but raise a little hell and damage a couple of chairs in the saloon. We'd just hold him ourselves, but we ain't really got no jail."

"No jail?" Cole responded. "Where have you got him locked up?"

"In the smokehouse behind the stables," Mort said. "He ain't goin' anywhere. That smokehouse is built outta solid logs with a padlock on the door, and we got members of the vigilance committee takin' turns watchin' him till the army comes to get him." He paused then and watched Cole for a few seconds. "What are you lookin' for them fellers for?" It seemed to him that the young man was deep in serious thought.

"They owe me something," he said, and that was as far as he cared to go with it. What they owed him were their lives, and he had vowed on Ann's grave that he would accept nothing less. Ready to leave, he paid for his purchases, then hesitated before putting his money away. "If that little coffeepot was a dollar, I'd buy it."

Mort grinned as he responded, "Well, you gimme a pretty good order, so I might let you have it for a dollar and a quarter."

"Done," Cole said. "I'll take it."

Mort walked outside with him and helped carry his supplies. He stood watching as Cole filled his saddlebags until they could hold no more. "Looks like you need a sack for the rest of that stuff," Mort commented. "I'll getcha one." He went back inside, returning moments later with a cotton sack.

Cole tied it on his saddle. "Much obliged," he said.

Mort nodded and remarked, "You was down to just about nothin'. How much farther are you goin'?"

"Don't know," Cole answered honestly, then stepped up into the saddle before Mort could think of any more questions.

He turned Joe's head toward the stables at the end of the street and held the horse to a lively walk as he looked for the smokehouse Mort had mentioned. He had a lot to think about. The fact that one of the men who had murdered his wife and family was locked in a smokehouse no more than forty or fifty yards from him was causing him to struggle with indecision. It was unthinkable that a cold-blooded murderer might receive no more punishment than a short stay in the guardhouse at Fort Laramie. If what Mort had told him was true, that he was being held for nothing more than disturbing the peace and minor property damage, then it was very much likely that this would be the case.

The thought of waiting for the soldiers to show up, and then shooting Smiley when they let him out of the smokehouse, was tempting. He had to discard that idea, however, because it gave him little chance of escaping unharmed after taking the shot. And while it might give him the satisfaction of killing one of the outlaws, it might also mean that the other three would go unpunished.

On the other hand, if he simply followed the cavalry patrol back to Fort Laramie and waited for Smiley's release, the murderer's three accomplices would get even farther away by that time. He might never find them. He could choose to forget the one in order to make sure that the three did not get away, but he felt that the dead cried out to him that they all must die or vengeance would not be complete.

Perplexed, he sought a place to think about his decision, so he rode up the river about a quarter of a mile to a shady grove of cottonwoods and dismounted. While Joe grazed on the riverbank, Cole brushed a light dusting of snow from a log and sat down to decide what he was going to do.

* * *

It was well after sundown, and a moonless sky cloaked the cottonwoods in darkness when Cole rode Joe slowly out of the trees and headed back to town. To avoid being seen by anyone at the noisy saloon, he rode behind it until he came to the stables and the smokehouse.

Guiding Joe toward the rear of the smokehouse, he dismounted when he was within about twenty yards and pulled his rifle from the saddle sling. Mort Johnson had told him that there would be a guard at the makeshift jail at all times, so he skirted the building in the darkness until he saw a figure sitting by a fire in front of the door. Dropping to one knee, he watched the guard for a few minutes and decided that the man's main interest was simply to keep warm. He then turned his attention to the stables in front of the smokehouse and watched for a few minutes. There was no sign of anyone there. The only things stirring were a few horses left in the corral for the night. His mind made up, he rose to his feet, pulled his bandanna off his neck and retied it around his face, then walked boldly toward the smokehouse.

"Whoa!" Jonah Welch blurted, taken completely by surprise. "Is that you, Paul?" he asked, unable to make out the man's features in the dark. He struggled to get up out of his comfortable position by the fire, only to be met by the barrel of Cole's rifle against his forehead before he was halfway up. When he looked up to see the masked man hovering over him, he sank slowly back to a sitting position. Convinced that he was about to cross that dark divide that awaited all men, he pleaded, "For God's sake, mister, hold on. I've got a wife and young'uns. Whatever you're after, I ain't gonna give you no trouble."

"Unlock the door," Cole ordered. He had no intention of harming the man, so he hoped he was as scared as he seemed. "Smiley Dodd," he called, "you in there?"

"Hell yeah," Smiley answered, fully as surprised as his guard, Jonah Welch, had been. "Who is that?"

"A friend," Cole answered. Then he glared at Jonah when the trembling man failed to open the padlock. "Mister, I ain't got time to fool with you. Unlock that damn door."

Shaking with fright, Jonah whimpered, "I ain't got no key. Mort Johnson's got the key. He won't unlock it till he brings the prisoner some breakfast in the morning."

This was disappointing news to Cole, causing him to hesitate while he decided what to do. Determined to carry out his plan, however, he ordered Jonah to surrender the rifle beside him. "You wearin' a handgun?" he asked as he took the rifle from him. When Jonah opened his coat and showed him that he wasn't, Cole told him to get on his feet. "Turn around and put your hands on the wall." Jonah did as he was ordered and faced the front wall of the building with the palms of his hands flat against the logs. "You just stay that way," Cole said, "and maybe you won't get hurt."

"Did Slade send you?" Smiley called out impatiently. "Hurry up and get me outta here."

"Hold your horses," Cole told him. He tested the hinges on the smokehouse door. There were only two, and they were held in place by two nails each. It didn't surprise him. Smokehouses weren't built with imprisoning outlaws in mind. And whoever built it wasn't worrying about cured hams trying to break out. The hinges seemed to be firmly attached, but he felt sure they could be loosened with something to use for leverage. He looked around for a lever of some kind, but he could see nothing in the darkness. Then he remembered Jonah's rifle.

That might do it, he thought.

There was a large enough crack between the edge of the door and the doorframe to insert the barrel of the rifle, so he wedged it up as close to the top hinge as he could. It wasn't necessary to tell Smiley what to do. As soon as he saw what Cole was attempting, he put his shoulder to the door and tried to help.

Cole applied all the force he could muster behind the resisting hinge until, finally, the nails began to back out of the door frame. Smiley, becoming more excited with the considerable show of progress, increased his efforts, banging against the door like a bull. Suddenly the hinge pulled free of the frame, causing the door to sag away at the top.

Held now by only a bottom hinge and the padlocked clasp, the door hung open far enough for Smiley to step through the opening. "Hot damn!" he exclaimed, truly amazed to have been rescued. Anxious to complete his escape, he didn't take time to look closely at the masked stranger who had freed him. Instead he looked around frantically.

"Where's my horse?"

"There are some horses in the corral there," Cole said, nodding toward the back of the stables. "Pick one out."

"Pick one out?" Smiley retorted. "Hell, I want my horse and my saddle."

"We ain't got time for you to break into the tack room in the stable. I've got money to buy you a new outfit when we get away from here. We need to leave now, before the next fellow comes to relieve this guard. So just grab any horse with a bridle on it and let's go."

"You've got money?" Smiley replied, confused by the entire situation. He was still surprised that Slade and the others would bother to come back for him. "Who the hell are you, anyway?"

"I told you. A friend," Cole answered. "Now, let's not waste any more time here." He turned his attention to Jonah then, who was still standing flat against the wall. "You can step inside now and go sit in the back corner." Jonah obeyed immediately.

"Shoot the son of a bitch!" Smiley blurted. "He'll tell 'em which way we went."

"No, he won't," Cole said. "He's gonna stay put in that smokehouse till we're outta sight, 'cause he knows I'll shoot him if he sticks his nose out in the light of that fire. Ain't that right, mister?"

"Yes, sir," Jonah replied. "I ain't in no hurry to get shot."

"And I can see that fire for a long way," Cole continued. "If I shoot him before you get a horse, we'll have half the town runnin' out here to see what's goin' on. So get goin'."

Smiley wasn't tickled with the plan. He wanted his horse and saddle. He was fond of the buckskin gelding he had stolen in Kansas. But on the other hand, the idea of buying a whole new outfit wasn't bad, either, so he ran to the corral and climbed over the rails. As luck would have it, his buckskin was among the horses there. He almost blurted out in surprise.

"Hell," he muttered, "I bet I can get my saddle, too." He paused to take a look around. There was no one around the place but the masked man and the scared little fellow in the smokehouse. There was a locked door to the barn inside the corral. "We'll spend that jasper's money on somethin' more pleasurable," he said, and kicked the door in.

Cole couldn't help wondering if he had overplayed his hand. Smiley was taking far too much time in the corral, and he could hear the sound of the outlaw's boots thudding against the door. Maybe he was too smart to be taken in by the simple ruse and was figuring on running out the other side of the barn. He decided to go in to search for him, but the gate to the corral opened just then, and Smiley burst out riding a buckskin horse, saddle and all. "Let's make tracks!" he blurted to Cole as he rode by.

Cole had no choice but to turn Joe and gallop after him, but before he did, he emptied the cartridges from Jonah's rifle, just in case he decided to take a parting shot. "I'd be careful about using this rifle if I was you," he called out to the man inside. "I bent the barrel a little bit on that door, and it might split on you if you try to shoot it." There was no sound or reply from inside the dark smokehouse, so Cole gave Joe a firm nudge and set off after Smiley.

Anxious to put as much ground behind him as possible, Smiley held the buckskin to a reckless gallop over the darkened prairie, with Cole giving close chase. They maintained the pace for almost two miles, until finally Cole shouted for him to hold up.

"It don't make much sense to run the horses to death," he told him. "If we don't walk 'em for a spell, you and me are gonna be on foot with a posse after us." Smiley couldn't disagree, so he reluctantly dismounted and led his horse beside Cole.

"Who'd you say you was?" Smiley asked again.

"I'm an old friend of Slade's from way back," Cole replied. "He sent word for me to come get you outta that smokehouse."

"Slade ain't ever said nothin' about knowin' somebody around here. Seems kinda funny he ain't even mentioned it. How'd he have time to send word to you?"

"You ask too damn many questions," Cole said. "You're out of that smokehouse, ain't you?"

"Yeah, I reckon," Smiley replied, still finding his jailbreak more and more strange. "How long you gonna keep that bandanna tied around your face?"

"I forgot I had it on," Cole lied. "I couldn't take a chance on that fellow back there recognizin' me." He pulled it down just below his chin, counting on the night to mask his features, and hoping Smiley didn't recognize him at once.

Although confused by the sudden appearance of a strange rescuer whom he had had no knowledge of before, Smiley did not suspect foul play. In fact, he took little notice of Cole's face as they led the horses in the darkness.

"They took my rifle," he complained. "It wasn't in the saddle sling. I'm gonna have to get another one, first chance I get. We shoulda took that feller's back there."

"The barrel was bent," Cole said.

Smiley held up a pistol for Cole to see. "They didn't get this .44 I had in my saddlebag, though." He checked the cylinder to make sure it was loaded. As they continued walking while the horses caught their breath, Cole was trying to decide the best way to find out where Slade and the other two were going when they fled Johnstown. In a few moments, however, Smiley asked the question "Where the hell are Slade and the boys? Where are we supposed to meet 'em?"

Cole had to think fast. "He said you'd know. That's all he told me. Said you'd know where they're headin'."

"I'd know?" Smiley responded. "How the hell would I know?" He thought for a minute before speculating. "Well, we was plannin' on headin' up in the mountains after we left Cheyenne to lie up awhile, but I don't know where he figures we'll catch up to him." He scratched his shaggy whiskers thoughtfully. "Best I can figure, he must be plannin' on goin' back to Buzzard's Roost, up in the mountains. At least, that's where we was talkin' about goin'. Reckon that's where he meant?"

"I reckon," Cole replied. Hoping to get more specific directions to Buzzard's Roost, a place he had never heard of, he pressed for more information. "I've heard of that place, but I ain't ever been there. I ain't sure I could find it, if I was on my own."

"Easy enough," Smiley said. "Follow the creek up from the river where Lem Dawson's tradin' post sets. . . ."

He paused abruptly, suddenly sensing something wrong, and he realized that he had not been able to get a close look at this stranger who said Slade sent him. It seemed to him that any friend of Slade's would know where Buzzard's Roost was. And ever since he had pulled his bandanna off, the man had kept his face turned aside, never facing him head-on.

"Wait a minute," Smiley said, straining to get a better look at his benefactor. "Ain't I seen you someplace before?" It struck him then. "You're the bastard that shot Frank Cowen in that hotel dining room." He hesitated as he formed the picture in his mind. "That was you!" He jerked the .44 from his belt and aimed it at Cole but wasn't quick enough to beat the bullet already on its way from Cole's rifle. He folded over when the slug tore into his belly, causing him to fire his pistol into the ground at his feet. Even as he dropped to his knees, he tried to pull the trigger again, but Cole knocked the weapon from his hand.

Helpless now, his eyes glazed with the searing pain in his gut, he gasped, "Why?"

"Those people you and your friends killed on the Chugwater, they were my family, my wife—and you animals slaughtered them, that's why." No longer able to remain on his knees, Smiley keeled over to land on his side, his pudgy face twisted in a painful snarl. "You're dyin'," Cole said. "You might as well tell me what river Lem Dawson's tradin' post is on. Maybe that'll help make up some for your sins."

"Go to hell," Smiley choked out with a mouthful of blood. "You broke me out so you could kill me?"

"That's a fact," Cole said. "And I'll find the other three sooner or later," he stated stoically. "Tell me where to find them, and I'll put an end to your sufferin'."

"Go to hell," Smiley repeated.

Cole studied the dying man's face for a few moments. There was no compassion in his heart for him. "Have it your way," he said. "Maybe you'll die before the coyotes and the buzzards start to feed on your worthless carcass."

He cranked another cartridge into the chamber

and put another slug in Smiley's midsection to make sure he died, although not too fast. He didn't feel that it was right for the murderer to slip easily into death.

Even though one more of the killers had paid the ultimate price for his sins, there was no feeling of solace for the determined executioner. The fact that he had been transformed into a killing machine with no purpose beyond the fulfillment of total vengeance was of no moral consequence to him. His thoughts turned immediately to the unfinished business he had sworn to complete. He had hoped to learn more regarding the possible whereabouts of Slade Corbett, the man called Tom, and the Mexican, but at least he had one clue to work on. Smiley had said that their plan had been to go up in the mountains.

As cold as it had already been, it seemed odd to him that they would be heading up in the mountains. But if that was true, it could be anywhere north or west of where he now stood. The closest mountains would be the Laramie Range, directly west. And if that had been their intended destination, then maybe the trading post was on the Laramie River. He could think of no better option than to proceed on that assumption. There was little doubt that a posse from Johnstown would soon be on its way, but they would most likely wait until daylight to have any hopes of following his tracks. And just like the posse, Cole would have to wait until sunup for any hope of finding tracks left by Slade and the others. With those facts in mind, he decided there was no risk to camp where he was until dawn. So he picked up Smiley's weapons, tied a lead rope on his horse, and rode downstream until he found a campsite that suited him.

He surprised himself by falling asleep soon after making his camp, waking only after the first rays of sunshine began infiltrating the mist rising from the river. Startled as he was by the fact that he had slept through the remainder of the night, his automatic reaction upon opening his eyes was to reach for his rifle to defend himself. His sudden move was met with bored indifference on the part of Joe, as the Morgan and the buckskin grazed peacefully on the riverbank. When there appeared to be no cause for urgency on his part, Cole decided to rekindle the fire and make some coffee.

When he had finished his coffee, he saddled the horses and rode back up the river to the site of the execution. Just as he had suspected, Smiley was only a few yards from where he had left him, no doubt having tried to crawl away from the spot. His corpse stared up at Cole in eternal agony, evidence of his final hours. With no feelings of compassion or conscience, Cole relieved the body of its gun belt and searched its clothing for anything he might have use for. The decision to be made now was whether or not to go upriver or down in hopes of finding Lem Dawson's trading post.

Chapter 5

Two entire days were wasted riding up and down the river, upstream on the first day, then downstream on the second. There was no trading post to be found, and he had to conclude that if Lem Dawson's place was on this river, then it had to be a hell of a way from the crossing where he now stood. Bitter frustration threatened to overcome him, because there was no reasonable way to decide which way to go, and no certainty that the trading post was even on this river. Maybe he hadn't gone far enough north. Maybe Dawson's store was on the Platte. That would make more sense, if the man was looking for more trade. There would be a lot more travelers on the Platte.

Reluctant to start out in the wrong direction, he decided to camp where he was, even though there were still a couple of hours of daylight left. So he unsaddled the horses and gathered wood for a fire. When his stomach suddenly reminded him that he had forgotten to eat again, he unwrapped the major portion of the antelope haunch, which was all that was left of his kill. He had packed it in a sack filled with snow to keep it fresh, so he hoped it hadn't spoiled.

If it has, he thought, *it'll just come back up and I'll have an empty stomach again, no worse off than I am now.* With that in mind, he fashioned a leaning spit out of green cottonwood branches to roast it over the fire.

He had no idea how long he had sat there by the fire, his mind lost in his loneliness for his wife. Somewhere in the darkness of the prairie, he heard the howl of a coyote, and it caused him to realize that he had become a relentless hunter as well. It was a role he had never wished to play, but driven by his grief, his every thought seemed to be a desire to kill.

"Hello the camp! Mind if I come in?"

Abruptly shaken from his trance, Cole dropped the strip of antelope he had been eating, grabbed his rifle, and rolled away from the firelight. He had been taken completely by surprise. There had not been a sound to alert him that he had company, not so much as a nicker from the horses. The voice had come from the stand of trees close to the riverbank, but as yet, he could not see anyone in the fading evening light. "Come on out where I can see you," he yelled back, his Henry trained on the spot where he had heard the voice.

"You ain't aimin' to shoot me, are ya?"

"Not if you're peaceable," Cole answered, surprised again when this time the voice came from another spot in the trees, close to the horses.

"I'm peaceable," the man said, and stepped out from behind a cottonwood.

"Then come on in," Cole said, still holding his rifle ready to fire.

Cole watched as his surprise guest approached the fire. A short stump of a man, he strode easily toward him on a pair of legs bowed as if they had been formed around a barrel. Clothed in animal skins from head to toe, he might have been mistaken for an Indian were it not for the heavy gray beard covering most of an elfish face burned red by the sun.

"Good evenin' to ya, friend," the man said. "I caught the smell of that meat roastin' when I come up the river just now. Thought I'd best see who was doin' the cookin'. I almost run up on a Sioux huntin' party a ways up the river, and they ain't been too friendly lately."

"You're welcome to share some of this antelope," Cole offered. "This haunch is all I've got left, but it's more'n enough for both of us."

"Why, thank you kindly," he said. "My name's Harley Branch. Don't reckon you've got any coffee, have you? I ain't had no coffee in quite a spell."

"I might," Cole replied, thinking his brand-new coffeepot was obvious enough, sitting in the coals of the fire. "Cole Bonner," he said. "You got a cup?"

"Sure do," Harley said. "I'll go get it—left it on my saddle."

Cole watched the odd little man as he walked back toward Joe and the buckskin, grazing near the water's edge. In the fading light, he could see that there was now an extra horse munching grass next to them.

Damn! he thought. *It's a good thing he ain't a horse thief. If he was, I'd be on foot now.*

Normally sharp of ear, he scolded himself for not being more alert. In a few seconds, Harley returned with a tin cup. Without hesitating, he picked up the coffeepot and poured himself a cup. Swishing the pot around a couple of times before returning it, he said, "Feels a tad light. Reckon I got the last cup?" He gave Cole a wide grin. "Ain't a very big pot to start with, is it?"

"I don't usually have guests for supper," Cole said. Looking the little man over carefully now, he could see that he was not wearing any weapons, so he decided he wasn't up to any mischief and was just intent upon taking advantage of free food and coffee. "I'll fill it with some more water. That was just the first pot with those grounds."

"Here, I'll do that," Harley said. "I reckon that's the least I oughta do since you're furnishin' the coffee." He went at once to the water's edge and scooped more of the dark river water into the pot, being careful not to lose any of the remaining grounds. When he returned, he placed the pot in the coals again, pulled a strip of the roasting meat off the spit, and settled himself beside the fire to eat it with his coffee.

"'Preciate the hospitality," he said as he helped himself to another strip of meat. "Antelope's good eatin'. I'm partial to elk, but there ain't no elk in this part of the country. Bighorns, there's elk up in them mountains. I need to get up that way again." He finally paused in his rambling recitation to study his impassive host for a few moments. "I swear, young feller, I reckon I've been rattlin' on like a magpie, ain't I? It's been a while since I've had a human being to talk to. So, where are you headin', Mr. Cole Bonner? Fort Laramie?"

"No," Cole replied. "Is that where you're headin'?"

"Oh, I don't know," Harley replied. "Maybe I'll end

up there or somewhere else. I hadn't thought about it that much. I got a little camp back up in the mountains, but I got tired of talkin' to myself. Thought I might go visit some Crow friends of mine before winter set in too hard to get through the passes. Sometimes I hunt down this way, and once in a while I'll ride on over to Fort Laramie. I can trade my hides there." He poured himself another cup of coffee. "I need to get over to the fort pretty soon, though. I forgot how good coffee tastes, 'cause I've been out awhile."

Cole figured he'd save Harley the trouble of asking for a handout. "I just bought some coffee beans in Johnstown. I can let you have some."

"Well, that's mighty neighborly of you," he said. "Maybe we can make a trade. You said this antelope was the last meat you've got. I've got a packhorse below the riverbank on the other side of your horses, and he's totin' two mule deer I was fixin' to skin and butcher just as soon as I could set up a camp and get me a fire goin'. Whaddaya say you gimme a hand and I'll share the meat with you, fifty-fifty?"

Harley's suggestion served to alter Cole's opinion of him. The little man was not a beggar after all. The offer of a supply of deer meat was generous indeed. "All right," Cole quickly agreed. "How far have you been totin' those deer? I didn't hear any gunshots, and I've been here for a couple of hours."

"'Bout five miles, I reckon. You didn't hear no gunshots 'cause these two deer was shot with bow and arrows."

Cole was impressed. "And you managed to get close enough to shoot two of 'em? That's pretty damn good."

Harley grinned. "I didn't say *I* shot 'em. Like I just said, I almost run up on a Sioux huntin' party. They was trailing a good-sized herd of mule deer. They killed two of 'em and left 'em while they went after the rest. The poor things looked so lonesome a-layin' there, I didn't have the heart to leave 'em."

"You stole deer that a Sioux huntin' party killed?" Cole couldn't believe his ears. He unconsciously looked over his shoulder, half expecting to see a band of angry Indians bearing down upon them. "And now you led 'em straight to me?"

"Hell, they've done it to me before," Harley said. "Besides, it'll save me some cartridges." There was no mistaking the concern he saw in Cole's eyes, so he tried to reassure him. "If you're worried about me leadin' 'em here, there ain't no need to. I was real careful about not leavin' my trail—crossed over the river a couple of times. And dark as it is, they couldn't hardly follow a trail till mornin', anyway. That's the reason I was waitin' so late to make camp. I wanted to make sure I got far enough away from them Sioux before I went to work on them carcasses." When Cole still looked a little skeptical, Harley continued. "Them boys are a little piece offa their usual range this far over on the Laramie. This is mostly Crow country, so they've got to mind they don't get caught too close to ol' Medicine Bear's village. That's where I was headin' when I saw your camp."

That was even more news to Cole. "There's an Indian village near this spot?"

"Yeah, but they's Crow, friendly with white men," Harley assured him.

"Damn," Cole swore softly, realizing how lost he

was, with no idea where to look for the three men he sought. "We might as well get started with that butcherin'," he said with a shrug.

Harley grinned happily. "Now you're talkin'. We'll cut out some fresh meat for a couple of days and smoke the rest of it for jerky." He was still pleased that he had met someone to talk to. He had been a long time alone, and Cole Bonner seemed like a man you could turn your back on. Harley decided that right off. "I'll go get my packhorse," he said, but paused a moment. "You never said where you was headin'."

"I'm lookin' for Lem Dawson's tradin' post," Cole said.

Harley hesitated, thinking that maybe he had been wrong about the broad-shouldered young man, and he remembered thinking that it was a little strange that there were two saddles lying near the fire.

What, he wondered, happened to the fellow who sat in the other saddle?

"Lem Dawson, huh? You a friend of Lem's?"

"Never met the man," Cole answered. "I ain't really lookin' for him. I'm lookin' for the tradin' post. I've got some business near there, and I was thinkin' it might be on this river, but I ain't found it yet."

"You won't, neither," Harley said, thinking he might have jumped to the wrong assumption. Maybe Cole was a lawman. "This is the Laramie River. Lem Dawson's place is on the North Laramie."

"You know where it is?"

"I know where ever'thin' is in this part of the territory," Harley replied. "You help me get this meat cured, and I'll take you there."

He knew he should not have doubted his instincts. There was no way this young man could be part of that murderous scum that hung out at Lem Dawson's place. "I'm thinkin' you're a lawman. Is that right?"

"Hell no," Cole replied at once. "Whatever gave you that idea?"

"Just took a notion," Harley said, still convinced he had guessed right.

Most likely one of them secret government detectives, he thought. *Don't surprise me that he denies it. He don't want nobody to know his secret.*

They worked late into the night, butchering the deer, roasting some of the meat and smoke-curing the rest until Harley determined it would not spoil. The next morning they packed the meat on the extra horses. Watching Cole trying to fashion a makeshift version of a packsaddle for the buckskin, Harley finally had to make an observation. "Don't usually see somebody usin' a ridin' saddle on their packhorse," he commented dryly.

"It didn't start out as a packhorse," Cole replied, but offered no further explanation.

"I figured somebody had to have been settin' in it, but I didn't say anythin' about it. Ain't none of my business."

But you just did, didn't you? Cole thought. The task that he had sworn himself to accomplish was no one's business but his, and he felt no desire to make it known to every person he happened to meet along the way.

"It was makin' do just fine," he said, referring to the saddle. "I'll just have to rig up a couple more knots to tie this extra meat on. I reckon I'd best get it done so we can get the hell outta here." He shot a sideways glance at Harley. "Just in case you didn't cover your trail as good as you said. I expect there's gonna be a party of angry Sioux hunters lookin' for the feller who stole their meat."

"You might be right about that," Harley admitted. "But we ain't but about five miles from that Crow village I told you about. We wouldn't have to worry about no Sioux huntin' party there in Medicine Bear's camp."

"You said you could take me to Lem Dawson's tradin' post," Cole insisted. "That's where I need to go."

"I was just sayin'," Harley was quick to reply. "I'll take you to Dawson's, like I said."

He studied the intense young man's face as he finished tying up his rough-fashioned packsaddle. Granted, he had known Cole for a very brief time, but he couldn't help noticing that Cole had never cracked a smile. There had to be something weighing heavily on his mind. And if it had to do with Lem Dawson and his kind, it might be serious trouble Cole was riding into.

Ordinarily Harley would think only about distancing himself from whatever trouble the intense young stranger was heading for. But he had a feeling about Cole Bonner, a feeling that basically he was a good man. Harley was not ready to give up the notion that Cole was a secret government agent, but maybe there was something more involved, something personal, and it had to do with Lem Dawson, or the rats that hung around him. In good conscience, he couldn't hold his tongue any longer.

"I expect you know best," Harley started out. "I

said I'd take you to Dawson's place, so that I will. And I reckon you know the kind of men you'll most likely run into when you get there. I don't know what you're aimin' to do, but if you're thinkin' about stirrin' up any trouble with that bunch he usually has around him, you're gonna need more men."

Cole realized then that Harley might be having second thoughts about acting as his guide. "All I'm askin' you to do is to show me where the tradin' post is," he quickly assured him. "Like I said, I've got no business to settle with Lem Dawson—don't know the man. I just need to find his store. When I find that, I'll know how to get to the place I wanna go."

Harley scratched his head thoughtfully, confused by the roundabout explanation he had just heard. Why didn't he just say where it was he wanted to go? He thought about Dawson's store. There wasn't any place anywhere around it. That's why outlaws hung around there. Then it struck him.

"Buzzard's Roost!" he blurted. "You're lookin' to find Buzzard's Roost, ain't you?"

"You know it?" Cole asked, surprised. He had figured it to be a secret hideout that only a few outlaws knew about.

"Hell, I know about ever'thin' in this part of the territory. I told you that." He reined his horse to a stop. "What I don't know is why you're wantin' to go there, and I ain't sure if I wanna take you. If you're part of that sorry bunch that hides out up that mountain, then I reckon we'd best part company right here, and you can find it on your own." He dropped his hand to rest on the pistol he wore, just as a precaution against a violent response.

Seeing his reaction, Cole was at once alarmed that

he was about to lose his guide. He was already far behind the three men he was after. He couldn't afford to lose more time. From the beginning, he had decided to tell no one that he intended to avenge the deaths of the people who meant the most to him. He still thought that was best, but knowing he might save precious time if Harley accompanied him, he reluctantly told him why he wanted to find Buzzard's Roost.

"There were four of the murderers who left my place on Chugwater Creek," Cole concluded. "I caught up with one of them at a place called Johnstown. That's where the empty saddle came from. There are three more that I have to catch up with before my wife and the rest of my family can rest in peace."

"Good Lord in heaven . . ." Harley drew out a long, slow exclamation after hearing of the massacre of Cole's family. He said nothing more for a long moment while he thought about what he had just heard. "That is a sorry piece of news. I'll take you there, if you're determined that's what you need to do. I damn sure don't blame you for wantin' to kill them bastards. I'm just hopin' you ain't bitin' off more'n you can chew, and I'd hate to see you end up in the ground with your wife. These are dangerous men, sounds to me, and you say you've settled with two of 'em. Maybe that's enough to pay for what they done." He could see in Cole's face that it wasn't. "All right, then, we'll go. We're about half a day from the North Laramie, and Lem Dawson's place is a short half day upriver from where we'll strike it."

"I appreciate it, Harley. If you can lead me through these hills between the two rivers, you don't have to take me all the way to the tradin' post. Just head me in the right direction, and then you can be done with me and get along to wherever you were headin' before."

"I was on my way to Medicine Bear's village," Harley said. "Figured on winterin' with 'em, instead of spendin' the winter by my lonesome. Them two mule deer was gonna be a present to the old chief, but seems to me that somebody needs to help you get your ass in trouble. So I'll take you to Lem's place."

It took a bit longer than Harley had predicted, owing to a heavy snowfall during the night. "Well, yonder it is," Harley finally pointed out when he pulled his horse up short of a sharp bend in the narrow river, just as the sun was sinking behind the mountains to the west.

Cole urged Joe forward a few paces to get a better look at the weathered log cabin sitting in the trees lining the bank of the river. Behind the cabin, there were two outbuildings, and off to one side, a barn with a small corral. Unaware of the tightening of the muscles in his arms and the increase in the beating of his heart, Cole looked hard at the simple building as if he was trying to see inside it.

"There's a stream on the other side of the cabin," Harley said. "The trail you're lookin' for follows that stream up the mountain."

"As hard as this place is to find, why do they need another hideout up the mountain?" Cole asked.

"Dawson's been here a long time," Harley said. "The Crows told the army about his tradin' post, and the fact that it was a hideout for outlaws on the run. Ever'thin' was fine till a cavalry patrol paid him a visit one day, lookin' for some fellers that killed some folks over at that hog ranch at Fort Laramie. After that, Lem built him a new place up on the side of that mountain. The army don't know about that one. Ain't no way up but that narrow trail along the stream, and if the law does find it, whoever's up there can go down the other side of the mountain."

"Much obliged," Cole said, never taking his eyes off the cabin. "I can go the rest of the way by myself."

"I don't know if you're plannin' on goin' in the store or not," Harley said. "But if you ain't, and you don't want Lem to know you're goin' up that trail to Buzzard's Roost, I'd advise you to ride up this ravine, then cut across to strike the trail by the stream half-way up. That way, you'll be above Lem's place, and nobody'll see where you're goin'."

Cole nodded. "That makes sense to me," he said, "but I thought you said there ain't but one way up."

"Well, there ain't for most folks," Harley said. "But I don't count myself with most folks."

Cole almost smiled when he turned to thank the crusty little man again for his help.

"I'll tell you what," Harley said, "I'll ride up this ravine with you, and I'll hold your extra horse while you cut across to Buzzard's Roost. As fast as the snow's pilin' up on that slope, you'll have your hands full without havin' to tend to a packhorse."

His offer drew a wry smile from Cole. "If things don't go the way I want, then you'll have a good horse, right?"

"Why, I hadn't thought of it that way," Harley lied. In fact, he gave Cole very little chance of coming back alive, and the buckskin looked like a good horse.

"Well, I'd just as soon you got the buckskin, instead of one of them," Cole said. "Let's go." He snorted contemptuously when it occurred to him that the horse had belonged to the late Smiley Dodd. He nudged Joe then and followed Harley up the ravine.

After a climb that brought them to a rocky ledge about one hundred and fifty feet above the trading post, Harley pulled his horses over against the slope to let Cole pass. "I'll wait for you here," he told him when Cole handed him the buckskin's lead rope as Joe edged past.

Cole paused long enough to ask, "What am I lookin' for up there?"

"There's a little clearing about fifty yards up the trail big enough to graze a couple of horses when it ain't covered up with snow. Over against a rock-faced cliff they've fixed up a place that started out as a tent, but they built a shack at the end of it. So it's half shack and half tent now. At least that's what they had the last time I saw it, about six months ago. That's about all I can tell you about it. I ain't never been no closer to it than that ridge on the mountain above it." Cole nodded and turned Joe toward the stream. "Boy, you be real careful," Harley said, genuinely concerned for the young man's safety. "Just because you got *right* on your side don't mean you ain't gonna end up with your ass shot full of holes."

Cole didn't reply to Harley's warning, his mind already fixated on the hideout he was stalking. He rode along the ledge until he came to the stream and the trail beside it. The trail was narrow, but it was not too steep to go up on horseback, so he continued on until first getting a glimpse of the clearing Harley had described before dismounting. Figuring it would be safer to go the rest of the way on foot, he pulled his rifle and looped Joe's reins around a bush.

* * *

To keep from burning his fingers on the little red-hot iron stove, Porter Lewis used a stick of stove wood to open the firebox. Thinking how grateful he was that Lem had toted the little stove up the mountain, he put the last few sticks of wood in the fire. Before the stove, all the cooking had to be done over a fire outside the shack. Of course, the added benefit was a warm shack to sleep in. Now it was like staying in a hotel. And there was no charge except, of course, guests were expected to spend a generous amount of money in Lem's store.

With those thoughts in mind, he told himself that he was going to have to go outside and carry in enough firewood to last him through the night. And that reminded him that he was going to complain to Lem Dawson that the last boys who used the hideout didn't replace the firewood they had used. That was a firm rule that Lem had established when he brought the stove up the mountain.

Porter sat down on the roughly fashioned bunk to pull his boots on, and as he did, he wondered if the authorities were still looking for him in Colorado. He figured they would have given up by now, but since that damn fool bank teller had to make a play to stop him—and wound up getting himself shot—they might have sent a marshal and posse into Wyoming. Fort Collins was not that far away.

They'd play hell finding me in this place, he told himself. There ain't but a handful of people who know about Buzzard's Roost, and they're all outlaws.

"I'll hole up here for a couple more days. Then I'll head back down to Cheyenne," he said. "That's a good place to ride the winter out, and I've got plenty of money, thanks to them generous folks at the bank in Fort Collins." He laughed at his joke, got to his feet, and went out to get the wood.

"Lazy sons of bitches," Porter muttered as he picked among the last of a stack of firewood. He was going to have to cut more than his share in the morning.

"Hold real steady. This Henry rifle has got a hair trigger." The low warning came from out of the darkness.

Porter froze, still holding an armload of wood. Caught in a helpless position, he naturally thought the law had tracked him down.

"Take it easy," he pleaded. "There ain't no call to shoot nobody."

"Turn around so I can get a good look at you. Do it nice and slow."

Porter turned slowly around to face Cole and the Henry rifle aimed at him. There was no recognition on the part of either man. Porter was still left with the thought that he had been caught by a marshal, while Cole realized he was not one of the men he sought.

"Who else is here?" Cole demanded, although there were only two horses tied in the trees.

"Ain't nobody here but me," Porter said.

"I'm lookin' for Slade Corbett," Cole said. "You know him?"

"Yeah," Porter answered, wondering what this had to do with him, "I know him, at least I know *of* him."

"Has he been here?"

"Hell, I don't know," Porter replied, getting more confused by the moment. "Not since I've been here, he ain't." He remained frozen, with an armload of fire-wood, while Cole tried to decide what he should do now. Finally Porter became perplexed to the point where he felt compelled to ask, "Are you arrestin' me, or not?"

"I'm not a lawman," Cole answered matter-of-factly. "Go on and take your wood in the shack." He turned abruptly and went quickly down the path to retrieve his horse, leaving a totally astonished bank robber behind him.

Since night had fallen quickly over the mountain, Cole did not step up into the saddle, deeming it safer to lead Joe down the darkened trail. When he got to the ledge, he found Harley waiting there as he had promised. "Damned if I ain't glad to see you," the little man said. "I'm 'bout to freeze to death. I'da built me a fire, but I was afraid somebody'd see it down below." He waited for Cole to report his findings, but not for more than a few seconds before asking, "What happened up there? I didn't hear no gunshots or nothin'."

"They weren't there," Cole replied.

"Whaddaya gonna do now?"

"I don't know," Cole said, factually. "Maybe I'll go see this Lem Dawson feller. See if I can find out anything from him."

Harley shrugged. "Don't know if it'd do you any good or not. Worth a try, I reckon, but let's wait till mornin', get offa this mountain, and make camp. Even if you found out somethin' tonight, you couldn't do nothin' about it till mornin'."

"I reckon you're right," Cole said, somewhat surprised that Harley was still planning to stay with him.

Chapter 6

"Somebody's comin'," Zeke Pritchard announced. Standing in the door of the trading post, he watched the two riders approaching. "Two riders leadin' two horses," he continued. A small-time horse thief and cattle rustler, Zeke didn't suspect the law was after him, but it was always best to identify visitors to Lem's store. When they got a little closer, he was able to recognize one of them. "That's that old coot that roams all over these parts. What's his name?"

"Harley," Lem Dawson said. "Harley Branch?"

"Yeah, that's him," Zeke said. "I don't know who that is with him. I ain't never seen him before, and that buckskin he's leadin' is totin' an empty saddle. You don't reckon he's a lawman, do ya?"

Lem wasn't interested enough to get up from his chair by the stove and go to the door to have a look for himself. There were none of his usual guests at his establishment at the present—only Zeke and Porter Lewis, who was up in Buzzard's Roost. So he wasn't concerned about warning anyone. Porter said he had shot a bank teller, but Lem doubted any law enforcement officers in Colorado Territory would come this far, even if they knew about his place. He was only slightly curious about who might be riding with Harley Branch. And as far as Harley was concerned, he was probably looking to trade some ragged old pelts for whiskey. It was unusual that he had someone with him, however, since Harley was always a loner. When the two riders pulled up in front of the store, Zeke left his position by the door and walked back to stand by the counter.

Cole took a good look around him as he dismounted before the log structure. The aging logs were in need of attention in several areas of the walls, where the clay chinking had fallen away. There had been a couple of additions built onto the original and it was easy to tell which one was the latest. There appeared to be no one around, no other horses at the hitching rail, so Cole followed Harley into the store, ducking his head to keep from bumping it on the lintel.

Inside, the room was as dark as a cave, and it took him a few minutes to adjust his eyes. There were two men in the store, one leaning against the counter, the other sitting in a rocking chair beside a tall iron stove. In no hurry to greet them, the man sitting in the chair spoke after a few moments.

"Harley Branch, it's been a while since you've showed up around here. I thought maybe you was dead, maybe you was scalped by some of them Sioux Injuns." He got up and walked over to stand by the counter with Zeke.

"I just come by to see if the soldiers had burned this place down," Harley returned.

"Huh," Lem grunted. "There ain't nothin' here the army's interested in—just an honest businessman tryin' to get by." He turned his attention toward Cole. "Who's your friend?" Not waiting for an answer, he said, "Mister, you ain't particular who you ride with, are you?" Cole made no reply, so Lem turned back to Harley. "What can I do for you, Harley? You lookin' to trade off some pelts?"

"Nope," Harley said. "I'm just ridin' along with Cole. He's tryin' to catch up with some of your friends."

"Is that so?" Lem replied. "And who might that be?" He took a closer look at Cole then, his natural suspicion aroused.

"Slade Corbett," Cole answered quickly, lest Harley might blurt the real reason he was looking for Corbett. "I was supposed to meet him here, but I got held up when Smiley Dodd and I ran into a little trouble in a place called Johnstown. We had to run for it when they got up a posse after us, and Smiley didn't make it. That's his horse out there beside mine."

Lem scratched his chin under his whiskers while he considered what Cole said. The story sounded like a reasonable explanation for the empty saddle Zeke reported when they first rode up. Still, he was cautious about supplying strangers with any information regarding his customers. "You didn't miss Slade by much," he said. "He was here, all right, but he didn't stay—him and Tom Larsen and Sanchez came in one night and they was gone the next mornin'." He watched Cole's reaction closely. "Funny, he didn't say nothin' about meetin' anybody."

Sanchez, Cole repeated to himself. Now the Mexican had a name. It was time to think fast. "He wasn't likely to have said anything about it till I showed up.

We were gonna talk over a little piece of business that didn't include Tom and the Mexican, and he wasn't sure what they'd think about that." Cole could see that Dawson was chewing that over in his head. "I reckon I'll catch up with him somewhere. Where did he say he was headin' when he left here?"

Still cautious, Dawson said, "He didn't say where he was headed. He just lit out."

"Yeah, he did, Lem," Zeke began, before Dawson cut him off with a sharp elbow in his ribs.

"He didn't say where he was goin'," Dawson insisted. "It wasn't no business of mine, anyway."

"That's a fact," Zeke said. "Come to think of it, they didn't say where they was headin'."

"You boys needin' some supplies?" Dawson asked. He pointed to Cole's rifle. "I've got cartridges for that Henry you're carryin'."

"Reckon not," Cole said. "I'm pretty well supplied right now, and we need to get on our way."

"Damn," Dawson said. "It's hard for a man to make a livin' offa boys like you and Slade."

"Reckon maybe we could take time for a little drink, couldn't we, Cole?" Harley had been eyeing a full bottle of whiskey sitting on a shelf behind the counter. "I swear, it's been a while since I've had any of that poison Lem sells."

Cole had no interest in a drink. His mind was working on where to look for Slade Corbett and his two friends. But he realized that he at least owed Harley a drink of whiskey for bringing him to the trading post.

"Sure, why not?" he replied. "We ain't in that big a hurry."

This was not exactly true. He was in a desperate hurry, but he didn't know where to search for those he sought. One thing he was certain of, however, was that both Lem Dawson and Zeke Pritchard knew where Slade was heading when he left the trading post. There was little doubt that Zeke was the weak link in the chain of silence that outlaws abided by. "I'll stand good for a couple of drinks for my friend here," Cole told Lem.

"What about yourself?" Lem asked, reaching behind him for the bottle.

"Nothin' for me," Cole said.

"Nothin'?" Lem echoed, as if finding it hard to believe. A man who didn't want a drink of whiskey was a man you couldn't trust, as far as he was concerned. "Don't you need a snort of somethin' to warm your insides on a day like this?"

"Reckon not," Cole replied.

"Well, I need somethin' to warm my insides," Zeke spoke up. "I'm fixin' to go out to the barn and fork some hay down for the horses, and it's cold out there."

"You've already run up an account that you ain't paid for," Lem said. "I'm cuttin' you off till you come up with what you owe me."

"I swear, Lem, you know I'm good for it," Zeke whined. "Come spring, I'll catch up with it."

"Come spring, you'll still be settin' around here talkin' about what you're gonna do while you're still forkin' hay and sloppin' the hogs just to pay for your grub," Lem told him, and poured Harley's drink.

"I'll stand good for one drink for your friend," Cole said, and motioned for Lem to pour another.

"Why, that's mighty neighborly of you, mister," Zeke said. He picked up the glass as soon as Lem poured it, tossed it back, and smacked his lips in appreciation. "Damn, I needed that. Thanks again, mister."

"Don't mention it," Cole said. He looked at Harley then and said, "I reckon we're ready to leave now."

Mystified by his young friend's generosity, Harley finished his second drink and turned to follow Cole, who was already walking toward the door.

Outside, Harley asked, "I thank you kindly for the whiskey, but I'm kinda buffaloed on why you bought a drink for that piece of horse dung in there."

"I bought you a couple of drinks because you've done me a big favor. I bought him a drink because he's *gonna* do me one." He offered no further explanation as he stepped up into the saddle and turned Joe away from the hitching rail. Harley followed as Cole rode up the trail that had led them to the trading post earlier, not waiting for the stumpy little man to lead as usual. When they had turned onto the river trail and were out of sight of the store, Cole reined Joe back and waited for Harley to catch up.

"Where are you headed?" Harley asked.

"I'm goin' to cut back down there by the barn," Cole told him. "That fellow—what was his name, Zeke?—said he was fixin' to go down to the barn to fork some hay. I wanna have a little talk with him."

Harley didn't have to ask why. "I reckon I'll hold the buckskin for you while you have your talk." He figured he wasn't going to be of any help in whatever Cole had in mind, so he had just as soon wait it out.

"That's what I figured," Cole said. "Maybe I won't make you wait as long as last time."

"He don't have to treat me like a damn loafer Injun," Zeke Pritchard muttered to himself as he swung the barn door open and climbed up into the hayloft. He had come upon some hard times lately, and he had tried to explain to Lem that he was just waiting for some of the old regulars to show up. Then he'd join up with them and be working again. But nothing was going to happen until spring. Lem should know that as well as anybody. Then the stage lines would be running and settlers coming. There would be plenty of opportunities for an experienced road agent like himself to come into some money. And he wouldn't have to do chores just for grub.

After tossing a pile of hay down to the two stalls in Lem's barn, Zeke climbed down the ladder. As he stepped off the last rung, he turned to encounter the formidable presence of Cole Bonner. His natural impulse was to try to step back, but the ladder to the hayloft was there to stop him, and he found his nose on a level with the bigger man's chest. "What the hell . . . ?" he exclaimed, and tried to move to the side, only to be grabbed by the collar and held firm.

"Zeke," Cole said, his voice low and threatening, "I'm here to collect on that favor you owe me for that drink of whiskey."

"What favor?" Zeke blurted, quivering with uncertainty.

"Let me explain somethin' to you, Zeke. I've got somethin' I've got to do, and I'm gonna kill any man that stands in my way. Now, all I want from you is just a little piece of information. That's all, but if I don't get it, then I'm gonna be mad as hell, and that ain't gonna be good for anybody I'm mad at. So you think about that when I ask you one simple question."

Uncertainty gave way to full-blown terror as Zeke was struck with the thought that he was in the clutches of a conscienceless killer. "I don't know nothin' about anything, man! I swear to God!"

"It's real simple, Zeke. I ask you one question, you answer it, and I'll be gone. And nobody will know you said anything. Ain't that simple enough?" He tightened up on the frightened man's collar. "But if it turns out that you told me a lie, then I ain't gonna be this friendly when I come back for you." He paused a few moments to let that sink in. "Now, Slade Corbett told Lem where he and his friends were headin' when he left here. Where was it?" Zeke's eyes looked about to pop out as he stared speechless in fright, causing Cole to jerk him up closer to his face. "I'm about to lose my patience with you. It's a simple question."

When Zeke still did not answer, seeming to be rendered mute by a fear of retaliation by Lem Dawson if he did, Cole threw him violently to the stable floor. "That's it," he said. "I'm done with you." He leveled his rifle at the terrified man and cocked it.

"Wait!" Zeke gasped, finally finding his voice. "Crow Creek Crossin'! They said they was goin' to Crow Creek Crossin'!" Cole made no sign of relenting, still holding the Henry on the frightened man. "They said that was a good place to wait out the winter," Zeke pleaded. Cole released the hammer on his rifle, turned away, and started for the door. Realizing that the threat to his life was evidently over, Zeke implored, "You ain't gonna say nothin' to Lem, are you? I answered your question."

"I hope to hell I never see the son of a bitch again," Cole growled as he passed through the barn door.

"Hell, I ain't surprised," Harley said when Cole told him where Slade Corbett and his friends went. "Crow Creek Crossin', huh? They don't call it that no more."

"I know," Cole said. "It's Cheyenne now."

"That's right. I forget," Harley replied. "Like I said, I ain't surprised that bunch went there to winter. They got ever'thin' three outlaws are lookin' for. From what I've heard of that place, the railroad people had to stop when the cold weather set in. They couldn't get up the first big hill west of the crossin', so they quit till spring. Most of the railroad men are still there with no place to go, and every gambler, saloon keeper, whore, outlaw, and drifter in the territory are holed up there, too."

"What you heard is a pretty accurate picture of the town," Cole said. He thought of the first encounter he had had with Slade Corbett and his gang.

"I reckon we didn't have to waste your time askin' Zeke where Corbett went," Harley said. "Shoulda figured that's where he'd head for."

"Maybe so," Cole agreed, although he had to admit he was a little surprised, for the last time Corbett was in Cheyenne, he had fled with a posse on his tail. Cole supposed the fact that the three outlaws were bold enough to return lent credence to the reports that a lawless breed had overrun the town that winter. "But that's where I'm headin' now," Cole continued. "What are you gonna do? Go to that Crow village you started to before you met up with me? It ain't that far from here, is it?"

"No, it ain't far," Harley said. "It's where the Laramie and the North Laramie come together—half a day, maybe more. But to tell you the truth, I'm thinkin' 'bout ridin' on down to Crow Creek Crossin' with you. I ain't been there since they changed it to Cheyenne. I ain't never been to a circus, and I reckon that's about as close as I'll ever get to one."

He didn't express it, but there was also some curiosity about what Cole was going to do when he got there. He had to admit that he felt a fascination about the seldom-smiling man he had joined up with, who professed to have only one purpose in his life. According to what Cole had reluctantly confessed, three of the original six men who had destroyed his world were dead, two by his hand. And he seemed to look no further into the future than the deaths of the remaining three.

Harley considered himself a good judge of men, and Cole Bonner struck him as having been made of good stock. It was a waste of life to dedicate himself to vengeance, especially when the odds might favor those he sought to execute. The thing that bothered him about the young man was his lack of a fear of dying. It was one thing to be fearless and brave, but even for the bold there was a natural desire to survive. He sensed that Cole's loss had been so great that he no longer cared if he lived or died, as long as he could survive long enough to kill those who destroyed his life. Ordinarily Harley would let a man insistent upon committing suicide go his own way, but he felt that Cole Bonner was worth salvaging.

"Course, you might not want no company," Harley finally allowed.

Cole looked at the gnarly little man wearing buckskins, and wondered for a few moments why he would want to tag along with him. This quest was his business alone, and he couldn't understand why Harley would want any part of it. He shrugged after a moment and said, "I don't see any reason why you can't go with me, if that's what you wanna do—as long as you know somebody's gonna end up dead before I'm through. Might not be a good idea to stay close to me."

"I'll cut out if it gets too hot for me," Harley said.

"Fair enough," Cole concluded. "Let's get movin'."

Two and a half days of hard riding brought them to the outer buildings of Cheyenne, some of them still under construction. The street, filled with people, had been churned into a quagmire of snow and mud as horses and wagons plowed up and down past the saloons and shops, general stores and brothels—the toddling town of Cheyenne had them all. Amazed by the growth of the town since he had last been there, Harley sat on his horse, taking in the busy scene on that cold winter day. If ever a town looked like a hot-bed of the wild and wicked, Cheyenne was it. He wondered if he should have elected to ride on up to Medicine Bear's camp, instead of partnering with Cole. He glanced over at the relentless searcher, his face a mask of granite, as he glared at the busy street, looking as if he was peering into every door.

"Whatcha aimin' to do now?" Harley asked.

"I expect we're gonna have to stable our horses first thing," Cole told him. When Harley confessed that he didn't have the money to pay for that luxury, Cole said he didn't expect that he did. "I'll pay for boardin' the horses while we're here. I wanna get Joe and the buckskin some grain and rest 'em up ready to go when I need 'em. I expect you want the same for your horses."

"Well, I reckon," Harley replied, "although my horses ain't used to gettin' grain to eat. And I didn't expect you to pay for me. I figured we'd camp outside town somewhere."

"I need to be in town, and the horses need decent feed for a change." Cole ended the discussion. He nudged Joe with his heels and started down the street toward the stables at the other end.

"Well, I'll be . . . ," Leon Bloodworth started when Cole and Harley led their horses inside the stable. "I wondered if I'd see you back in town again, after the way we treated you the last time." He grinned at Harley. "He had to shoot his way outta the hotel dinin' room, and then Jim Thompson threw him in jail for the night." He turned his attention back to Cole then. "I expect you've been workin' pretty hard on that piece of land you bought up on the Chugwater."

"I see you took to wearin' a gun," Cole said in reply, having no desire to relate the tragic events that had destroyed his life.

"Had to," Bloodworth said. "Had to wear it for my health. It ain't only the railroad crew that's causin' all the trouble. It's the dad-blamed riffraff that follows 'em. I swear, it seems like every road agent and murderer has headed to Cheyenne this winter. What brings you back to town?"

"I'm lookin' for some old friends of mine," Cole said. "I heard they're back in town."

Bloodworth knew right away who Cole was referring to. "They're here, all right—big as life, like they own the town—but if I was you, I believe I'd stay clear of 'em. They ain't nothin' but trouble, and they ain't likely to forget that you shot that feller that was with 'em."

"I woulda thought the sheriff would arrest the three of them as soon as they showed up here," Cole said. He had been expecting to have to figure a way to get to them while they were in jail.

"He mighta, if we had a sheriff. Jim Thompson was gunned down in the middle of the street a few days ago. Funny thing, those fellers you had the fight with showed up the next day. Jim's deputy decided to retire from the law business right after that. Left us in a mess. You interested in the job?"

"Reckon not," Cole replied. "But I am interested in finding those three outlaws."

Bloodworth frowned thoughtfully, realizing that Cole was deadly serious. "Well, that won't be a hard job. They sure as hell ain't makin' theirselves scarce. They've took to hangin' around the Sundown Saloon. You can find one of 'em or all three of 'em there about any time of day."

"What about the vigilance committee you told me about?" Cole asked.

Bloodworth shook his head. "Well, we still aim to take our town back, but we suffered a couple of deaths that slowed us down, and we've got to get our backbones up again. I'll tell you the truth, most of us that rode with that posse weren't all that disappointed that we didn't catch up with 'em." He shook his head slowly. "And now we've got the sons of bitches back in town, actin' like it's their town."

"Well, Harley and I need to put our horses up while we're in town. They've been rode hard for the last couple of days." He paused to take a look around him. "Looks like you're pretty full up. You got room for four more horses?"

"I'll make room for you," Bloodworth said, eyeing the solemn young man intensely. "And if you're thinkin' on gettin' rid of some of that riffraff, I won't charge you nothin'."

"Can't get a better deal than that," Harley spoke up for the first time.

Cole only nodded. "Sundown Saloon, huh?"

"That's right," Bloodworth replied, certain he had correctly read the look in Cole's eyes. But he couldn't help wondering why a young man with a pretty little wife and a fine family would risk standing up to three hardened gunmen like Slade Corbett and his two partners. "Be careful, and good huntin'."

Outside the stable, Harley remarked, "He don't know about what happened to your wife."

"Reckon not," Cole said. It didn't surprise him. The only way anyone in Cheyenne could know would have been from Walter Hodge, John Cochran's friend and neighbor on the Chugwater. Evidently Walter hadn't been into town since the massacre. Cole could easily understand why he had thought it wise to avoid Cheyenne and stay close by his family.

Tom Larsen studied his cards carefully, a pair of jacks and the ten of clubs. He discarded the nine of spades and the six of hearts. "I'll take two," he said, and watched the dealer as he dealt two cards. The dealer moved quickly to the player on Larsen's left, casual in his handling of the deck of cards, too casual in Larsen's opinion. He was convinced the gambler was dealing off the bottom, so his gaze was intense when the gambler dealt himself three cards. *Damn you,* Larsen thought, *you're pretty damn slick. I ain't caught you yet, but I know you're dealing off the bottom of that deck.* The gambler had won too many pots to call it pure luck since they'd started playing two hours before. Slade and

Sanchez were still up in the room at the hotel, sleeping off a drunk from the night just past, but Larsen never allowed himself to drink until incapacitated like his partners. It was that policy that kept his mind and reflexes sharp. And now his instincts told him the gambler was definitely cheating, even if he had not been able to catch his sleight of hand.

Larsen picked up the two cards, a ten of hearts and the deuce of clubs, which gave him two pairs, jacks and tens. He watched the dealer carefully as he opened the bidding. When it came around to him, Larsen called, and frowned sullenly when the dealer spread three sevens on the table. It was all the justification Larsen needed to call him out. "That's the last time I'm gonna let you get away with that bottom deal," he announced stoically.

There was an immediate hush in the crowded saloon as Larsen sat staring into the gambler's eyes, waiting for his response. The other two players at the table backed their chairs away, anticipating the trouble that was sure to follow. A faint smile appeared on Larsen's face, as he recognized the familiar blanching of the gambler's features that betrayed the fear that Larsen's fixed stare created.

"You're wrong, my friend," the gambler protested weakly. "I've just had a streak of good luck."

"You're not only a cheat, but a liar, too," Larsen told him, his tone calm and threatening. "Now, just shove that pile of cash over to the center of the table, and get your no-good ass outta here." The thin smile was still firmly in place as he waited to see if the gambler had the guts to meet his challenge. "A damn poor cheat, to boot," he said, adding fuel to the fire, and giving the man no choice but to fight or slink out in shame.

The gambler hesitated, nervously fidgeting with the cash on the table before him, obviously weighing his chances. All eyes were on him, waiting to see if he would hand over the money and turn tail and run. He knew that Larsen wore a .44 six-shooter in a holster. Seated up close to the table, as Larsen was, the gambler decided it would be too awkward for Larsen to draw it before he could reach the revolver that he wore in a shoulder holster. Although he was still unnerved by the insolent glare in Larsen's eyes, the gambler's common sense told him he had the advantage. Gaining some confidence then, he said, "You're gonna have to back up your words or apologize. Which is it gonna be?"

They made their moves at almost the same time. The gambler had been correct in his estimate of the time it would take for Larsen to make the awkward draw from his chair. He did not allow for the possibility that Larsen had a double-barrel derringer lying in his lap, however, a habit he always employed when playing cards with strangers. Two quick shots under the table ripped into the gambler's gut before he could reach inside his coat. Larsen was immediately on his feet, his .44 now in his hand. He walked around the table and kicked the gambler's chair over, dumping the fatally wounded man on the floor. He stood over him for a moment before reaching down to relieve him of his revolver. Then he looked around the room at the witnesses to the shooting. "He tried to draw on me," he claimed, loud enough for everyone to hear. "Anybody could see that, and he got what he deserved. Anybody see it any different?"

"Yeah, I did."

"Who said that?" Larsen demanded, his brow

furrowed in anger as he turned, scanning the room, searching for the person foolish enough to refute his word. His gaze stopped when it fell upon the tall young man holding a Henry rifle near the door. "Who the hell are you?" he started, but it struck him almost as soon as he said it. "You, you son of a bitch! You shot Frank Cowen!"

"That's right," Cole replied solemnly. "I shot Smiley Dodd, too. And now it's your turn. I'm sendin' you straight to hell for killin' those folks on the Chugwater."

"The hell you are!" Larsen blurted, shocked to think Cole knew about the murders. He raised the weapon already drawn from its holster to silence his accuser. It was almost a draw, but Cole was a fraction of a second faster. His rifle already leveled, he hit Larsen in the middle of his chest, knocking the stunned man backward to land on the table and then slide to the floor. Cole moved quickly to make sure Larsen was dead. He pulled the table aside too late to avoid the pistol aimed at him. Larsen's final effort before fading from consciousness was to pull the trigger, sending a .44 slug into Cole's side.

Staggered, Cole fought to keep his feet, willing himself to confirm the kill. He cranked another round into the chamber and sent the fatal bullet through Larsen's brain.

"Where are the other two?" he demanded of anyone, determined to complete his task, only vaguely aware of Harley, who had rushed to his side to help him stay on his feet.

"They're up in the hotel!" someone shouted in answer.

Defying the bullet wound in his side to stop him,

he pushed toward the door, ignoring Harley's pleading for him to sit down and wait for the doctor. The crowd in the saloon emptied out to follow him into the street, where their numbers increased as bystanders outside ran to see what the shooting was about. In no time at all, a mob of spectators was created, all eager to witness the confrontation.

Young Claude Campbell, who helped his father in the hotel's stables, ran ahead of the mob to tell his father the news. He burst through the door just as Slade and Sanchez came down the stairs. "They shot him!" Claude exclaimed to his father, who was behind the desk. Then seeing Slade and Sanchez, he yelled, "A feller shot that friend of yours, and he's coming after you!"

Sanchez leaped several feet over the stair railing before reaching the bottom step and rushed to the front door. "It's a lynch mob!" he exclaimed, mistaking the intent of the crowd of spectators.

"Vigilantes!" Slade concluded immediately, thinking the townspeople had gotten their vigilance committee together again. "Let's get the hell outta here!" There was no need to repeat it. Slade grabbed a handful of Claude's shirt collar. "Get our horses saddled and bring 'em to the back of the hotel!" Then he bounded up the stairs after Sanchez, who was already at the top, with Arthur Campbell yelling after him that their bill hadn't been paid.

Accustomed to fast exits, the two outlaws were down the back steps in minutes, certain they were only seconds away from a necktie party. In too much a hurry to wait for Claude to bring the horses from the small hotel stable, they ran in and took over the task of saddling up. "Are you sure they shot Tom Larsen?" Slade asked as he worked feverishly to tighten the girth.

"Yes, sir," Claude exclaimed. "Some big stranger. Shot him with a rifle. Then your friend shot him, and he didn't even slow down. He just walked over and shot your friend in the head."

"Damn marshal, I bet," Sanchez blurted. "We got to get the hell outta here."

As soon as they were saddled, they jumped on their horses and galloped out the back into a snow flurry. Had he known it was only one man coming after him, Slade would not have run, especially when the man was already staggered with Larsen's bullet in his side. But he was convinced that a lawman had come to town and had managed to organize the vigilance committee again. And it sounded as though he was not dead set upon merely capturing the three of them. Tom Larsen was one hell of a tough hombre, fast with a gun, and with nerves of steel. If this lawman took Larsen down, he was nobody to take lightly. To run was the only choice Slade and Sanchez had.

Chapter 7

The mob of spectators drew up before the front door of the hotel, all eyes on the grim avenger as he forced himself to remain on his feet, determined to complete the vengeance the dead demanded. Harley Branch stayed at his side, ready to support him if he faltered, knowing all the while that Cole might well be walking to his death. But he also knew that Cole would not listen to reason when he was so close to finishing the task that relentlessly drove him.

Inside the door, Cole stumbled back against the jamb, almost falling, as he desperately scanned the small lobby. Gaping wide-eyed at the wounded man whose blood-soaked shirt could be seen inside his open coat, Arthur Campbell blurted, "They're gone!"

"Where?" Cole forced through a painful grimace.

"They lit out the back when they heard you were coming," young Claude answered.

Cole turned to Harley. "I've gotta get back to the stable to get my horse."

"The hell you are," Harley replied, determined that he was not going to let him kill himself in his desire for revenge. "You can't even stand up on your own, and you're still losin' blood. You're goin' to the doctor."

"Take him to my room." Harley looked toward the dining room door to see Mary Lou standing there.

"No," Cole replied. "I can't do that. I'll lose 'em."

"You've already lost them," Mary Lou said. "Your friend is right, you can't even stand up on your own."

Taking charge of the situation, she told Claude, "Go fetch Doc Marion. Bring him to my room." Turning back to Harley then, she said, "Come on, my room's behind the kitchen."

She slid up under Cole's arm and she and Harley walked the protesting man down the hall to the back door. By the time they arrived at the small wing behind the kitchen that housed a couple of rooms for Mary Lou and Maggie Whitehouse, Cole was out on his feet and supported almost entirely by Mary Lou and Harley. He could make no further protest, and dropped exhausted on the bed when they tried to lower him gently.

"He's heavier than he looks," Mary Lou remarked, then went to a cupboard and pulled an old blanket out. "Here," she told Harley, "roll him over on his side so I can get this blanket under him. He's gonna bleed all over my good spread."

When they settled him on his back again, she decided that wouldn't do. "Let's sit him up and get his coat off him. The doctor ain't gonna be able to treat him like that."

When that was accomplished, she told Harley to build a fire in the stove while she pulled Cole's boots off. "Might as well get him outta that shirt, too," she said. "It's soaked through his underwear."

By the time they were able to remove all of his blood-soaked clothes, so the ugly wound could be fully exposed, she and Harley had stripped him down to his socks. She got a clean cloth and pressed it on the wound, which was still bleeding when Dr. Frederick Marion arrived and took over. Not especially noted for a sense of humor, Doc Marion was not pleased to have been summoned in the middle of his dinner.

"Damn fool gunmen," he grumbled, "they don't ever learn that they're not children playing with guns." He paused to ask Mary Lou, "How's that shoulder of yours coming along?"

"Fine and dandy," she replied, and rotated her shoulder to demonstrate her recovery.

He took the cloth from her and examined Cole's wound. She stepped back out of his way to let him work.

"It looks pretty bad, doesn't it?" Mary Lou said to Harley. Harley just shook his head, concerned. "I guess you, or someone, needs to ride up to tell his wife what happened. I expect she'll want to be with him." Before Harley could reply, she added, "Better tell her we tried to hold a blanket over him when we took his underwear off."

She grinned mischievously.

"I don't reckon she'll care much," Harley said. He then told her what had happened to Cole's wife, her sister and her sister's husband, and their children. "That's the reason he came here lookin' for Slade Corbett and the other two. There was six of 'em to start with. Cole got Tom Larsen today, so there ain't but two of 'em left now, and he ain't gonna stop till he gets ever' last one of 'em." He paused to look at the unconscious man. "Or they get him."

"My God," Mary Lou gasped, stunned by the horrible news. With no words to express her shock, she simply repeated, "My God."

Overhearing the conversation between Mary Lou and Harley, Doc Marion softened his opinion of his patient. "I'll do what I can for him," he told them, "but he's tore up pretty bad. I'd say just leave the bullet in him, but I'm afraid it's gonna cause him a lot of trouble if it moves around in there. So I'm gonna try to dig it out of him, and he's gonna be in poor condition for a good while, depending on how strong a constitution he has. What I need to know now is how long he can stay here, or if he's got to be moved somewhere else."

"I don't know where else to take him," Harley said.

"He can stay right where he is," Mary Lou volunteered. "There's no need to move him, so you go right ahead and do your work on him, Doc. I've got a perfectly good sofa that'll do for me."

"You sure about that?" Doc asked.

"You bet. He's a decent man, and it sounds like he deserves a chance to get well. I'll just go talk to Maggie to see if I've lost my job, and then I'll be back to give you any help I can."

As Doc Marion had predicted, the work was long and tedious, going well past suppertime. Maggie had dropped by later in the afternoon to bring in a pot of coffee from the hotel kitchen and to tell Mary Lou that she could handle the supper crowd without her for one night. Doc appreciated it, because Mary Lou was helping a great deal to assist him. Harley could do little beyond keeping the fire going in the stove so they wouldn't freeze to death. Doc was able to remove the bullet, but his biggest problem was to stop the bleeding. When he had stopped all he could, he sewed up the resulting incision and pronounced the patient now in the hands of God.

"I'm gonna leave you a bottle of laudanum," he told Mary Lou. "When he wakes up—if he wakes up—give him a slug of it. He's gonna be in a lot of pain, so let him have it anytime he wants it."

Maggie and her cook came in just as the doctor was preparing to leave. They were each carrying a tray of food, the leftovers from supper. "Thought you folks might be hungry," she said. "I know you missed supper. How's the patient? Is he gonna make it?"

"We'll have to wait and see," Doc said while looking over the plates of food on the trays.

"Does that include me?" Harley asked. "It sure smells good."

"Of course it includes you," Maggie told him. "Help yourself. There's plenty."

Doc sat down at Mary Lou's tiny table and attacked the beef stew and soup beans with an unusual amount of gusto, worthy of admiration by the cooks. "I love to see a man who appreciates my cooking," Maggie said as she watched him reach for another biscuit.

"My compliments, madam," Doc said gallantly when he had finished drowning the last biscuit with his coffee and got up to leave. "I've been fortunate in a marriage that's lasted twenty years as of this past summer. Mrs. Marion is a lovely companion, but unfortunately, cooking is not one of her strongest qualities, and she can't bake a biscuit fit for a dog." He looked up quickly. "I wouldn't want my words to get back to her, dear woman that she is. And if I can depend upon you ladies to never repeat what I just said, then I'll consider that fine supper as payment of my fee for this operation."

Maggie's eyes opened wide with astonishment, but Mary Lou threw her head back and laughed heartily. "Your words are safe with us," she said. "We'll take 'em to the grave." She closed the door behind him and turned to look at the man stretched out on her bed. It struck her then that the doctor's humorous departure was rather macabre, considering the young man's feeble hold on his life. She stood over him, watching his painful battle, evident even while he slept, and it struck her that he would probably not make it through the night.

"It's a damn shame," she muttered.

"What is?" Maggie asked.

"Nothing," Mary Lou answered. "Here, I'll help you with those dishes."

When they started out the door, Harley asked Mary Lou, "Is it all right if I stay here?"

"Yeah, it's all right," she said. "We'll make it for one night. If he pulls through tonight, I'll most likely let you men have my room and I'll move in with Maggie. I'll stay with you tonight in case he needs something during the night."

"Much obliged, ma'am," Harley said. "I'll keep an eye on him till you get back. Then I reckon I'd best go down to the stables and get our saddlebags."

Mary Lou and Maggie picked up the rest of the dishes and took them to the kitchen. "Sitting by his bed like a faithful old hound dog," Mary Lou commented, referring to Harley.

"I guess they've been riding together for a long time," Maggie said. "Maybe they're kin."

"Maybe, but the old fellow wasn't with him when he hit town the first time."

The subject of their speculation was at that moment questioning the reason he was standing by Cole so faithfully.

I oughta be in ol' Medicine Bear's village right now, he thought. *Maybe sitting by the fire in Yellow Calf's lodge, eating his wife's pemmican.* He surprised himself with his interest in the young man's welfare. Cole had been dealt a tough hand to play, and it just seemed a shame for him to have to deal with it all by himself.

I reckon I'm just getting soft in the heart in my old age, he thought.

The patient was alive the next morning, but he appeared to be in no better condition than the night before. The only noticeable difference, as far as he was concerned, was the awareness of the considerable pain inside him. He was also aware of the people around him and the helplessness his wound had caused him.

When consciousness first came that morning, he had attempted to get up from the bed, only to fall back with the pain that resulted. He rolled his head to the side on the pillow to see Harley asleep in his bedroll on the floor. Near the window, he saw Mary Lou, bundled in a blanket on the sofa. It struck him then that while they all slept, Slade Corbett and Sanchez were getting farther and farther away. The thought was enough to cause him to make a greater effort to get up from the bed, thinking that once on his feet, he would be able to remain upright.

Gritting his teeth, he braced himself to muster all the force he could put behind him. He succeeded in getting his feet planted on the floor, only to feel his knees give way and land him crumpled up on his side on the cold wooden floor.

"You damn fool!" Harley exclaimed, having been awakened by the crash of Cole's considerable bulk on the hard floor. "You tryin' to bust up ever'thin' the doctor fixed inside you?" He scrambled up to come to Cole's aid, with help from Mary Lou, who was also roused from a sound sleep by Cole's attempt to get up.

"Are you gonna be a problem patient for me?" Mary Lou scolded as she and Harley helped him back on the bed.

"I can't lie around here on your bed," Cole protested.

"Well, you sure as hell aren't in any shape to go anywhere," Mary Lou said. "I don't know why you think you can get on a horse when you can't even stand up." She stepped back and gave him a stern look, hands on her hips. "You're just gonna have to realize that you've got to give yourself time to heal. Otherwise, you might as well just shoot yourself and get it over with."

Harley nodded in agreement. "She's pretty much tellin' you like it is," he said. "You've got to let yourself heal."

After his attempt to get out of bed, Cole could not convince himself that they were wrong. It was not easy to accept. Slade Corbett and Sanchez were escaping him again, running free to God knows where. He thought of Ann, and the way he had found her body, naked and burned, and he closed his eyes tightly, trying to rid his mind of the picture. But it would not go away. In fact, it was never very far from his conscious mind. He apologized to her silently for the thousandth time, and renewed his vow to track down every last one who violated her and took her from him.

Mary Lou stood near the bed, looking down at the suffering man, his tightly closed eyelids quivering with the troubling thoughts racing through his brain. She looked at his tightly clenched fists, and decided that he was fighting a terrible battle in his mind. She whispered to Harley, who was standing by her, "It must have been pretty bad, finding his wife and the others the way he did."

"Yessum," Harley whispered in reply, "I expect it was."

"Were you with him when he found her?"

"No, ma'am. I hadn't even met up with him till after that happened."

His answer surprised her. He seemed so much the devoted companion that, like Maggie, she had assumed their association had been one of many years. Returning her gaze to the wounded man, she wished that she could do something to ease his mind and let him rest peacefully. She reached down to gently lay her hand upon his brow, but the touch of it caused a violent reaction. His body became immediately tense and his eyes jerked open to glare at her defiantly. It was just for a moment and then his gaze softened when he realized where he was. She was struck by the man she saw in that brief moment, however. She remembered the easygoing young man who had shown concern for her treatment at the hands of Slade Corbett that night in the dining room. He had been ready to gallantly come to her aid. The man she just saw in this brief second was not the same man. The original had been replaced by a cold executioner. It was a tragic transformation.

"Easy, Cole," she said softly, and placed her hand back on his forehead. She glanced at Harley and said, "He's got a fever. Doc said he might have. I'll get some water and a cloth and see if I can't cool him off a little. Doc said he'd come by to check on him when he got a chance this morning."

Mary Lou took an extra day from her duties in the dining room to look after her patient. After that, Cole appeared to be making some progress, so she moved into Maggie's room and returned to the dining room, leaving Harley to act as Cole's nurse with her frequent visits to check on him. It would be several days before Cole was strong enough to make the short journey to the outhouse behind the hotel—an accomplishment most appreciated by Harley, who had had the dubious responsibility of emptying the chamber pot. It was progress for the patient, however, enough to make him anxious to vacate Mary Lou's room, in spite of her assurance that she was in no hurry to evict him.

To the relief of both Mary Lou and Harley, Cole no longer pressed to resume his hunt for the two murderers. More than anyone, he was aware of his weakness in recovery, and he was no longer prone to overestimate his ability to ignore his wound. The result of these circumstances left him in a state of morbid suspension, frustrated by his weakened condition, yet anxious to pick up a trail now as cold as the wintry plains he could see from Mary Lou's window.

Although his recovery seemed painfully slow to him, Doc Marion was satisfied that his patient was improving rapidly, and confessed that he had harbored some doubts because of the seriousness of the wound. He attributed it to the patient's strong constitution. Harley was inclined to believe that Cole's refusal to die before his wife's death was avenged had as much to do with his recovery as his constitution.

"Can you ride?" Harley asked when Cole told him that it was time they vacated Mary Lou's room.

"I reckon so," Cole answered. "I ain't too strong yet, but I think I can stay in the saddle till we find us a place to camp." He had offered to pay for his and Harley's room and board, but she had refused it.

She told him that he had better keep what money he had, knowing that he was going to need every cent of it, since he had no apparent means of acquiring more. "It's no hardship on me," she said. "And as far as your food is concerned, I've been feeding you and Harley on leftovers from the hotel kitchen."

Harley had enjoyed the stay in the warm room behind the kitchen, but he could see that Cole was serious about leaving. "Where are you thinkin' about goin'?" he asked. "It's a bad time of year to build a winter camp, especially when one of us is likely gonna be doin' all the work."

"I see what you mean," Cole said. He hesitated for a few moments. He owed Harley a lot. The little man had chosen to stand by him when he could have gone his own way at any time. "Maybe you figure you've done all you can to help me," he finally said. "If you're wantin' to get on with whatever you were plannin' to do before we hooked up, I figure I owe you some money for your time."

Harley merely shook his head slowly, as if perplexed by the offer of money. "You don't owe me any money. I've got a better idea. Why don't we just ride on up to Medicine Bear's village on the Laramie? I've got friends in that camp, and we can winter there. If you get your strength back, and wanna leave before spring, that's up to you. But right now that's the best thing to do, instead of freezin' our asses off holed up somewhere on this open prairie."

Cole thought it over for no more than a few moments before agreeing. "You're right. I expect we'd better tell Mary Lou she can move back in her room," he said.

"Hot damn," Harley exclaimed. "Now you're talkin' sense. We've hung around this damn town long enough." He had enjoyed the use of the warm room, but it was just as cozy in Yellow Calf's tipi.

Mary Lou had mixed emotions upon receiving the news that her patient was leaving. She had become comfortable having him around, although he never seemed to relax his somber attitude, never smiling, his thoughts never far from the tragedy that tormented him. When completely honest with herself, she had to admit that she would miss him.

Hell, she thought, *I'll even miss his ol' hound dog, Harley.*

Cole knew she would refuse payment for his care, as she had the room and board, so he left fifty dollars on a shelf in her cupboard. He was certain she deserved more than that, but fifty dollars was a substantial chunk of the money he had left. So it was generous in that respect. Their saddlebags packed, Cole and Harley went by the dining room to tell the two women they were leaving.

"You know you don't have to go, don't you?" Mary Lou asked earnestly. "You can stay till spring if you want to."

"I owe you too much as it is," Cole said. "I don't wanna put you out any further. I just hope you know how much I appreciate you takin' care of me."

"You sure you're well enough to go?" she asked, realizing at that moment just how much she really was going to miss him, although hard-pressed to understand why. Maybe, she thought, it was simply having a man around, even one that required so much care.

"Yes, I'm sure," he replied.

"Cole." She looked into his eyes earnestly. "It's time to forget about taking your revenge on that murdering trash. If you don't, you're just gonna drive yourself crazy. Ann wouldn't want you to do that. You've already settled the debt. Let the other two find their own way to hell. That's where they're gonna end up sooner or later, without you to personally send them." He patiently heard her out, but his stoic countenance told her that she was just wasting words. "Well," she finally relented, "you're gonna do what you're gonna do." Then on impulse, she stepped up and kissed him on the cheek. "Take care of him, Harley," she said to the grinning stump of a man behind him.

"Yes, ma'am," Harley responded.

* * *

While Cole and Harley rode north out of Cheyenne, the two outlaws who had fled the town were some forty-five miles south in Colorado Territory. Slade Corbett and Jose Sanchez sat beside the stove in a log cabin high up in the foothills of the Front Range of the Rocky Mountains. Another cabin had been built beside the one they occupied, empty now, which was not unusual at this time of the year when the mountain passes were closed by the snow. Constructed over several years' time by fugitives from justice as a place to hide out from the law, it had become known as Rat's Nest.

Like Lem Dawson's Buzzard's Roost in the Laramie Mountains, Rat's Nest was well known among road agents, stage robbers, train robbers, and other men of low character on the run from the law. High up in the hills, on the Cache La Poudre River, it was never visited by honest men, even if they knew of its existence.

At this time, in the dead of winter, there were no other outlaws hiding out in Rat's Nest. It was hard to find, and easy to defend. In order to reach it, a person had to follow a series of old game trails that followed the river up through rocky gorges where the Cache La Poudre formed dangerous rapids in its hurry to reach the valley below. To reach the clearing where the cabins stood, a person had to pass between the walls of a rock passage, wide enough for only one horse at a time. Because of this, the part-time residents of Rat's Nest felt safe from the long arm of the law, but at this time of the year, it could also seem like a prison of sorts.

"Helluva note," Slade complained. "There's a lot of

places I druther spend the winter than this damn mountain."

He looked at Sanchez, calmly sharpening his knife on a whetstone, and he wasn't sure he could pass the entire winter with no company but Sanchez. It had not been an issue when the other men were around.

I might end up shooting the bastard before spring gets here, he thought.

"We're gonna have to go down the river to Fort Collins to get more supplies, before a real storm closes us in up here," he told Sanchez. "There ain't a damn thing left to eat after we finish up the coffee and bacon."

Still brooding, Slade had been unable to get over the fact that a lawman had somehow found them in Cheyenne, and Sanchez was tired of talking about it. As far as he was concerned, the marshal found them, and killed Tom Larsen, but the two of them got away, so the one who did not was just unlucky.

"Well, we gotta go down to Fort Collins tomorrow and get supplies," Slade told him. "Before you drink up all the coffee we got left," he added.

The remark brought forth nothing more than a smirk and a shrug from Sanchez.

"Afternoon, fellows," a thin clerk with a shock of black hair and a matching mustache offered when Slade and Sanchez walked into the small store north of the town of Fort Collins. "Kinda bad day to be travelin', ain't it?"

"That's a fact," Slade replied, "but there ain't a helluva lot a man can do about the weather, is there?"

The clerk laughed. "Can't argue with that. What can I do for you boys?"

Slade called off a list of supplies that they needed while Sanchez walked back to the door and stared at a building about fifty yards down the road. There were several horses tied to the rail in front of it.

"What's that place down yonder?" he asked the clerk. "Is that a saloon?"

"Sure is," the clerk said. "Clyde Simpson's place. He just ain't put a sign up yet."

"Maybe we'll go down there and give him a little business," Sanchez said. "Whaddaya say, Slade?"

"Sounds like a good idea to me," Slade replied. "I could use a little drink to warm my insides."

"You fellows are new in town, ain'tcha? Leastways, you ain't ever been in here before."

At once leery of anyone asking questions, Slade quickly said, "We're just passin' through." He wasn't sure if any of the townsfolk knew about the existence of Rat's Nest. "We've been doin' a little prospectin', got us a little camp back up in the mountains."

"I expect you'll be payin' with dust," the clerk said, moving over to a pair of scales on the counter.

"Cash money," Slade said. The clerk seemed surprised, and made no comment, but he would have bet that the two had never stuck a shovel in the ground. When he glanced up to meet Slade's deadly cold gaze, he decided it best not to ask any more questions. "Thank you, gentlemen. 'Preciate your business."

Outside, they secured their supplies on the horses, then led them down to the saloon and tied them to the corner post of the porch, next to the hitching rail. From habit, they both took a few moments to look over the horses already tied at the rail, checking not only the quality of the horses, but also the saddles. One of the identifying points of a U.S. marshal was the fine horse he usually rode. The horses they saw there were merely ordinary, some pretty good mounts, others poor to fair. One of them looked to have been ridden long and hard, but nothing about the saddle rig caused them to think it could belong to a lawman. Even so, Slade paused in the door to look the room over before walking in.

"Welcome, men. What'll it be?" The bartender, a heavyset man with beefy arms and a close-cropped beard, stood awaiting their pleasure.

"Somethin' that ain't been watered down," Slade replied. "Rye, if you got it."

There was a group of four men standing at the end of the bar. Their loud discussion was difficult not to hear, and Slade's attention was captured at once by a tall, thin man who was doing most of the talking. Slade didn't wait for his drink to be poured. Instead he moved down the bar to join the conversation. The thin man paused to look Slade over before deciding it best to be neighborly.

"Howdy," he said.

"Howdy," Slade said. "Go on with what you was sayin'."

"I was just tellin' these fellers about a shootin' up in Cheyenne," the thin man said.

"Me and my partner was in Cheyenne not too long ago," Slade told him. "Who got shot?"

Aware now of the topic of conversation, Sanchez picked up the shot glasses and moved down to listen in on the discussion. He handed Slade his drink and leaned on the bar, waiting for the man to continue.

Recognizing a potential for violence in the faces of the two strangers, the man narrating the story hesitated for a moment before deciding they were just interested because they had just come from Cheyenne.

"Well, like I was tellin' these fellers, there was a shootin' in the saloon over a card game, and a couple of men got shot. One of 'em said the feller settin' across the table from him was dealin' off the bottom. The other feller called him on it and went for his gun. But the one that said he was cheatin' cut him down with a derringer he was holdin' in his lap."

So that's what started it, Slade thought, knowing that it sounded like Tom Larsen's style.

"You said there were two men shot," he said. "Who shot the other one?"

"Some jasper who just walked in the door, went over to the table, and shot that other feller twice, once in the chest and once in the head."

"Just walked in and shot him?" Slade asked. "Didn't say nothin' to him, just shot him?"

"Well, he did say somethin' to him, but I couldn't hear what it was. The other feller looked like he knew him. He yelled somethin' at him, but I didn't understand what he said. He got off a shot, hit that stranger in the side, but it didn't even slow him down."

"Was he a lawman?" Slade asked. "Was he wearin' a badge?"

"Nah, he weren't no lawman. I reckon he just had somethin' to settle with that feller." He paused then, recalling the rest of the incident. "And that ain't all. With blood runnin' out of a hole in his side, he walked out of the saloon and started toward the hotel, looking to settle somebody else's hash. Damn nigh the whole town went with him, just to see the show. I was in the crowd, too, but whoever he was lookin' for had already took off." He paused to chuckle. "Good thing, I reckon, 'cause he was sure in a killin' mood."

Slade was stunned as he realized what he had just heard. He turned to meet Sanchez's eyes, and saw that he was struck with the same realization. There was no lawman, and there was no vigilante posse. They had run from one man—one wounded man at that! The thought of it was enough to infuriate him. He picked up his empty glass and moved back down the bar, away from the group of men. When Sanchez joined him, he said, "I'm goin' back to Cheyenne to kill that son of a bitch." He banged his glass on the bar and motioned for the bartender to fill it. He tossed it down his throat as soon as it was filled, the burn of his fury overpowering the sting of the alcohol.

Sanchez was more chagrined than furious. As far as he was concerned, the killing of Tom Larsen was no great loss to him. He didn't like him anyway.

"To hell with him," he said. "It ain't worth the ride back up there to get him." He took another drink, then asked, "Who the hell is he, anyway?" There could be a hell of a lot of people who had a reason to come after them, but this one sounded like a crazy man. It was best to avoid crazy people; they were too unpredictable.

"I don't know," Slade answered, knowing they had not left any witnesses to their crimes. He cast an accusing glance at Sanchez, thinking that he might have talked carelessly in a saloon. Sanchez was prone to boast about his exploits.

"Maybe somebody let their whiskey do the talkin'."

Aware that it was an accusation, Sanchez replied,

"Maybe. Maybe it was you that talked too much." It didn't occur to either man that the silent witness who testified to the massacre of the family on the Chugwater was the body of Skinner Roche.

"The hell you say," Slade retorted. "You know better'n that." He looked Sanchez straight in the eye for a long moment, as if daring him to disagree. "I'm goin' back to Cheyenne," he repeated. "There ain't no one man who can run me outta town."

Sanchez shrugged, still not as incensed over the incident as his partner. "If we ain't gonna stay here in that hole up on the mountain, why don't we just go on out to Ogallala or down to Texas to wait out this winter?"

"And have that son of a bitch keep doggin' our trail? I don't know how he knew we were in Cheyenne. That mouthy kid in the saloon said he was a stranger. And I don't know why he's after us, but I'll know I don't have to worry about him after I put a bullet in his brain. So you go to Ogallala, or Texas, or any other place you're of a mind to. I'm goin' to Cheyenne to kill that son of a bitch."

Sanchez thought it over for a few moments before deciding. "What the hell?" he finally said. "Cheyenne's a helluva lot closer than Ogallala—might as well go there as any place." He shrugged again. "It's a helluva lot better place to spend the winter than here. We don't even have to ride back up that damn slippery little trail to the cabin," he said.

Sanchez was right. They had all their possessions with them on their horses, plus the supplies they had just bought, so they set out on a trail to the north as soon as they finished their whiskey.

Chapter 8

It was a long three days in the saddle, but Cole managed to gut it out, even though the ride resulted in causing some bleeding from the wound in his side. The trip was made no easier by the winter storm that swept across the Wyoming prairie, bringing blinding snow at times. They pushed on in spite of it, relying upon Harley's unusual sense of direction. Although he would never admit it to Harley, Cole thought he might regret the decision to leave the comfort of Mary Lou's room behind the hotel kitchen. Feed for their horses was of major concern, owing to the heavy covering of snow, so a good portion of their time in camp was spent in peeling the bark from cottonwood branches to feed them. This was when they were lucky enough to find a creek or stream bordered by the trees.

The bulk of the camp-keeping was performed by Harley, a chore he seemed to do cheerfully, most of the time quietly singing some little song to himself. He seemed to know only a few lines of any song, for Cole never heard him sing one from start to finish. And with a voice low and raspy, he could be mistaken for a man in pain. There was very little that Cole could do to help with the chores of making camp. Still extremely weak, he did the best he could, but the cold seemed to freeze the recovery of his wound. Harley was satisfied with just Cole's ability to remain in the saddle all day. At night by the fire, Cole would question Harley regarding the reception they might receive at the Crow village.

"How do you know they'll take both of us in?"

The question caused Harley to grin confidently. "Because they're my friends. I've been winterin' with them Crows for more'n six years, and a friend of mine is a friend of theirs. You'll see."

Harley's predictions turned out to be factual, for the entire village came forth to greet the gnarly little man upon their arrival at the camp near the banks of the Laramie River. Nestled in a wide turn of the river about a mile west of the confluence with the North Laramie, the village was protected from the wintry winds by a thick border of cottonwoods.

As Harley had promised, Cole was received cordially, and he and Harley were welcomed into Yellow Calf's lodge. His wife, Moon Shadow, made him a bed of blankets, and Yellow Calf sent for the medicine man to take a look at Cole's wound.

After Cole was put to bed, Yellow Calf said, "We must have a dance to welcome our friend, Thunder Mouse, back to our village," referring to Harley by the name the Crow had given him.

It was a name given partially in jest, because of Harley's small stature contrasted with his bold voice, but it was an affectionate label, for he was held in high esteem by the Crow village.

Walking Owl unwrapped the bandage Mary Lou had tied around Cole's body and examined the healing wound in his side. Making comments as he looked at the stitches left by Doc Marion, he nodded as if he approved. Cole did not protest, although he had little faith in the medicine man's expertise. He didn't understand Walking Owl's comments, since they were in the Crow tongue, even though Harley, who was standing by, told him everything was all right. He figured it would be an insult to decline the medicine man's help. Harley told him that Walking Owl possessed special spiritual powers. The Crow word for it was *maxpé*, Harley told him, and he was more than a simple doctor.

Exhausted by the ride from Cheyenne, he really didn't care what they did to him as long as they let him sleep. So when Walking Owl left to make up a poultice, Cole barely noticed. When he returned to place it over the wound and rewrapped the bandage, Cole was fast asleep.

When the medicine man left, Yellow Calf came back in and stood watching the sleeping white man for a few moments before speaking to Harley.

"Walking Owl said your friend is strong. He will soon be well."

"His body is strong," Harley said, speaking in the Crow tongue. "I worry about his head." He then related the circumstances that led to Cole's wound. "His mind is sick with revenge against those who killed his wife. I fear he will try to go back on the warpath before his body is ready."

Yellow Calf understood then why Harley worried

about his friend. "A man must do what his medicine tells him to do. You say he has killed all but two of the men who murdered his people. I think he must be a powerful warrior. If his medicine is strong, he will do what is right for him. You and I are too old to tell the young warriors what they should do. They do not listen anyway. Let us sit by the fire and smoke the pipe, eat the fresh-killed deer meat, and drink the coffee you got at Fort Laramie."

"As always," Harley said, "you speak with the wisdom of your years."

He respected Yellow Calf's words, but he was not inclined to sit by the fire while Cole pushed himself to seek out Slade Corbett before he was fully healed and back to strength. He wished that there was some way he could persuade Cole to consider his debt paid and let his mind heal as well as his body.

Things would be a whole lot easier if I hadn't taken such a strong liking to that boy, he told himself.

Cole slept through the night, oblivious of the celebratory feast held to welcome Harley back to the village. He awoke the next morning in the predawn hours, before the sun rose above the eastern plains. Feeling stronger than he had in the days preceding his arrival in the Crow village, he lay there in his blankets for a while listening for sounds that would tell him someone else was awake. He turned his head to see if there was any sign of life from Harley, but the little man was deep in sleep, his breathing heavy and noisy. Looking toward the opposite side of the tipi, he saw Yellow Calf and Moon Shadow bundled together, also fast asleep.

He lay there a little longer before deciding he would do something about the nagging reminder that it had been a while since he had answered nature's call. He felt a sharp pain in his side when he sat up, much like a knife piercing his insides, but when he paused to examine his bandage, there was no sign of bleeding. Rolling over on his knees, he pushed himself up on his feet, trying not to disturb the others still sleeping.

Once on his feet, he experienced a few seconds of dizziness, but his brain soon righted itself so that he was steady again. Confident then that he wouldn't stumble over anybody, he wrapped the blanket around his shoulders and walked carefully toward the entry flap.

Outside the tipi, he looked around him at the sleeping village—a great circle of lodges seated on the snow-covered ground, churned with the many tracks of people and horses. Near the center of the village, the smoldering remains of a great campfire could be seen, dying evidence of the celebration of the night before. Farther down the river, beyond the village, the horse herd pawed in the snow to get to the grass beneath. Joe and the buckskin were among the Indian ponies there. It was a peaceful sight, and for a brief moment, he was unaware of the bitterness in his heart. But it soon returned to remind him that he had not succeeded in righting the monstrous wrong that had been done to those he held dear. He walked toward the cottonwoods bordering the river, seeking privacy, even though there was no one about who might see him.

Since it appeared that he was the only person awake in the camp, he stopped to relieve himself as soon as he reached the outer trees. When he had finished, he considered the dull throbbing he now felt in his wound, thinking it was more aptly described as discomfort than outright pain. He was satisfied that he was rapidly healing and would soon be ready to ride again. Pulling his blanket up tighter around his shoulders, he walked over to the bank of the river and stood gazing at the dark body of water, gently moving past him in the misty morning light. He heard the faint splashing of a fish or a muskrat under the dark bank. Feeling slightly dizzy again, he brushed the snow from a dead log and sat down to await the sunrise.

As he sat there, he was suddenly aware of a pair of dark eyes peering at him from the solid white of the snow-covered bluff on the opposite side of the river. Startled, he stared back at the eyes, astonished when they moved and the white mass began to take shape, separating itself from the veil of white snow. As it moved closer to the water's edge, its entire form became distinct. It was a large wolf, its fur solid white. Suddenly it struck, snatching some prey from the edge of the river. Cole was not sure what it was, perhaps a muskrat or some other varmint. He had not even seen it there. The white wolf paused to look back at the man, staring at him for a few moments before scrambling back up the bank, his prey locked in his powerful jaws, and disappearing into the whiteness of the predawn.

In the next instant he was aware of the bright rays of the sun stealing across the snowy prairie, its light glistening silver and gold as it announced another day. Cole suddenly realized that he had been asleep before the sun's rays awakened him, but for how long? He got to his feet and stared across the river at the opposite bank for signs of the kill he had witnessed.

Was there really a white wolf? Or had he dreamed the whole thing? Was there any such thing as a totally white wolf? He had never seen one. He would have liked to cross the river to look more closely for sign of the encounter, but there was no way to cross without getting wet. He would have to wait until later and cross on horseback.

Aware now of sounds of the village awakening, he turned away from the river, still not sure if he had actually seen what he thought he had.

It had to have been a dream, he thought, but it had seemed so real, and he had no idea that he had fallen asleep.

He had been wide-awake before that. Maybe he was feverish again and was hallucinating. He placed his hand on his forehead as if feeling for a fever. His forehead was cold. The whole episode was troubling, and he paused and turned to look back at the river-bank, to make sure he could find the exact spot again.

When he got back to the tipi, he met Moon Shadow on her way out to attend to her morning needs. "I come back," she said. "I cook food."

"Yes, ma'am," Cole said. "Thank you, ma'am."

She paused to give him a closer look. "Good," she said. "Get strong. Walk good." She then hurried off to the privacy of the trees.

"I was startin' to wonder if somethin' grabbed you," Harley said, still sitting in his blanket. "You was gone a long time." Like Moon Shadow, he scrutinized Cole closely. "You look like you're feelin' some better."

"Yeah, I think I am," Cole said. "At least I'm pretty sure I ain't gonna die right away." Yellow Calf turned to look at him as well. He had been feeding sticks into the fire to rekindle the small flame struggling to survive. He nodded his agreement.

"I'm damn glad we've got some coffee in our packs," Harley said. "Moon Shadow said they ain't had none in quite a while. Let's get that little coffeepot of your'n out and get some started. I swear I don't believe I can get goin' this mornin' without no coffee."

"I expect we oughta share what we've got with Moon Shadow," Cole said. "We ain't got a helluva lot, but I've still got some money. If we can get to a tradin' post somewhere, I'll buy some more. Oughta give 'em somethin' for takin' care of me."

"Closest place is Fort Laramie," Harley said. "If you look as much better tomorrow as you do this mornin', maybe we can take a little ride over there in a few days." He got up from his bed then. "Moon Shadow's gonna build a fire outside to cook on, but I'll take that coffeepot and fill it at the river. I gotta go pee anyway." He grinned as Cole handed him the pot. "I'll try to remember which vessel I'm emptyin' and which one I'm fillin' up so I don't get 'em mixed up and make the coffee too strong to drink." He was still laughing at his joke as he went out the entrance.

Cole's coffeepot was refilled two more times before the four of them had enough to go with the pemmican Moon Shadow prepared. As the three men sat by the fire finishing their coffee, Cole couldn't help thinking about the strange dream he had had by the river.

"I think I'll saddle Joe and take a little ride across the river," he said.

"What for?" Harley asked, thinking his young

friend might be asking too much of his body too soon. "What's over there you wanna see?"

"I'm just curious about something," Cole said. "Besides, I don't wanna let Joe get too lazy."

"Hell, he ain't been with the rest of the ponies but a day," Harley said. "He don't need no exercise, and neither do you. You'd better let that wound heal, boy."

"You're gettin' like an old mother hen," Cole said, getting slightly irritated by Harley's questions. "I just, by God, wanna ride across the river. That's as far as I'm goin'. All right?" His tone must have been a little sharper than he intended, for Harley's heavy eyebrows suddenly drooped as if his feelings had been hurt. Cole quickly tried to repair the damage. "I just don't wanna get to lyin' around too much—figure it's better to be on my feet." Harley looked at him as if he were talking out of his head. "You ever see a white wolf?" Cole suddenly blurted. He knew as soon as it came out of his mouth, he was going to have to explain.

Harley didn't react as Cole expected. Instead he fixed a steady gaze upon his young friend and replied, "No, I ain't never seen one, but that don't mean there ain't any. Why did you ask me that?"

"What the hell?" Cole said, and gave in to Harley's curiosity. "You'll probably think I'm loco." He went on to tell Harley about his strange dream experience that morning. "I know I was just dreamin', but it was so real and I'm gonna have to go over to that bluff on the other side to see for myself."

"Solid white, huh?" Harley asked. "That'd be somethin', all right. Hell, I'll help you saddle up and go with you."

* * *

"You sure this is the spot?" Harley asked as he and Cole searched the bluff.

"Yep, I'm sure," Cole said. "Right below this tree with the dead limb hangin' just off the ground." He stood there staring at the open space down to the water's edge.

"Well, there ain't no tracks here now, 'cept mine and your'n," Harley said. "Reckon you're right. You were dreamin'."

When they returned to the village, Walking Owl was sitting by the fire, talking to Yellow Calf. Having overheard Cole and Harley's conversation earlier, Yellow Calf had repeated it to the medicine man. He looked up at Cole and said, "It is not my place to tell you what to do, but I heard you telling Thunder Mouse about your dream. I thought it might be a message to you, so I told Walking Owl about it, and he thinks it might be so."

Cole shrugged and said, "It was just a dream I had. It didn't really make any sense." He was surprised that they would be interested, and he was inclined to let it go at that.

"The spirits sometime send a man a message to tell him the path he must walk," Walking Owl said. "The spirit usually takes the form of an animal or a bird. Our young men go in search of their path when they are still boys, but any man can talk to the spirits no matter how old he is. When a young Crow boy is ready, he will cleanse his body in the sweat lodge. Then he will go out into the prairie or the mountains, alone, without food and water for four days. Then his mind and body will be ready to receive his vision. I think that the spirits sent the white wolf to talk to you, even though you did not know to do these things. But your body was weakened by your wound, making your mind more ready to accept your vision. If it was not so, then the spirits would not have caused you to come to me."

Cole was skeptical. "I don't know about that," he said. He was aware of the ritual of young boys, out in the wilderness somewhere, starving themselves until they collapsed, hoping to get a vision. It was how many of them picked the name they wanted to be called. It was a little beyond Cole's imagination. "I saw a white wolf, but he didn't tell me anything," he insisted.

"Maybe the wolf did not talk to you with words, but maybe it told you what it wanted you to know. You did not listen with your heart," Walking Owl said. "Will you tell me your dream?"

Cole hesitated before declining, thinking too much had been made of a simple dream already. But since he was a guest in the village, and Walking Owl had administered to his wound, he didn't want to appear rude. And Harley had told him that Walking Owl was a *maxpé* man, so he didn't want to insult him. He glanced at Harley, who nodded his encouragement to cooperate.

"Why, sure," Cole said, "if that's what you want, I'll tell it."

"Leave out nothing," Walking Owl said. "Tell me everything you saw in the dream."

Cole thought for a minute, trying to recall every move he had made that morning when he walked down to the river. "Tell you the truth, I have a hard time remembering when I was awake and when I went to sleep." He went on to relate the dream, starting with the two dark eyes on a veil of white.

When he had finished, Walking Owl nodded solemnly but said nothing for a long moment. When he spoke, he told Cole that he wanted to meditate and hold the dream in his head for a while.

"That's it?" Cole asked. "That all you wanted?" He assumed that was the end of the matter. When he and Harley unsaddled their horses, he remarked to his pint-sized partner, "Remind me not to talk to you about my dreams anymore."

"That ain't the end of it," Harley said with a chuckle. "Walkin' Owl's the medicine man. Dreams and such, that's his business. I know you don't believe in all the Injun magic and spirit stuff, but I'm tellin' you they know a lotta things that the white man don't."

Another day saw Cole improving even more, regaining most of his strength and favoring his wound less than the day before. He slept later than usual, awakened by the gravelly voice of Harley, singing one of his many little ditties.

" 'Someone stole the big dog, and I wish they'd bring him back. Big dog jumped over the fence, little dog through the crack, Lord, Lord. . . .' "

He lay there for a while, remembering how Ann used to sing while she did her chores. It brought him no comfort.

Harley knew that his friend's thoughts were returning to the quest he had sworn himself to complete, so he endeavored to take Cole's mind off Slade Corbett.

"I'm thinkin' you're lookin' fit enough to ride over to Fort Laramie. There's a tradin' post near there. It ain't but half a day's ride—probably do you good to get your blood flowin' again. Like you said yesterday, we need to stock up on some supplies, so I don't mind helpin' you spend some of your money."

"I appreciate your help," Cole grunted. "I'd like to test my side anyway, see how half a day in the saddle feels." Thoughts of his dream and Walking Owl's interpretation of it had already slipped from his mind.

It struck Harley as significant that this was the first time he remembered seeing Cole approach even a chuckle, maybe in the entire time he had known him—if the grunt could be interpreted as humor. "Well, let's go saddle up before the mornin' gets away from us."

On their way to the horse herd, they met Walking Owl coming from his tipi. "I have thought hard on your vision, White Wolf," he said to Cole.

"White Wolf?" Cole responded.

"Yes," Walking Owl said. "That is your Crow name, I think. If you want me to, I will tell you what your dream tells me."

"Course he wants to hear what you have to say about it," Harley quickly interjected, afraid Cole might reject the offer of guidance and insult Walking Owl. "Don't you, Cole?"

It was not difficult to interpret the tense expression Harley was aiming at him, so Cole said, "That's a fact. I would be honored to have your advice."

There was an immediate look of relief on Harley's face. "Why don't you set down now and talk? We can go to the tradin' post later on when you're finished."

"Good," Walking Owl said. "Come. We will go to my tipi." He turned and walked away, leaving Cole no choice but to follow him.

"I'll go get the horses saddled, White Wolf," Harley said softly enough not to be heard by the departing medicine man, a huge grin spreading his whiskers.

"You do that, Thunder Mouse," Cole snorted. "Take my buckskin as a packhorse. Saddle him, too. Maybe I can sell that saddle at Fort Laramie."

Walking Owl welcomed him into his tipi, where he lit a pipe, offered it to the four directions, then handed it to Cole. Not really sure what his proper response should be, Cole repeated the medicine man's actions. Walking Owl seemed pleased, and proceeded to tell him what he was sure the dream meant.

"The spirit of the wolf came to you to show you your medicine path," he said. "He would have come to you sooner, but he knew that you did not understand the meaning of spiritual visions. So he waited until you came here where I could read your vision for you. Like the wolf, you are a hunter. Because the wolf was white, with no dark markings at all, it means to tell you that you must kill only those who do evil, for your heart must be pure. As long as you walk this path, the white wolf will give you strength and courage, and your medicine will be strong. You should take the name White Wolf for your Crow medicine name." He paused and sat back. "That is all I have to say."

Cole wished that Harley had told him if there was any ceremonial custom he would be expected to follow at the conclusion of the medicine man's interpretation. The reading seemed pretty simple to him, one anyone could have come up with, but he nodded gravely and thanked Walking Owl for delivering the message. He got to his feet then and went to help Harley with the horses.

So now he had an Indian name.

He couldn't really say that he believed everything Walking Owl had told him, but at least White Wolf was a hell of a lot better than Thunder Mouse.

It was not a long ride to Fort Laramie, but it was enough to convince Cole that he was strong enough to ride any distance. Harley had hoped to get his mind off the grim task that drove him relentlessly with a visit to the busy army post. Cole was not interested in anything the fort had to offer, however, preferring to make his purchases at the trading post, then inquire about the possible sale of his extra saddle. Finding no potential interest at the trading post, or the sutler's store at the fort, he finally sold the saddle to the owner of a stable outside the fort. It was for considerably less than he thought the saddle was worth, but knowing he had no use for two saddles, he took the offer. Once that was done, he was ready to return to the Crow village.

"I was thinkin' we just might stay over for the night and do a little drinkin'," Harley complained when Cole secured the supplies on the buckskin, using the new pack rig he'd gotten as part of the sale of the saddle. He nodded thoughtfully as Cole covered the load with a bearskin coat he had purchased along with the supplies.

"I'm feelin' fit to ride," Cole told him, "and we've got enough daylight left to make it back before dark." Seeing the obvious disappointment in Harley's face, he said, "If you ain't ready to leave, I'll give you enough money to buy a few drinks. I can find my way back with no problem." Harley looked uncertain, so Cole suggested, "Tell you what, I'll buy you a bottle and you can take it with you."

Harley's expression changed to one of accusation. "You're thinkin' 'bout goin' after them two bastards again, ain'tcha?" He was afraid his friend had that in mind when he bought the bearskin coat.

Cole nodded. "I'm fit enough to go right now."

"I wish you'd wait till spring before you go on the hunt again," Harley said. "You'll be a helluva lot more fit then."

"Maybe, but I reckon I've got to go now. There ain't no tellin' where they'll be by spring. I've lost too much time as it is."

Harley hesitated, biting his lip in his reluctance to speak his mind. "Partner, I've come to think a lot of you, but I'm feelin' winter in my bones more and more. What I mean is, I ain't goin' with you this time."

"I hadn't really figured on it," Cole said, his expression never changing. "I thought you'd stay in the Crow camp all along. There ain't no sense in you riskin' your neck along with mine."

"Hell, Cole, you know it ain't 'cause I'm worried 'bout my neck. I'm just gettin' too damn old to be of much help, and like I said, the cold is startin' to get into my bones. I don't want you to think I've gone slack on you."

Cole gave him one of his rare smiles. "I know that, partner. I never thought for a minute that you had. This thing I've got to do is mine alone. I've already gotten you mixed up in it more than I should have. Anyway, Walkin' Owl told me that I was supposed to go after Corbett by myself." It was a lie, but he thought it might make Harley feel better about not going with him. "So don't give it another thought."

Harley seemed relieved to have gotten the matter said.

"Well, you know I hope you have good huntin'." He didn't want to tell Cole that part of his decision not to accompany him was the reluctance to see his young friend killed. He flashed a big grin then. "I'll take you up on that bottle of whiskey, and we'll ride on back tonight."

Chapter 9

"Where are you thinkin' about headin'?" Harley asked as he watched Cole checking the ropes on his packhorse one last time. The little man was finally resigned to the fact that Cole was setting out after Slade Corbett, in spite of another attempt to change his mind. "Them two outlaws could be anywhere— might be halfway to Texas by now. You ain't got a snowball's chance in hell of findin' 'em."

"Maybe you're right," Cole replied stoically. "But I've got even less of a chance of findin' 'em sittin' around this village all winter." Satisfied that his pack was secure, he answered Harley's question. "Cheyenne was where I lost 'em, so I reckon Cheyenne's where I'll start lookin' to pick up their trail."

Yellow Calf, Walking Owl, and Medicine Bear, along with several more of the village, came out to wish him good hunting on his journey. The medicine man agreed with Harley in the belief that Cole should give his wound more time to heal properly, but he understood the young man's sense of what he must do. After thanking his hosts, Cole stepped up into the saddle. A moment before turning the Morgan toward the river, he paused when Harley suddenly stepped up and extended his hand.

"You be damn careful, partner," Harley said, then stepped back to watch him ride out of the camp, a foreboding thought striking him that he might never see the determined young man again.

When the others returned to their tipis, he remained there, watching his friend as he led the buckskin across the river, passing by the spot on the bank where they had searched for tracks left by a white wolf. He shook his head sadly, for he feared there was nothing but tragedy awaiting the young man. For several long moments, he stood there after Cole had ridden out of sight before turning to go back to Yellow Calf's lodge.

Mary Lou Cagle stood in the kitchen door, her attention captured by two men who had just walked into the dining room.

"Well, I'll be damned," she murmured. "I don't believe the nerve of that pair of murderers." She turned back toward the kitchen where Maggie was drying a stack of dishes. "You're not gonna believe who just showed up in the dining room," she said.

"Who?" Maggie asked, aware of the astonishment in Mary Lou's tone.

"That son of a bitch Slade Corbett and the other son of a bitch—whatever his name is," Mary Lou answered.

"No!" Maggie replied in disbelief, and walked to the door to see for herself.

"Well, you know we should have expected it," Mary Lou said, disgusted. "They know there ain't anybody in town that'll stop them, now that Jim Thompson's dead and his deputy quit."

"This deputy wasn't around long enough to even learn his name," Maggie said. "How do these outlaws find out so soon, anyway?"

"Huh," Mary Lou snorted, "I know what my guess would be."

She and Maggie *had* expected trouble with the sudden absence of any semblance of law enforcement, but they had hoped that it would be confined to the riffraff brought in by the railroad. Most of the merchants expected the town's swollen population to be gone when the weather improved and the railroad could push the tracks farther west. They just wondered if the town could survive until spring.

"I wonder if Leon Bloodworth knows those two are back in town," Maggie wondered aloud, still stunned by their blatant disregard for the law. She knew that the stable owner had been trying to get the merchants together to re-form the vigilance committee now that there was an absolute lack of any official law in town.

"He'll find out soon enough," Mary Lou said as she watched Corbett and Sanchez swagger over to a table in the dining room. "Whaddaya think we oughta do about them? Think I should tell them we don't serve their kind? They can get something to eat in one of the saloons."

Patrons at the two tables close to them got up and headed for the door, their supper unfinished. Minutes later, the other diners departed, leaving no one in the dining room but the two outlaws.

"No," Maggie said. "I'm afraid if you do that, they're liable to tear up the place. Maybe it's best to go ahead and serve them. Then they might just go on about their business. There's no sense in making them mad."

"All right," Mary Lou said. "I'll go wait on them." She released a long weary sigh and started toward the table.

"There she is," Slade drawled when she approached. "I was wonderin' if I was gonna have to go back yonder in the kitchen to look for you. Hell, that's the main reason I came back to this pigsty, to see you again. Ain't that right, Sanchez?" Sanchez's response was a sarcastic sneer.

Mary Lou had cautioned herself not to get into a conversation with Slade Corbett, but seeing his mocking grin, she could not control her disgust for the monster. "You've got your nerve coming back in here. You're running all our customers out. What do you want, anyway?"

"One thing for sure," Corbett told her, "is a helluva lot more respect outta you." Mary Lou snorted her derision. He ignored it and continued. "Me and Sanchez want some supper, and I wanna know where that friend of yours is. You know, the coward with the Henry rifle. I heard he was lookin' for me. I'm lookin' for him now, so where's he hidin' out?"

"How the hell would I know?" Mary Lou replied. "Even if I did know, I wouldn't tell you, and that's a fact. Whaddaya want with him, anyway? You've already slaughtered his whole family. Ain't that enough for you two murderers?"

"What the hell are you talkin' about?" Slade questioned. "We ain't murdered nobody."

"You know what I'm talking about," Mary Lou came back, thoroughly into her revulsion for the two murderers. "That family you and your gang of garbage massacred on Chugwater Creek," she charged. "Why do you think he came after you?"

Stunned by the accusation, Corbett was left speechless for a moment before demanding, "Who told you we had anything to do with that?" Then thinking it best to claim ignorance of the incident, he said, "I didn't know there was anybody killed on the Chugwater. We ain't been up that way in a year. That mouth of yours is liable to get you into more trouble than you're set to handle."

Realizing that she had already said too much for her own good, Mary Lou decided it best to hold her sharp tongue before she became their next victim. "Maggie says I gotta feed you," she blurted. "You want supper? Six bits each."

Corbett hesitated, still shocked that she knew about the little party he and his gang had had at that farm on the Chugwater. He glanced at Sanchez, to gauge his reaction to the accusation, but was met with the insolent sneer his partner always wore.

"Yeah, we want supper," he answered her. "And we want it quick." Favoring him with an expression of contempt, she turned and went into the kitchen.

When she had gone, Corbett said, "So now we know why that son of a bitch came after us. He ain't no lawman at all. He's just a crybaby sodbuster tryin' to get back at us for killin' his wife and family—just a damn farmer that don't know when to just thank his lucky stars he wasn't home when we hit his place."

"He shot Tom Larsen," Sanchez reminded him, not ready to take the rifleman lightly.

"Maybe so," Slade conceded. "But you know damn well he had to catch Tom by surprise—snuck up on him when he was playin' cards, or shot him from a safe distance. Hell, he was usin' a damn rifle. He most likely shot Tom from the front door, and Tom never saw him."

"Tom got a shot in him," Sanchez reminded him again. He was not prone to dismiss Tom Larsen's killer as a simple grieving farmer.

Sanchez's remark was not enough to alter Corbett's opinion of the man stalking them. "Right," he responded. "The son of a bitch got shot. He's run off somewhere to hide—might be dead already." Their speculation was interrupted then by the arrival of Mary Lou at the table with their coffee. Filled with the confidence then that the *lawman* they had fled was now running for his life, Corbett questioned her again. "Now, how 'bout you tell me where that stud is that shot a friend of ours? Is he still in town?"

"No," Mary Lou replied, thankful that he wasn't.

"How bad was he shot?"

"I don't know. I'm not a doctor," she answered. "Now, if you're gonna eat, stop asking me questions, so I can go to the kitchen and get your supper."

"Somebody's been tellin' you the wrong story 'bout us," Slade said, still trying to convince her she was wrong. "Hell, killin' peaceful folks ain't our style. Is it, Sanchez?" Sanchez merely grunted in reply.

"Is that so?" Mary Lou responded. "I remember how quick you got outta town when you heard what Cole Bonner had done for your friend and was coming for you."

"Is that his name?" Corbett replied. "Sounds like

you know him pretty well." He waited for her to respond, but when she didn't, he continued. "Me and Sanchez left town so there wouldn't be no more killin'. 'Cause we'da had to take care of that crazy son of a bitch, and some innocent folks mighta got hurt—like the time you got shot when that feller got Frank Cowen." He didn't realize that the man who shot Cowen was the same man who now stalked him. Recalling that incident, he commented, "Musta not been too bad. You look like you're doin' all right." Mary Lou declined to respond.

Seeing no useful purpose to the conversation between Corbett and the woman, Sanchez interrupted. "Go get the food—too much talk. I'm hungry."

"You know," Corbett said to Sanchez when Mary Lou went into the kitchen, "the feller that shot Frank— reckon he's the same one that shot Tom?"

Sanchez gave it a thought. "Could be," he allowed. Then his face twisted with an evil grin. "Be kinda funny if he is—gettin' shot served him right for kil- lin' Frank."

Further conversation on the possibility was inter- rupted by the arrival of supper, but the possibility served to convince Sanchez that it was more than a simple farmer they were to be concerned with.

Mary Lou placed a bowl of thick soup before each of them. Slade picked up his spoon and stirred it around. "Looks pretty good. You didn't spit in it, did you?" He gave her a malevolent grin while Sanchez dug in immediately.

"Now, why didn't I think of that?" she replied, and turned to go back to the kitchen, smiling to herself, since she had done that very thing just moments before.

When she returned to the kitchen, it was to find Arthur Campbell talking furtively to Maggie, having slipped in through the back door. He looked up when Mary Lou walked in, and whispered, "What are they doing?"

"Eating," Mary Lou replied matter-of-factly, wondering what he had expected.

"They came into the hotel," Campbell said. "I didn't have much choice. I had to give them a room. I sent Claude down to the stable to tell Leon."

Maggie became upset immediately. "If you men are thinking about getting the Gunnysack Gang together to do something with those two, you do it outside my dining room. I've had more than my share of damage because of that man and his gang."

"By the time Leon gets a posse together, they'll most likely be out of your dining room—might be in the Sundown Saloon. That's where they liked to hang out before." He slipped over to the edge of the door to get a peek at the two outlaws. "Sitting there big as life," he whispered, "like they had nothing to worry about." He watched for a moment more before speculating, "It would be pretty easy to shoot both of them while they're sitting there eating—do the whole town a favor." He spent a moment more thinking about the danger to the person who tried it and happened to miss. Withdrawing carefully from the edge of the door, he said, "I'd best get out of here and go meet with Leon and the others."

"What are you planning to do about them?" Maggie persisted, still concerned about her dining room, especially after hearing his speculation.

"I don't know," Campbell said. "I'll meet with the others and I reckon we'll have to decide the best way to handle it." He went out the back door then. "It's best if we act as a committee and not one man on his own."

In the time it took Arthur Campbell to hurry down to Bloodworth's stable, only two other members of the vigilance committee had shown up. Arthur found Bloodworth talking to Jesse Springer, the blacksmith, and Douglas Green, who owned Green's Dry Goods. "We're gonna need more than the four of us to take those two gunmen," Green said.

"Four of us against two of them," Springer said. "Seems like enough of us to me."

"Four merchants with wives and children, against two hell-raising gunmen." Green was quick to differ. "We need more than the four of us. We at least oughta send for Gordon Luck."

"Hell, Douglas," Springer scoffed. "They're in the dinin' room now where we can surprise 'em. It would take too long to ride out to the sawmill to get Gordon. We've hung a few hell-raisers before who thought they were too big to worry about the law in our town. These two ain't no different."

"The hell they're not," Green insisted. "Those two are in the business of killing. And there were a helluva lot more of us on those occasions, if you'll recall."

Gordon Luck had been at the forefront of every lynching in town, and Green would have been a lot more confident with him to lead them. A powerful man, with shoulder-length sandy hair and a trim beard to match, Gordon was a natural leader, as well as the minister of the town's newly established Baptist church. Far from being humble in his religious beliefs, he conducted himself as a soldier in the Lord's service. His Sunday sermons contained more than a few casual references to the evil that had descended upon Crow Creek Crossing with the coming of the railroad, and the duty for all citizens to take up the sword against it.

"If you ain't got the stomach for it, I reckon the three of us can do the job," Springer chided Green.

"Hold on," Leon Bloodworth stepped in. "It don't do no good for you two to have a catfight right now. John, I understand what Douglas is sayin'. It would be a whole lot safer if there were more of us to go take those two down. I'm glad that you're willin' to go after 'em with just us here now, but let's wait a little bit to see who else shows up. I've sent my boy, Marvin, to tell some of the others about the meetin'."

Some minutes later, Marvin returned with Alvin Tucker right behind him. "I figured we could count on Alvin," Bloodworth remarked when the rawboned proprietor of the saddle shop walked in, carrying a double-barreled shotgun. Along with Gordon Luck, Tucker had played a leading role in every hanging carried out by the Gunnysack Gang, and he looked eager to stage another one. "What about Swartz?" Bloodworth asked his son.

"I told him," Marvin said, "but he said he couldn't come right now, 'cause they already stopped in his place before they went to the hotel. And he said he oughta stay there in case they come back."

"Hell, five of us is enough to take care of two lowdown gunmen," Tucker said.

"That's what I've been tryin' to tell 'em," Springer said. "We've got enough for a committee. Ain't even no use to wear masks. We're actin' in the name of the law." He looked directly at Douglas Green to see if he was going to object. When Green did not, Springer went on. "All right, then, let's decide how we're gonna do this."

The discussion went on for a quarter of an hour, with some difference of opinion over whether to try to take Corbett and Sanchez alive, then hang them, or to surprise them in a blaze of gunfire and be done with it. "You say they're in Maggie's dining room?" Tucker asked Arthur Campbell.

"Well, they were when I left," Campbell said. "I reckon they're still there."

"Then I say let's jump 'em while they're settin' there stuffin' their gullets," Tucker said. "Don't give 'em a chance to reach for their guns."

"I reckon that's the safest way to do it," Bloodworth said. "If all five of us go in shootin', I don't expect they'll be ready for that. I'm for it."

"Anybody got any objections?" Tucker asked, again looking at Green. No one said anything. "All right, everybody's in. It's important that every one of us shoots the bastards. We don't want to give 'em any chance to fight. Agreed?" Everyone nodded. "All right, then, let's go show the sons of bitches who owns this town!"

"I didn't bring my gun," Arthur Campbell said. "I wasn't sure we were gonna do something like this right away."

"Well, what the hell did you think we were meetin' for?" Springer blurted. "I swear, Arthur."

"Never mind," Bloodworth said. "I've got an extra gun in the feed room. He can use that."

He hurried to the feed room in the middle of the stable and took a .44 handgun and holster off a peg by the door. Before handing it to Campbell, he checked the cylinder to see if it was loaded. Campbell strapped the gun belt around his waist, looking slightly uncomfortable as he did so, causing Springer to look at Tucker and shake his head in doubt.

"Now," Bloodworth said, "everybody ready? Let's go."

The short-staffed version of the Gunnysack Gang had taken longer to make their decision to act than they realized, for the two they came to assassinate had finished their supper and were preparing to leave the dining room.

"You can just run us a bill," Slade told Mary Lou when she asked them to pay. "We'll settle up at the end of the week."

"The hell we will," Mary Lou said. "We don't run credit lines here. You were supposed to pay before you ate anyway."

"We'll settle up at the end of the week," Slade repeated emphatically. Then he smiled wickedly and said, "If you've got to have it now, you can come up to the room to collect it. I might even give you a little bit extra."

His suggestion caused a feeling of nausea in the pit of her stomach. She did not say anything for a few moments, knowing that there was nothing she could do to make them pay for their meal. Mary Lou looked with contempt from Slade's lascivious grin to Sanchez's crude sneer. Knowing the evil they had done, and what they were capable of when no one was around to stop them, she was suddenly overcome by a deep feeling of fear. Concerned for her safety, she spun on her heel and fled to the kitchen to find Maggie kneeling behind the table, her shotgun aimed at the door. With no gun of her own, Mary Lou grabbed a butcher knife from the table and stood behind Maggie. Prepared to defend themselves, they waited for one of the men to appear in the doorway.

Sanchez had started toward the kitchen when Slade suddenly stopped him. He had taken a quick look out the window to discover five heavily armed men walking around the building toward the back door.

"Hold on, Sanchez," he said. "I think we got company comin' to see us." He stepped up closer to the window for a better look. "Ain't that the son of a bitch that runs the hotel?"

Sanchez moved to the other side of the window to see for himself.

"Yeah," he said, "that's him, and the man that owns the stable. Looks like some of the fine citizens of Cheyenne are plannin' to pay us a little visit." Like Corbett, Sanchez had no fear of a hastily formed handful of the town's businessmen. They were a far cry from an angry lynch mob.

"Well, now," Slade said, "that's right neighborly, ain't it? Let's get ready to welcome them." He watched from the window until they disappeared around the corner of the building. "They're comin' through the kitchen. Let's turn a couple of these tables over."

They worked quickly, turning two tables over to serve as barriers. Once that was done, Slade directed Sanchez to one corner of the large room while he went to the opposite one. They both knelt down behind the corner tables and chairs and waited.

Maggie gasped, startled, when the back door opened and Jesse Springer led four of the town's businessmen into her kitchen, signaling her to remain silent. Whispering quietly, she was at once alarmed as she tried to tell him to take the fight outside, even as they tiptoed around her with their weapons drawn, intent upon attacking.

"It's too late now," he told her. "You and Mary Lou best find you a place to hide till it's over."

"You're too late to surprise them," Mary Lou warned. "They saw you through the window and turned a couple of the tables over to use for cover. Why in hell didn't you come up the alley?"

"That woulda been the smart thing to do," Alvin Tucker whispered. "But we didn't. Anyway, them tables ain't gonna be much cover when we hit 'em all at once." He turned to the others in the posse. "Hit 'em with everything you've got, as fast as you can shoot." He looked at Springer and received a nod to show he was ready. "Me and Springer will lead the charge. They won't know what hit 'em."

They inched up closer around the doorway, taking care not to show themselves through the open door too soon.

"Everybody ready?" Tucker whispered. "Let's go!" he yelled then as he and Springer charged through the doorway, blasting away at the two overturned tables on the other side of the room. Like a cavalry assault on an enemy position, the five-man vigilante posse unleashed a blistering barrage, knocking great chunks of wood from the two tables and splitting the tops in their fury.

They realized too late that there was no one behind the tables and they had blundered into a trap. Tucker and Springer were cut down almost instantly by gunshots from the corners of the room. The resulting panic to escape the lethal return fire led to a rush to retreat, but not before Arthur Campbell caught a round in his left thigh and Leon Bloodworth was hit in the shoulder. The only member of the posse who escaped with no wounds was Douglas Green by virtue of his tendency to hang behind during an attack. Consumed by fright when the tide of the battle turned immediately in favor of the two outlaws, he sought a place to hide. Seeing the pantry door, he plunged inside where Maggie and Mary Lou had taken refuge. Bloodworth and Campbell, limping along as best they could, escaped out the back door.

As suddenly as it started, the shooting stopped, and in a few seconds, the three hiding in the pantry could hear the sound of heavy boots in the kitchen, walking toward the back door.

"Yonder!" Slade blurted as he caught sight of Campbell rounding the back corner of the rooms behind the kitchen. His exclamation was followed at once by a couple of shots. "Too late, they're gone. Don't matter. We'll find 'em and finish the job." He saw that as no problem since the vigilantes had not bothered to wear masks. He recognized both men as the owner of the hotel and the operator of the stables.

Inside the pantry Douglas Green squeezed between the two women, trying to hide himself behind them. When they tried to resist his efforts, he pleaded, "Please, they won't hurt you women, but they'll kill me. I can hide behind your skirts if you'll stand together." It was easy to feel contempt for the man's cowardice, but difficult not to feel sorry for him, for he was probably right.

So they stood close together while he squatted on the floor behind their skirts, trembling in fright, as the sound of the outlaws' boots could be heard when they walked back toward the dining room. Then they stopped and came back to stand before the pantry door. Suddenly the door was jerked open to reveal Slade Corbett standing there with his .44 aimed at them. There was no shot fired, however, as a cruel sneer spread across his unshaven face.

"Well, well," he said, smirking, "lookee here, Sanchez. The ladies didn't run out on us after all." He took a step backward and holstered his pistol. "Come on outta there, ladies. We wouldn't want nothin' to happen to you."

"Shoot them!" Sanchez insisted. "We don't leave no witnesses."

"Why not?" Slade replied. "Hell, we need witnesses. They saw that bunch try to kill us. We just defended ourselves. We didn't start it." He found it amusing that it was actually the case. "Besides, we don't wanna kill the cook, and we might find some better use for 'em, too." Turning back to the women, he repeated, "Come on outta there." He took another step back when the two women hesitated. "We ain't gonna hurtcha."

Conscious of the frightened man trembling behind them, they moved out of the pantry, staying as close together as possible, hoping to shield him from view.

"Make us some coffee, and cut a big slice of that pie on the counter there. Shootin' cowards makes me hungry," Slade declared, confident that there would be no further attacks from the citizens of Cheyenne, and riding high after repelling the citizens' attack. Mary Lou and Maggie stepped quickly out of the pantry and closed the door behind them. Too busy enjoying the confrontation just finished to think about taking a closer look inside the pantry, the two outlaws pulled a couple of chairs up to the kitchen table to await their dessert, unconcerned about the crowd of spectators gathering outside the hotel, curious to see what the gunshots were about.

"Ain't none of 'em got brass enough to come in to find out what the noise was," Slade gloated, knowing that he and Sanchez had just destroyed the only semblance of law and order in the whole town. "We'll let them three that got away set on it for a while. We got all the time in the world to settle with them—let 'em sweat for a spell."

Forced to sit there in the kitchen while the two outlaws had pie and coffee, Mary Lou and Maggie could only hope that they would eventually finish and leave them in peace. Realizing just how defenseless she was if the depraved monsters decided to press her beyond the harmless flirting stage, Mary Lou wanted to run. But she could not in good conscience leave Maggie to deal with them alone.

After consuming his dried apple pie, Sanchez drew a long skinning knife and began cleaning his fingernails with the tip of it, all the while leering at her as if undressing her with his eyes. Suddenly she was surprised by a question from Corbett.

"Where do you sleep? I know you ain't got no husband. I reckon I'll bunk in with you tonight. Where do you live?"

"I don't remember giving you an invitation," Mary Lou replied, as boldly as she could affect.

"I don't need no invitation," Slade said. "You'll be better off when you get it straight in your head that you're lucky I claimed you. Sanchez here, he don't leave 'em in too good a shape. Now, me, I know how to treat a lady, long as she don't give me no hard time. So you might as well tell me where you live so I won't have to beat it outta you."

"All right," Mary Lou said. "I live two miles north of town on the Lodgepole Creek Road."

Slade smiled smugly. "Now, you know that's a damn lie. You live right here in town. Where? In the hotel?" Mary Lou didn't answer. "That's what I thought," he said. "Which room number?" Still, she refused to answer. "Listen, you damn bitch, I ain't got time to play games with you." He grabbed her by her wrist and pulled her up close to him, his fist drawn back to strike her.

"Wait!" Maggie yelled. "She lives upstairs in the hotel, room number four at the back of the hall." She knew that room was vacant, and had been since the last guest knocked the stove over and burned a big patch in the floor.

Slade backhanded Mary Lou, almost knocking her down. "If you had just told me that, you wouldn'ta got smacked. That ain't but two doors down from my room. That'll be real handy." She steeled herself to keep her mouth shut, afraid that Maggie had put herself in danger by trying to help her. "Now, let me tell you how things are gonna be while I'm in town," Slade continued, convinced that he now owned it. "I like to do a little drinkin' and playin' cards. And when I'm done with that, I want my woman waitin' for me. So I'll be knockin' on your door tonight, and if you ain't there, I'll track you down. And, missy, when I find you, it ain't gonna be pleasant. Do you understand me?" When she didn't answer, he grabbed her by her throat and shook her. "Do you!"

"Yes, damn it," she cried, "I understand you."

"Good," he said, and released her. "Come on, Sanchez, let's go get a drink."

The two women stood staring at the door after they had gone, still stunned by all that had taken place, scarcely able to believe it had actually happened. The world had gone completely loco to let an evil force like those two take over an entire town. Looking through the open door, they could see the bodies of Jesse Springer and Alvin Tucker, and knew that there was no one left to protect them, or any of the other decent people in the town.

"You shouldn't have told him I was living in the hotel," Mary Lou said.

"You sure as hell couldn't tell him where your room is," Maggie replied. "And he looked like he was about to beat it outta you."

"But now he's got a reason to come after you," Mary Lou said. "What are you gonna do?"

"I've got my shotgun, and I'm gonna keep it by my side from now on," Maggie said. "It's gonna cost him plenty if he comes after me. I'm too old to worry about that piece of slime bothering me, anyway. I'm more worried about you. Have you got a gun?"

"Yes, I've got a Colt revolver in my room, and I'll use it before I let that monster touch me again."

She reached up and felt the bruise already forming on her cheek. Her natural sense of survival told her to run, but there was no place to run to. Everything she owned was in her room behind the kitchen. She had no horse, and no one to help her. With Jim Thompson dead, there was no one to go to for help. And in the dining room, there were just the three women, she and Maggie and Beulah, Maggie's part-time cook. "What are you going to do about the dining room?" Mary Lou wondered then.

"I'm gonna close it, I guess," Maggie said. "I don't see how I can try to keep it open as long as the hood-lums have taken over the town."

"Corbett talked like he expected you to cook for him."

"He can cook for himself," Maggie said, "or take his meals at the Sundown Saloon. When Beulah shows up in the morning, I'm gonna send her home."

Her cook had been fortunate to have just gone home before Corbett and Sanchez came in. Further discussion was interrupted then by the squeaking of the hinges as the pantry door was cautiously eased open. In the aftermath of the violence, they had for-gotten the frightened man still hiding in the pantry.

They both turned to gaze at the timid storekeeper as he peeked out of the partially opened door, reluc-tant to come out until positively sure the killers had gone.

"Come on out, Mr. Green," Mary Lou told him. "They're gone." He came forward then, holding his shotgun in front of him in an effort to hide the exten-sive wet stain spreading on his trousers. Intent upon fleeing, he headed straight for the back door. "Wait a minute," Mary Lou said. "You can at least give us a hand getting these two bodies out of the dining room."

"I'm sorry. I can't," he said. "I've got to get home. You two oughta be able to drag them out the front door so Harvey White can pick them up and prepare them for burial."

"Yeah, you'd better hurry home," Maggie mocked. "Your family might need somebody to protect them."

"God help them if they do," Mary Lou added as he slipped out the door. She turned to look at the two bodies again and sighed. "Well, let's drag them outta the dining room. There's nothing more we can do with them. Maybe we can send one of those fools still standing around in the street to go get Harvey."

Chapter 10

"It ain't that bad," Doc Marion said when he wrapped a bandage around Arthur Campbell's thigh. "You're gonna be limping around for a few days, but the bullet's out, and it doesn't look like it's infected. Now, I'm gonna give you the same advice I just gave Leon Bloodworth. Find yourself someplace to hide for a few days, because those outlaws will most likely come looking for you. Whatever possessed you damn fools to go after those two murderers without wearing sacks on your heads or some kinda masks?"

"I reckon we were pretty sure we were gonna rub the two of 'em out, so we wouldn't need the sacks," Campbell confessed meekly.

"Damn it, Arthur, you weren't tangling with a couple of drunk railroad men. You boys should have known better than to go head-on with the likes of Slade Corbett and that animal riding with him." Doc shook his head, exasperated. "Well, you and Leon had better get the hell outta town for a few days, and maybe they'll leave. I sent somebody to tell Paul over at the telegraph office to wire Fort Laramie about the trouble we've got here. Maybe they'll send troops down here to help us out."

"I've already thought about it," Campbell said. "Me and Leon are gonna hole up at Boyd Mather's ranch till this blows over. My wife's already packing up some things we'll need. She's going with me. My boy, Claude, can handle the desk at the hotel. I told him not to tell those bastards he's my son. I just wish to hell they hadn't taken a room in the hotel."

Doc tied a knot in the bandage and gave it a light pat with his hand. "Try to keep that bandage clean. Now, get going before they come here looking for you. They know you're shot, right?"

"Right," Campbell answered.

Doc shook his head, worried about the outcome of the bungled attack.

Benny Swartz stood behind the bar at the Sundown Saloon talking to his bartender, Jake Short, while keeping a nervous eye on the two men sitting at the back corner table.

"They ain't really caused no trouble," Jake said in response to Benny's question. "They just look like they're dead set on drinkin' all the whiskey in Cheyenne. The one wearin' the hat with the fancy silver hatband was tryin' to get some fellers to get a card game started. But it don't look like anybody wants to risk their necks playin' cards with those two. They've been talkin' pretty big about killin' Alvin Tucker and Jesse Springer, braggin' about how they shot 'em down when they jumped 'em over at the dining room."

"That was bad business," Benny muttered softly, thinking that it could have been him if he hadn't begged out of it. Looking at the nearly empty whiskey bottle on the table, he asked, "How much do they owe us?"

"Oh, they're payin' for the whiskey they're drinkin'," Jake said. "Matter of fact, they've bought a few rounds for some of those railroad boys back there. I think they're showin' off, lettin' everybody see how much money they've got."

"Well, keep 'em happy, then, and maybe they'll leave all of it right here," Benny told him, never too fearful to think about a possible profit. "I've gotta go to the house now. I'll check back with you in a little while."

"What if they run outta money and ask for credit?"

"Same as anybody else," Benny said. "We don't sell whiskey on credit."

He went out the door then, leaving Jake to handle any trouble that might arise with the two gunmen. He hadn't been willing to confront them when the vigilance committee went to execute them, and he was reluctant to face them now more than ever. It was obvious that since the town's vigilantes had attacked them, Corbett and Sanchez felt they had a license to kill anybody and call it self-defense.

Benny's assessment of the situation was right on the mark, for the two were even then tiring of sitting in the saloon, drinking.

"Whaddaya say we take a walk down to the stables and shoot that son of a bitch that ran outta the dinin' room?" Slade suggested. "I've already got one bullet in him—might as well finish him off in case he gets his nerve up again."

"I not so sure it's your bullet in his shoulder," Sanchez said. "I think maybe I hit him."

"You probably think you got the other'n, too," Slade scoffed, "that hotel feller."

"Maybe," Sanchez said with a shrug.

Knowing how useless it was to argue the point with the stoic Sanchez, Slade just snorted derisively.

"Well, let's go see if we can find him. I don't want him sneakin' up on me and shootin' me in the back. I got a little business I gotta take care of back at the hotel, and if I drink much more of this damn whiskey, I ain't gonna be able to take care of her proper."

Already feeling the effects of too much alcohol, Sanchez was beginning to feel more like going straight to the hotel room and sleeping it off.

"To hell with that damn man at the stable. He's holed up somewhere like a dog, licking his wound. This town is ours to do what we damn please. Nobody wants to mess with us. They afraid they get what those other two got."

"We might own this town tonight, but tomorrow might be a different story," Slade said. "Some of the churchgoin' people of this town are gonna be stirred up by the killin' we done tonight, and they might work up a real lynchin' party, more'n just the two of us can cut down. I'm sayin' we need to get our business done tonight and maybe head back to Colorado tomorrow before a damn army patrol shows up lookin' for us."

"What about that son of a bitch that shot Tom Larsen? I thought that was why we came back here, because you wanted to kill him so bad."

"Well, I did come after him," Slade replied, a little irritated by Sanchez's remark. "But he's run off somewhere. I can't settle with him if he ain't here. If I knew where he ran to, I'd still go shoot the son of a bitch." Finished arguing with Sanchez about what they should do, Slade stated, "I'm goin' to look for that stable feller. I aim to make sure he don't come sneakin' up on me. You comin'?"

Without waiting for Sanchez's answer, he got up and headed for the door.

Sanchez shrugged indifferently. In his opinion, there was not much chance that either Bloodworth or Campbell would have the guts to come after them again.

"What the hell?" he decided, got up, and followed Slade out of the saloon, oblivious of the look of relief on the bartender's face as they passed by the bar.

Marvin Bloodworth froze when the two killers appeared in the open door of the stable. The young man was in the process of closing up for the night in the absence of his father, who was at that moment on his way to Boyd Mather's ranch with Arthur Campbell. Leon had told him to close the stable doors early and go home, but he had taken longer than he had anticipated feeding the horses boarded there. Caught unprepared now, he could think of nothing to say and just stood staring at the gunmen.

"Where's the man who owns this place?" Slade asked, aware of the young man's fright.

"He ain't here," Marvin finally managed, watching nervously as Sanchez strode past him to look in the stalls and tack room.

"Well, where is he?" Slade demanded.

"I don't know," Marvin said. "He just said he wouldn't be back for a spell."

Not surprised to hear it, Slade took a hard look at Marvin. "Who the hell are you? Is the owner your pa?"

"No, sir," Marvin lied. "I just work for him."

Slade was not convinced, for he thought the boy favored Bloodworth. "You know, boy, I don't like bein' lied to."

"I ain't lyin'," Marvin insisted, fearing for his life when Slade dropped his hand to rest on the handle of his handgun. He was spared further terror when Sanchez walked up then, coming from the back of the stalls.

"Nobody back there," Sanchez said. "I coulda told you that before we walked down here. That son of a bitch is running like a scared jackrabbit."

"I reckon," Slade said. "I'm goin' back to the hotel now."

He reminded himself that the five men who had attempted to kill Sanchez and him were not the only people in the town who would like to see them dead. He didn't like the thought that there might be a hidden rifle aimed at the two of them whenever they walked the streets. It was better to be inside the hotel. Besides, he had a social visit with the tall gal who waited tables in the dining room.

"We'll see if that feller I shot in the leg had the guts to show up," he told Sanchez.

Slade recognized the young man behind the desk in the hotel lobby as the boy who had told him Tom Larsen had been shot and the shooter was coming after him. He knew that he was the son of Arthur Campbell, the owner of the hotel.

"Where's your pa, boy?"

"He's left town," Claude answered. "I reckon you know why."

"Let's get one thing straight," Slade said, pointing his finger in Claude's face. "Your pa's lucky he ain't dead, like them other two that tried to kill us."

"If he don't run like a scared rabbit, he would be dead," Sanchez said, a contemptuous grin on his face. "Maybe you thinking about getting even."

"No, sir," Claude replied. "I ain't got no ideas about nothin'."

"Good," Slade said. "You'll live a lot longer that way." He was content to leave the boy unharmed, since he made no show of standing up for his father. "Now reach back there and give me a key to room number four."

Puzzled because he knew that his father had put the two outlaws in room two, Claude said, "We ain't usin' that room. What do you wanna get in that room for?"

"Boy, you're already startin' to get on my nerves," Slade warned him. "I know who's in that room. Gimme the damn key."

"There ain't nobody in room four," Claude insisted. He pointed to an empty letter slot behind him. "There ain't even no key in the box."

"You lyin' little bastard," Slade growled. He grabbed Claude by the shirt collar and jerked him halfway across the counter. "That bitch Mary Lou lives in that room. There ain't no key there because she's got it."

"No, she don't," Claude cried. "I swear she don't."

Confused by Slade's assertion, and growing more frightened by the minute, he tried to pull away from the outlaw's grasp. Slade shoved him violently, dumping him on the floor behind the desk. Amused by the confrontation between Slade and the boy, Sanchez stopped halfway up the steps and waited there to watch the outcome. Unnoticed by Claude or Slade, he eased his .44 out of his holster.

Leaving the boy lying on the floor behind the desk, Slade turned to follow Sanchez up the stairs. "I don't need a damn key," he announced angrily, unaware that Claude had reached for the bottom drawer of the desk where a revolver was always kept.

Intent all along to take vengeance upon the men who shot his father if given the opportunity, Claude slowly eased the drawer open and pulled the gun out. With his hand trembling with fear, he aimed it at the back of the man starting up the stairs and pulled the trigger.

At almost the same time, another shot rang out, this one from Sanchez, who anticipated such a possibility when Slade turned his back on the boy. The bullet slammed into the middle of Claude's chest, knocking him flat on his back. Slade, startled, dropped to his knees on the stairs after Claude's shot whistled harmlessly by his ear.

Furious at having come so close to taking a bullet in the back, Slade pulled his pistol and pumped three shots in the already dying boy. He turned then to unleash his fury on a grinning Sanchez.

"Damn you," he roared. "What the hell were you waiting for? I oughta shoot you for lettin' him get that shot off!"

"You oughta try," Sanchez replied, his .44 resting on the stair rail, his sinister grin still in place. He was obviously amused by his partner's flustered response to the near miss and, as usual, was ready to shoot again if Slade was foolish enough to let his anger get the best of him.

Smart enough to realize that Sanchez held the advantage, Slade forced himself to calm down. "Well, I reckon I shoulda been more careful about turnin' my back on the kid. I shoulda known he might wanna get back at me for shootin' his pa."

"He so damn scared he couldn't hold his hand steady enough to hit the side of the wall," Sanchez said. "I not worried about him hitting you."

"That's damn reassurin'," Slade said sarcastically. "Maybe next time it'll be the other way around." Bringing his mind back to the moment, he looked around the tiny lobby as if searching for bystanders, realizing then that the hotel was deserted. "We might as well take a look in the safe while we're at it."

He went back behind the desk and rolled Claude's body away from the small built-in safe.

"Damn," he cursed. It was unlocked and empty of all cash and valuables. He knelt there staring into the empty safe for a long moment, before getting to his feet and stating, "Well, I'm gonna go pay a little visit to Miss Mary Lou. I can't keep her waitin' much longer."

Sanchez grunted derisively. "I expect she excited as hell."

They went up the stairs to the second floor, continuing on past the door to room two before Slade stopped. "Where the hell are you goin'?"

Surprised, Sanchez said, "With you. You think you're the only one who got needs?"

"I'll be damned," Slade replied. "This is between

the woman and me. Hell, you ain't even talked to her."

"I ain't talked to my horse," Sanchez retorted, "but I still ride him."

"I don't need no company," Slade told him. "So you just go on in our room and I'll tell you when I'm done. Then I don't care what the hell you do with her."

Sanchez shrugged, indifferent, as he was about most things that pertained to killing, robbing, or women. "If that's the way you want it. You might need some help, though. She don't act like she's saddle-broke."

"Just wait for me in the room," Slade told him. Sanchez shrugged again and went into the room.

Slade waited until Sanchez had closed the door behind him before continuing down the hall to a door with the number four on it. Preferring to surprise Mary Lou if possible, he slowly turned the knob and pressed against the door, but it was locked.

"Damn!" he muttered lowly, and knocked politely. When there was no response from inside, he knocked a little harder. Still there was no response.

At once angry, he banged on the door with his fist and yelled, "Open this damn door, bitch!" He pictured her huddled in a corner, or behind the bed, praying that he would go away.

"Damn you! I'll break this door down!" Still there was nothing from inside the room. "It's just gonna be tougher on you," he warned. His temper out of control then, he stepped back, then slammed the door with his boot, as hard as he could manage. The door cracked but did not give way, so he repeated it again and again until the lock gave way and the door swung open.

Angry, but not to the point where he gambled with

his personal safety, he stepped back to the side when the door opened. With his pistol drawn, in the event she might be waiting with a gun pointed at him, he entered the room cautiously, looking right and left quickly, trying to see every corner where she might be waiting to ambush him. It struck him then that this was not her room and never had been. There was an odor of charred wood, and the room was dusty. The faint light from the oil lamp in the hallway shining through the open door revealed a large circle of burned-out floor where a stove had once sat.

"That lyin' bitch," he muttered, thinking of Maggie Whitehouse. "You just signed your death warrant, old lady."

Determined to find Mary Lou, he proceeded back up the hall, kicking in doors at each room he came to, his amorous mood replaced by the desire to punish. Sanchez came out of their room with gun drawn.

Seeing Slade storming around the corner to search the other hall, he bellowed, "What the hell's the matter with you?"

"They lied!" Slade complained. "She ain't in that room. I'll kill her when I find her, that old bitch, too!"

Slade's frustration brought a smile of amusement to Sanchez's face, and he followed along behind him as the enraged man destroyed door after door. All of the guest rooms were empty, having been evacuated when Arthur Campbell warned his guests of the possibility of the danger that might befall the hotel. While Slade ranted and raved, Sanchez took the opportunity to rummage through the various possessions that were carelessly left behind during the speedy exodus. He was disappointed to find nothing of value, however, with the exception of a man's pocket watch left on a dresser.

With no sign of Mary Lou on the second floor, Slade went back down to search the owner's living quarters on the first floor behind the lobby. His search was no more successful than before. Still angry, but calmer now, he said, "You know damn well she lives in this hotel somewhere. I hardly expect she moved out this quick."

Still highly amused by Slade's frustrations, Sanchez suggested an area that had not occurred to his partner. "There're a couple of rooms behind the kitchen. Maybe that's where them two women live."

"Yeah," Slade responded. "Damn right." The realization of the possibility brought a determined smile to his face. "That's where they are."

He kicked Arthur Campbell's favorite rocking chair out of his way and started back toward the lobby.

"Let's go call on the ladies," he told Sanchez.

Gunshots temporarily interrupted a quickly convened meeting at the small freight office of Sam Vickers.

"Those shots came from the hotel," Gordon Luck said. He stepped to the window and peered up the street. "They've gone back to the hotel and it sounds like they ain't through with their killin'. We need to see if the women in the dining room are all right." His main concern was for Mary Lou. "If we don't do something, and I mean pretty damn quick, they're gonna destroy the whole town."

His words were unnecessary, for each one of the six men who had responded to his call for action knew that what he said was true. Two of them, Douglas Green and Benny Swartz, were there out of guilt, determined to atone for their failure to support their slain neighbors earlier in the evening.

"With two of our people dead," Gordon continued, "and two others wounded, we can't hide behind our closed doors any longer. We've got to save our town."

He nodded toward Marvin Bloodworth, who had come to the sawmill to tell him that the two killers were looking for his father and Arthur Campbell with the intention of finishing them off.

"It's time to move now. You all heard what Marvin said. I just hope we're not too late to keep them from killing anyone else."

"What are we waitin' for?" Sam exclaimed. "I'm ready. Let's go get the bastards!"

Armed with handguns and rifles, plus the belief that the fate of the town hinged upon their actions on this night, the six men filed out of the freight office and hurried toward the hotel.

Pausing for just a moment to decide which of the two rooms behind the kitchen might likely be the one occupied by Mary Lou, Slade speculated that hers was probably not the one closest to the dining room. That, he figured, was probably Maggie Whitehouse's, since she managed the dining facility.

Without bothering to knock this time, he tried the door before kicking it in to bang noisily against the wall.

"Ain't no use you hidin'," he called out, cautiously extending his arm in the open doorway, holding the lantern he took from the hallway.

When there was no answer from within, he pushed a little farther inside the door. There appeared to be no one in the darkened room. Holding the lantern before him, he looked around the room, convinced that it was, indeed, her room, judging by the articles of clothing on the bed and the personal trinkets on a dresser.

He started to leave, but stopped when it occurred to him that she might be hiding under the bed. "Ha!" he exclaimed, grabbed a corner of the bed, and turned it upside down. Finding nothing under the bed but a wooden box with a couple of blankets inside, he looked about him for something to vent his anger upon. The closest object was a basin with a pitcher inside, sitting on a dry sink. In a fit of rage, he reached out and raked the pitcher off the sink, sending it and the pitcher crashing to the floor.

"Must be next door," Sanchez offered dryly, having become weary of Slade's passionate pursuit of the woman, and amused by the angry man's display of temper.

The sound of the intruders next door was easily heard by the two women who had taken refuge in Maggie's room. Huddled in the corner of the room, beside the dry sink, Mary Lou and Maggie cringed in fear, hoping that the two killers would go away after breaking into Mary Lou's room and finding it empty. In case they didn't, they had pulled Maggie's heavy chest of drawers over before the door. And if that didn't stop them, the women were ready to defend themselves, Maggie with her shotgun and Mary Lou with her revolver. There was nothing more they could do at this point, but wait and pray, each woman's heart beating so loudly that she feared it could be heard in the hall outside. In the next instant, both hearts stopped for a terrified moment when they heard the crash of a boot against the door.

When the doorjamb finally split and the door opened an inch or two, only to be stopped by the chest of drawers, it brought a satisfied smile to Slade's face. "We found 'em," he told Sanchez

"I found you!" he called out loudly. "And now you're gonna find out what happens to bitches that waste my time." He pressed his shoulder against the door and pushed. The chest moved a few inches. "Gimme a hand," he told Sanchez.

The sullen Sanchez stepped up beside him and the two of them strained against the door until they succeeded in shoving the chest a few feet backward before it toppled over. It was now much more difficult to move any farther since it was flat on the floor. Still, there was enough room to get through the partially opened door.

Unable to wait any longer, Slade threw caution to the wind and pushed through the opening. He stood triumphantly for a moment, staring into the dark room, trying to locate the cowering women. It was only for a moment, however, for in the next instant, he was blinded by the muzzle flash of Maggie's shotgun, knocking him backward against the doorjamb.

Reeling from the blast of buckshot that tore holes in his face and chest, he was saved only when Sanchez grabbed the back of his collar and pulled him out of the room—but not before a bullet from Mary Lou's revolver caught him in the leg.

Being careful not to expose his body, Sanchez reached inside the door and emptied his .44 into the darkness, with no idea if he was hitting anyone or not. He hurried to reload as Slade staggered back into the hallway, too stunned to draw his weapon, but still on his feet. He was about to fire six more shots into the room when the door from the back of the kitchen opened and he found himself facing a group of vigilantes, led by Gordon Luck. The outlaws and vigilantes alike were stunned by the sudden confrontation, and both parties fired wildly. Those behind Luck scrambled back to take cover as Sanchez's .44 tore chunks out of the door. It gained him time enough to help Slade down the hall and through the outside door.

"Let's get outta here!" he shouted, backing away while still covering the kitchen door with his pistol. He took a hard look at Slade then. "That shotgun sure make a mess of you. You gonna make it?"

"Damn right," Slade said. "I sure as hell ain't gonna wait around here for no necktie party." Through sheer willpower alone, the wounded man stayed on his feet, knowing that if he didn't, he would surely be left behind.

"Get to the horses, then," Sanchez ordered. "I'll keep these boys busy while you saddle 'em." He paused, still keeping his eye on the kitchen door. "You *can* saddle 'em, can't you?"

He would have left Slade to fend for himself if his horse had been already saddled, but he found himself in a tight situation. He couldn't hold off the vigilantes and saddle his horse at the same time, so he had to trust that Slade could get it done. He took his eye off the door just long enough to see that Slade was painfully making his way toward the hotel stables. Then he turned back in time to see it being slowly eased open. A couple of quick shots caused the men inside to slam shut again. Thinking that would hold them at bay for a few minutes, he backed away toward the stable.

Inside the kitchen, the citizen's posse was temporarily stymied, unable to open the door without exposing themselves to the outlaws' gunfire. They looked to Gordon Luck to decide what to do.

"They're gonna try to run for it," Gordon said. "So they'll be headin' for the stables for their horses. We've got to get to some cover where we can get a clear shot at the stable door. If we hurry, we can get there before they have a chance to saddle up."

"What about Maggie and Mary Lou?" Benny asked. "We need to see if they're all right. There was a helluva lot of shootin'."

"That's right," Gordon replied hurriedly, chastising himself for having forgotten about the women. "We need to make sure they're safe."

He moved close to the door again and slowly eased it open a few inches. When there was no immediate gunfire from the hallway, he gradually pushed it the rest of the way.

"They've run for the stable!" he exclaimed, and turned to issue his orders. "Sam, you take Benny and Douglas and go see 'bout the women. The rest of us will go out the front door and try to get around back to catch 'em before they can get away."

There was no hesitation on the part of either party.

"Maggie!" Sam Vickers called from the hallway. "Are you all right?" In case she didn't recognize his voice, he yelled, "It's me, Sam Vickers. Are you women okay?"

"Yeah, we're all right, but they ain't." Maggie answered from the darkened room, more confident than frightened now. In a moment, she and Mary Lou came to the door, both holding their weapons before them triumphantly. "We shot one of 'em for sure. I don't know how bad, but I reckon we showed those two bastards that it ain't good for their health to mess with us," she boasted.

"Best for you to stay right here till we take care of those two killers," Sam told them. "We just wanted to make sure you were all right." He turned to Benny and Douglas. "Come on, boys, let's get to the stables to help Gordon."

While Sam, Douglas, and Benny followed the trail of bloodstains down the hallway to the outside door, Gordon Luck led the other two out the front door of the dining room and hustled around to the stables.

"Come on, boys," he exhorted them to hurry. "We're doin' the Lord's business, slayin' the evildoers in His name."

"Amen," Harold Chestnut, the postmaster, sang out, responding to the Baptist minister's urging, much as he did on Sunday mornings in the partially finished church.

Rounding the back corner of the rooms behind the kitchen, the trio of vigilantes was met with a blistering volley of rifle shots that drove them back behind the building.

"Jesus Christ!" Luck swore as he dived for cover, his crusade effectively stalled for the moment. "Anybody hit?" he asked. Luckily, no one had been. "The Lord's with us, men," he said. "He don't mind if you swear a little in the heat of battle," he added to excuse his taking of the Lord's name in vain.

"We ain't in too good a spot," Chestnut pointed out. It was a needless observation, for they were exposed to rifle fire from the hotel stables anytime they might try to advance beyond the corner of the building. "They can hold us off all day. Somebody needs to go around behind the stable to keep 'em from goin' out the back."

"Maybe," Luck said. "But Campbell don't ever use that door. It's got a padlock on it. Let's wait a minute or two and see what happens when Sam comes up from the other side of the building. "They can't hold us off in both directions. They can't stay there forever, so they're gonna have to make a run for it. And when they do, we'll cut 'em down like wheat."

Luck was wrong in his assumption, however, for Sanchez and Slade had a clear field of fire on both corners of the building that housed Mary Lou's and Maggie's rooms. Set up behind a double bale of hay, the two outlaws could throw enough rifle shots at the two corners to effectively discourage any thoughts of a charge. When Sanchez was satisfied that Slade, although bleeding profusely, was able to continue watching the vigilantes alone, he decided it would be a lot quicker if he saddled the horses instead of Slade. So he left him behind the bales while he went to take care of the horses.

Once he had both horses ready to go, Sanchez went to the back of the stable to confirm something he thought he remembered seeing before. His memory served him, for he found a back door to the stable. When he tried to push it open, he found that it was latched on the outside, and probably padlocked, since there were no signs on the dirt floor that indicated the door had been used recently. He studied the door for a moment before going to the tack room to look for something to use. Among a few tools in a corner of the room, he found what he was looking for and picked up an axe.

This'll do, he thought.

When he came out of the tack room, he paused to check on Slade. "You gonna make it?"

"I'm still here," Slade answered weakly.

"Well, you hold on. I gonna cut a way out the back," Sanchez said, and hurried to the back door. Slade didn't sound too good, so he figured he'd better be quick. He paused again when he heard Slade's rifle open fire when Sam Vickers showed up at the corner opposite the one Gordon Luck was using for cover.

Wasting no more time, he attacked the board where the hasp was bolted. Although still green, the board from Gordon Luck's sawmill was not difficult to chop. Once he got a small hole started, it gave him more room for the axe blade's bite. Then it was just a matter of chopping away until he finally cut the board in two. Once that was accomplished, he tossed the axe aside and shoved the door open, leaving the hasp, still padlocked, hanging on the short piece of board.

Returning to the front of the stable then, Sanchez crawled up behind the hay bales beside Slade. He took a good look at his partner to decide if it was worth his time and effort to be burdened with the wounded man.

"See anybody try to get around behind us?" he asked.

"No," Slade replied wearily. "There's about half a dozen of 'em, and they split up—half of 'em at one corner of that building, half of 'em on the other."

"All right," Sanchez decided. "We throw a bunch of lead at both corners. Then we gonna get the hell out of here. You ready?" Slade nodded. "You'd better be ready to ride," Sanchez said, "because when I go out that door, I not gonna be looking back to see where you are. *Comprende?*"

"I *comprende* all right," Slade replied, fully understanding his situation, and with the firm intention to put a bullet in his partner's back in the event he tried to leave him behind. Staying low to the floor of the stable so as not to be seen retreating, they crawled back between the stalls where the horses stood waiting. When Slade tried to step up in the saddle, his wounded leg failed him.

"Gimme a hand, damn it," he blurted.

Sanchez boosted him up in the saddle. "You gonna be able to stay on that horse?"

"Yeah," Slade said. "I'm all right when I'm in the saddle. My leg smarts a little when I put too much weight on it. That's all. You ain't got to worry about me. Let's go."

It was not entirely true. He was in a great deal of pain, more so from the shotgun blast than the pistol bullet in his leg as blood continued to seep out of the many open wounds covering his face and torso.

"They've stopped shootin'," Harold Chestnut said as they continued to watch for some sign of an attempt to escape. "It's been at least fifteen minutes without a shot. You reckon they got outta there some way without us seein' 'em?"

"Most likely they're just savin' their ammunition," Gordon Luck said. He strained to see into the dark entrance to the stable. "Maybe hopin' we'll think they're gone and charge in there. But they've got to come out that front door."

After another ten or fifteen minutes passed with still no gunfire, Sam Vickers called out from the other corner of the building, "Gordon! Whaddaya wanna do?"

"Just hold on a minute," Gordon yelled back. "They're up to somethin'. Keep your eye on that door." After a few minutes more, he realized that they were locked in a hopeless standoff. "We've got to make a move," he told Chestnut. "We can't sit here till mornin', waitin' for them to come out. Maybe somebody had better go around behind the stable and try to see inside."

"Hell, I'll go," Chestnut volunteered. "It beats sittin' here all night."

"All right," Luck said, "but be careful they don't see you. There're a couple of windows in the back. Maybe you can sneak up to one of 'em and see what they're up to."

"They won't see me," Chestnut said.

He backed away toward the front of the building, near the dining room door. Then he made his way around the saloon next door and followed the alley behind to the rear of the hotel stables.

Luck and the others waited and watched for what seemed like a long time, but in fact was only a few minutes before hearing Chestnut's voice calling out. It came from the inside of the stables.

"Gordon! They're gone! Come on in!"

Chapter II

The six-man posse stood dumbfounded in the back of the stable, gaping at the door swung wide open.

"It was locked, all right," Sam Vickers said, looking at the padlock still in place on the short piece of board.

"Well, I reckon that's my mistake," Gordon Luck said. He picked up the axe beside the door. "Looks like we coulda heard them choppin' away at that door."

"I'm not surprised," Benny Swartz said. "There was a helluva lot of shooting going on. It'da been hard to hear them chopping wood in all that."

Gordon walked through the open door and stood peering out into the darkness beyond for a few long moments. "Well, I see it as my duty to go after 'em. Anybody gonna ride with me?"

"I'll ride with you, Reverend," Chestnut spoke up immediately.

"Me, too," Vickers said. He was followed by the rest of the hastily formed posse.

"Good," Gordon said. "We'll start after 'em as soon as it's light. It ought'n be too hard a trail to follow."

As she did every morning, Beulah Watts showed up at the hotel just before sunrise to build a fire in the kitchen stove. On this morning, however,.she found Maggie and Mary Lou already hard at work, scrubbing the dining room floor. Surprised, she stood in the doorway between the kitchen and the dining room to stare. "Am I late for work?" she asked.

"No, we just had a little cleanup to do before we start breakfast this morning," Maggie told her. "You go right ahead. We're about through here."

Since it appeared that most of the scrubbing had been in one area of the floor, Beulah walked in to take a closer look. "That looks like bloodstains," she said. "What was it?"

"Blood," Mary Lou answered dryly. She let Maggie tell her cook what had happened after she left for home the night before.

"My stars!" Beulah gasped when Maggie told her about the three who had lost their lives. "Alvin Tucker and Jesse Springer—and Mr. Campbell's boy, Claude! Oh, dear me, and Mr. Campbell don't even know his boy is dead."

"And somebody's gonna have to go out to Mather's place and tell him," Mary Lou said.

Maggie went on to tell Beulah of the reception she and Mary Lou held for Slade Corbett and his sidekick when they tried to break into her room.

"It's a wonder you both ain't dead," Beulah exclaimed when she saw the splintered tabletops piled over in the corner and the bullet holes in the walls.

"Hell," Maggie boasted boldly, "it's a wonder Slade

Corbett and that scum riding with him ain't dead. He'll know better than to come around here again. Right, Mary Lou?"

"I hope so," Mary Lou replied, not so confident as her employer. She knew that she would fight to protect herself, but at the moment she was too weary to think about it. All but a couple of hours since Slade and Sanchez left had been spent putting Maggie's room and the dining room back in order after the damage the two predators had wrought.

"You want me to tote in some wood for the stove?" Beulah asked. "Are we gonna open for breakfast?"

"I reckon so," Maggie said. "A little shootin' and murderin' ain't gonna kill any appetites in this town. When everybody finds out Slade and Sanchez are gone, they'll be back wanting breakfast. A couple of our regulars won't be here for breakfast, though, Sam Vickers and Harold Chestnut. They're riding with the posse."

"That's about as good as we're gonna do," Mary Lou decided, looking at the patch of stains where Tucker's body had lain. "I'm gonna throw this dirty water out. Then I'm going back to my room to try to pull myself together to work today."

"Take a little nap if you need it," Maggie said. "Beulah and I can handle it this morning."

"No, I'll be back to help," Mary Lou insisted. "I'm just gonna go splash some water on my face and freshen up a little."

She stood for a few moments, holding the two halves of the basin that had sat on her dry sink before Slade Corbett raked it off onto the floor. It had been her mother's, and she pressed the two broken pieces together, trying to will them to be whole again. Over

in the corner, in a dozen pieces, lay the shattered
pitcher that had sat in the basin. She had very little of
value: some jewelry that the two outlaws had not
found; what little bit of money she had managed to
save, along with the fifty dollars Cole had left for her,
hidden under a board in the floor; and two nice
dresses, trimmed in fine lace, that were too nice to
wear for any occasion in Cheyenne.

One of them had served as her wedding dress
when she was young and naive enough to marry
Tyson Cagle, who had worked in his father's bank in
Omaha. How dashing Tyson had seemed to the innocent girl of sixteen. And after only twelve months of
marriage, when she was carrying his child, her dashing husband dashed off with a substantial sum of the
bank's money and the fourteen-year-old daughter of
the bank's vice president. No one knew where they
had fled, and nothing had been heard of either of
them ever again. She had been left three months
pregnant with no place to go but back to her father's
house, only to lose the baby one month later.

She sighed. She hadn't thought about that time in
her life for quite a while. After all, that was over four
years ago, and many things had happened in her life
since then. She was a different person from that innocent girl now, with a more callous attitude toward
whatever life placed in her path. She picked up the
wedding dress from the floor and held it before her at
arm's length. She could still wear it, she thought, but
it would now be a good deal tighter than when she
had stood before the preacher.

Deep in thought, she was suddenly distracted by a
soft sound behind her. She turned to discover a dark
form in the dim light of the hallway, a rifle hanging

casually in one hand. Startled then, she involuntarily gave a little cry of surprise.

"I didn't mean to scare you," the man said. "The door was open. I was just fixin' to knock."

"Cole?" Mary Lou questioned, not certain. "Cole Bonner?"

"Yes, ma'am, it's me," he answered. "What happened to your door?" he asked, just then realizing it was open because it had been split from the jamb.

"That'll take a little time to tell if you wanna know the whole story. What are you doing here? I wasn't sure we'd ever see you again. When you and Harley left Cheyenne, I thought you were going to spend the winter with Harley's Crow friends."

She told herself that she should have expected him, because it seemed that every time Slade Corbett showed up in town, Cole followed soon after.

"I reckon I'm not too good at lyin' around an Indian village when I have some unfinished business to tend to," he said.

"You're supposed to be resting up, letting that wound heal," she lectured him. "How is it? There hasn't been enough time for that wound to heal. Here, let me look at it." She stepped forward to see for herself, causing him to step backward.

"It's all right," he said. "It's healin' up just fine. What happened to your door?"

Instead of answering his question right away, she paused to look at him closely for a long moment, and it occurred to her that she cared about what happened to him. In fact, she cared very much, and it contradicted her insensitive attitude toward men in general. She realized then that he was staring at her, puzzled by her failure to answer him.

"It got kicked in," she finally answered. She went on then to tell him the whole story of Slade Corbett and Jose Sanchez's return to Cheyenne.

He listened patiently until she was finished before commenting. "So that's why there ain't anybody at the front desk. I thought that was kind of strange." He paused to decide what he should do. "The posse left this mornin' to go after 'em?" he asked.

"About an hour before you showed up like a ghost at my door," Mary Lou replied.

He had to stop again and think for a second. He had not expected to cross Slade's trail so soon. He was tired and hungry, but the trail was too fresh to tarry. By the look of the dark sky, it looked as if snow might fall at any minute. A six-man posse should leave an easy trail to follow, but even that could be quickly covered by a snowstorm.

"Have they got anybody that's good at trackin'?" he asked, for there was always the possibility that the posse could lose the tracks and lead him off the outlaws' trail.

"Sam Vickers calls himself a good tracker," Mary Lou said. "I don't really know. Shorty Doyle's with them. He might be a good one. He hunts a lot."

Cole considered that for a moment before his thoughts shifted to Joe. His horse needed to rest before he pushed him hard again. But he felt that he couldn't afford to get much farther behind the posse. Watching him closely, Mary Lou could see the indecision in his eyes.

"Cole," she pleaded, "you've got no business heading out after those men now. You look tired as hell to me. Why don't you give the men a chance to catch up with those two murderers? Slade Corbett is badly wounded. I know that for a fact, because Maggie and I both shot him. The hallway is covered with his blood. He might not make it very far as it is. There's no sense you killing yourself trying to catch up to a dying man. Gordon Luck is leading the posse. He's a good man. He'll catch up with them."

"Maybe," Cole said. "I've got to see for myself."

His conscience, and his solemn vow over Ann's grave, gave him no choice but to verify Slade Corbett's and Sanchez's death. His thoughts turned back to Joe again. The big Morgan had traveled hard since his camp more than twenty miles north of Cheyenne. Cole had planned to buy some grain for him and figured he'd have plenty of time to rest before starting out again. It had stood to reason that it would take some time to find anyone who could give him a clue as to where to start looking for Slade Corbett. He hadn't figured on picking up a hot trail as soon as he rode into town. But his common sense told him that it would be a mistake to push Joe beyond the horse's limit at any rate. He might find himself walking across a snowy prairie if he mistreated the horse. Finally he made the decision that he knew to be the right one.

"I've gotta let my horse rest before I can start out again," he said.

"Well, that sounds like a sensible thing to do," Mary Lou told him. "I'm thinking your horse isn't the only one that needs to rest." She gave him a critical look then. "When's the last time you've had something to eat?"

He had to pause a moment to recall. "Not long ago," he said. "Yesterday sometime."

She shook her head, exasperated with his neglect

for himself. "I was going to the pump to fill this bucket when you showed up. While I'm doing that, you can take your horse to the stable and unsaddle him. There ain't anybody in the stable, either, so go ahead and give him some grain. When you're done with that, come on in the dining room and I'll fix some breakfast for you. You can't go off to get yourself killed on an empty stomach."

"Yes, ma'am," he said. Something in her tone discouraged him from protesting, so he turned and walked to the outside door at the end of the hall. Mary Lou stepped out into the hallway to watch him depart.

One-track mind, she thought, then compared him to the husband she had known briefly, and wondered how it would be to have a man so dedicated to her by her side. She cautioned herself not to become any more interested in Cole Bonner. No woman was likely to drive the memory of Ann Bonner from his mind.

It mattered little, she thought then. *He's riding a trail that will probably lead him to his death, anyway. Don't give him a permanent hold on your heart.*

As fate chose to play it, Sanchez and Corbett fled the town of Cheyenne, heading straight north for a couple of miles. And had they continued on along that path, they might have chanced upon an encounter with the man who hunted them, for Cole had ridden that very road toward Cheyenne. It was not to be, however, because the two outlaws changed directions after riding only two miles, leaving the road to strike out on a more western course. Their trail was easily followed by the posse over the light blanket of snow that had fallen two days before. And while Cole ate the hearty breakfast Mary Lou prepared for him, Gordon Luck and his men paused to rest their horses at the two outlaws' camp of the night before.

"That son of a bitch is still bleedin' like a stuck hog," Sam Vickers said, pointing to several spots of blood in the snow.

"Maybe we won't be chasin' but one man before we're done," Shorty Doyle speculated. "Ol' Maggie blasted him head-on with that shotgun. Maybe he'll bleed out before much longer."

"Maybe so," Luck allowed as he looked over the campsite, trying to get a picture in his mind of the outlaws' desperation. "They coulda found a better place to camp. There ain't no water here, so they had to melt snow to make coffee, if they had any coffee. It wasn't much of a fire they built." He looked around him at the barren rock formations, not surprised that wood for a fire had been pretty difficult to find. The impressions in the snow close to the ashes gave him an idea that the wounded man was literally hugging the fire in an effort to keep from freezing. "I'm thinkin' they made camp here because Corbett couldn't go any farther without stoppin' to rest. So let's get after 'em. There's a good chance they might have to find someplace to hole up, if he can't go any farther."

After walking and leading their horses for half an hour, they climbed aboard again and continued following the obvious trail left by the outlaws.

It was the middle of the afternoon when they approached Chugwater Creek. "We'd best rest the horses for a while," Luck said. "We can water 'em and take time to make some coffee at the creek."

It was a welcome suggestion to the rest of the

posse. The afternoon had turned much colder with the sun hidden behind heavy clouds, which threatened the possibility of snow.

"That sure as hell suits me," Harold Chestnut said. "I'm so cold I can't hardly feel nothin' in my legs."

They were the last words he spoke before a .54-caliber slug knocked a hole in his chest, and he slid sideways from his saddle, dead before he hit the ground.

Startled by the crack of the Spencer carbine, the other five members of the posse panicked when Chestnut fell. There was no cover close by the treeless creek banks, and their efforts resulted in a tangle of horses as they tried to turn them in an attempt to retreat. The carbine spoke again and Douglas Green clutched his chest and fell to the ground beneath the horses' hooves, causing them to rear up to avoid his body. They were at the mercy of the unseen sniper, and one of the rearing horses screamed when it was struck in the neck. Sam Vickers was just able to jump from the saddle before the injured horse fell.

"Get back outta range!" Gordon Luck blared amid the yelling of the men and the screaming of the frightened horses. Finally able to get their horses untangled, the ambushed posse galloped in retreat with Vickers sprinting behind them on foot. Being the opportune target, he made it only thirty or forty yards before a bullet in the back ended his run.

At a full gallop, Gordon Luck led the other two survivors up a ravine between two rock formations, where he pulled his horse to a halt. Shorty Doyle and Benny Swartz were close on his heels, and they reined their horses to a sliding stop. Harold Chestnut's horse followed them into the ravine. Still in a state of shock, Swartz stared wide-eyed at Luck, making small whining noises, scarcely believing he was still alive. Shorty, wide-eyed as well, said the obvious.

"They bushwhacked us!"

"Where's Vickers?" Luck asked.

"He didn't make it," Shorty said. "I saw him go down. I was lookin' back for him to try to get him to swing up behind me, but he wasn't quick enough."

"I'll pray for him and the others, too," Luck said. "We've got to figure out what's the best thing to do now—three of us gone." He shook his head in disbelief, unable to understand how the Lord could let that happen when they were in the right. "We'll have to be more careful how we go from here."

"I'll tell you, Reverend, the best thing for me is to get the hell outta here before they decide to come after us to finish the job," Swartz said, having taken control of his emotions somewhat.

"You don't mean that, Benny," Luck said. "We owe it to the three good men who got shot down to punish their murderers. Sometimes the Lord works in mysterious ways, sacrificing some so that others might fulfill their destiny."

"Benny's right," Shorty said. "His ways is a little too mysterious to suit me. There ain't no use in the rest of us hangin' around here till they pick off every one of us. We ran 'em outta town. That's enough for me. I'm goin' with Benny."

"What about the ones we lost?" Luck said. "Sam Vickers, Harold Chestnut, and Douglas Green— they're our friends and neighbors. We can't just leave them here. Douglas has a wife and child. What will we tell them if we don't take him home?"

"Well, that is a problem, and somethin' we surely oughta do," Benny said. "It's a terrible thing that happened here today, but we can't go back there now. I reckon there's nothin' we can do for those poor souls but pray for 'em and maybe come back another day to get the bodies."

Luck wasn't happy with the prospect of abandoning the dead, but there was no question that it was tantamount to suicide to ride back toward that open creek bank to retrieve the bodies. Already burdened with a feeling of responsibility for their deaths, he didn't like the prospect of facing Douglas Green's widow. But he could think of no safe way to go back for the dead at this point.

"You two go on back to Cheyenne," he finally decided. "You're right. There's no way to pick up the dead without gettin' somebody else shot."

Benny didn't understand. "Well, what are you gonna do?"

"I'm gonna stay here and keep an eye on that creek bank," Luck told him. "I'm not leavin' our dead for the buzzards to fight over." When Shorty started to protest, Luck went on. "I'm not thinkin' about playin' the hero. I'm just hopin' to wait Corbett and the Mexican out. I figure they'll move on when they're sure we ain't gonna make another try, and we've turned tail and run. When they leave, I'll pick up Vickers and the others. Leave Harold's horse with me to carry the bodies."

"If that's what you think best," Shorty said, feeling no guilt for abandoning Luck. "Maybe me and Benny can round up a few more to come back and help you carry them back. We'll bring a wagon to haul 'em in."

It occurred to him that there was a strong possibility that they might find Luck among the dead if they did come back. But it was his decision to stay. Shorty looked at Swartz. "Let's go, Benny."

Luck watched them for a few moments as they rode out of the bottom of the ravine. Then he dismounted and crawled up to the rim to a point where he could see the three bodies lying out in the treeless apron before the creek.

A self-satisfied smile spread slowly across Sanchez's unshaven face.

Like shooting fish in a barrel, he thought as he watched the broad expanse of open range for any sign of a counterattack. Lying on his belly in the shallow trench he had fashioned in the creek bank, he reloaded the Spencer carbine he carried.

Come on, he thought. *I've got plenty more bullets.*

Behind him, closer to the water's edge, and shielded from view by a tangle of dead berry bushes, Slade lay close to the horses. Sanchez looked back at his wounded partner and scowled. Once the leader of the small band of outlaws that followed him, Slade was feared by every man who rode with him.

Look at him now, Sanchez thought. *He lies there like a slaughtered pig.*

Sanchez was convinced that he had effectively stopped any advance upon the creek as long as it was light. But as far as he could tell, there were three of the posse left taking cover in the ravine. There would be no more than a few hours of daylight left, and he did not like the possibility of the three sneaking up on him after dark. Slade would be of little value in defense of the camp, even though he claimed to need only a little rest. So Sanchez intended to leave the creek and find a better place to camp. He briefly considered the odds of successfully leaving his position on the bank and collecting the weapons and ammunition from the bodies. Regretfully he rejected the notion, thinking that he would then be the one subjected to sniper fire from the ravine.

Feeling certain now that the three in the ravine had no intention of risking their necks before darkness, Sanchez drew back from his position. Moving quickly back to Slade and the horses, he told the wounded man it was time to go.

"We got maybe two hours of daylight before those bastards try again. Best we be gone when they get here. You rested enough to ride?"

"Yeah," Slade grunted with a painful grimace. "I can ride."

Maybe, Sanchez thought, *but not good enough to suit me.* He had already decided that Slade would slow him down too much.

"Come on," he told him, "I help you to other side of creek. Then I get horses ready to ride."

Sanchez boosted Slade up to get a foot in the stirrup, then watched him as he groaned to throw his other leg over. It was enough to confirm Sanchez's decision. He was not one to care for a wounded comrade at any rate. He stepped up on his horse, took Slade's reins, and led his horse over to the other side of the Chugwater. Once across, he dismounted and said, "There, you on this side now, nice and dry. I help you down so you don't have to sit in the saddle while I go see if those bastards still behind those rocks." Slade was in too much pain to object, so he let Sanchez pull him out of the saddle again. "Damn, you still bleeding," Sanchez said. "You sit here, wrap this blanket around you, and take it easy till I get back." After Slade had seemed to settle himself against a large rock, Sanchez bobbed his head up and down a few times as if seriously thinking something over. Then he said, "I think I lead the horses over behind those bushes so they don't be easy to see."

Slade sat there, infuriated by the pain he was suffering, and frustrated by his inability to stop the bleeding. His shirt and trousers were soaked with blood from the many open wounds left by Maggie Whitehouse's shotgun, and the bullet wound in his thigh threatened to swell until it split. And having to be helped by the insensitive Sanchez was irritating at best.

If I could get on my horse without help, I'd shoot the son of a bitch, he thought. It occurred to him then that it had gotten awfully quiet.

"What the hell is takin' so long?" he called out. "We've got to move from here."

When there was no answer from beyond the clump of bushes, Slade turned to look, just in time to see Sanchez riding over a low rise, almost a quarter of a mile away, leading his horse behind him.

"Damn you!" Slade bellowed, realizing that he had been left to die.

He pulled his pistol from his holster and emptied it at the rapidly disappearing target, knowing it was useless since Sanchez was already beyond reasonable pistol range. Still, he hoped that one of the six shots might have been lucky enough to find its mark.

He remained there, sitting against the rock, fuming, his anger so intense that he didn't feel any sense of the numbing cold. Determined to live, and too mean to die, he stared out across the quiet creek, waiting for someone to come seek him, certain that they would. All he lived for now was the chance to take out his vengeance on someone.

Having heard the six pistol shots in rapid succession, Gordon Luck scrambled up the hill where the top of the ravine ended. There was no sign of anyone, but he knew now that they must still be on the banks of the creek somewhere. He was beginning to question his decision to remain in this spot. If they had not left yet, could it mean that they were waiting for darkness to come after him, and what were they shooting at? If it was their plan to stalk him, then it would be Sanchez, for it was doubtful that Corbett was able to. He was still turning it over in his mind when a small movement on the prairie caught his eye. He squinted, trying to see more clearly. Then he realized he was seeing two horses racing toward the horizon, close to a mile away and fading rapidly.

They were running again! But what were the shots he had heard? Without waiting any longer, he decided to take a chance that it hadn't been a trick to lure him out in the open.

With Chestnut's horse behind him, he rode back down to the foot of the ravine and waited there for a few minutes before leaving the protection of the rocks. When there were no shots fired from the creek, he dismounted and walked to Vickers' body, being careful to keep his horse between him and the creek. There were still no shots fired, so he walked down closer to the creek where the other two bodies lay. Again there were no additional shots fired. Satisfied that there was no one left, he began the chore of loading the dead on the horses. A powerful man, he managed to heft the bodies up, two of them on Harold Chestnut's horse, and the other on his. With his grim cargo secured, he started back to Cheyenne.

He had ridden about two miles when he spotted a lone rider coming his way. He assumed it was either Shorty or Benny on his way back to help with the dead, having felt a twinge of guilt for leaving them. In case it was not one of them, however, he made sure his rifle was riding easy in the saddle sling. As the rider approached, he realized it was not one of the ill-fated posse, but a man sitting tall in the saddle, a stranger to him, for he had never met Cole Bonner. Luck reined his horse back as the rider pulled up before him.

"You'd be Gordon Luck, I reckon," Cole said in greeting.

Surprised that the stranger knew him, Luck replied, "That's a fact. How'd you know that? I don't recall makin' your acquaintance."

"I met two of your friends back there a ways," Cole said. "They told me about the trouble you fellers had."

"Yeah, I'm afraid we came out on the short end when we caught up with those two outlaws. And if you're gonna keep ridin' the way you're headed, I oughta warn you that you might run up on 'em."

"That's what I'm hopin'," Cole said.

Luck studied the young stranger's face more closely. "You're Cole Bonner, ain't you?" Cole nodded in reply. Luck continued. "I've heard about you, and the task you've set for yourself. I reckon it don't make much sense to warn you to be careful. You sure oughta know who you're dealin' with."

"I reckon," Cole said. "Your two friends said Corbett and his partner are holed up at Chugwater Creek."

"Not no more," Luck said. "They've left there now. That's the only reason I was able to pick up our dead."

Cole took a second look at the bodies draped across the horses. "That's bad luck, all right. How far is it to the creek?"

"I'd say about two miles, maybe a little bit more," Luck estimated.

Cole squinted as he looked at the low clouds obscuring the sun, thinking that it must be close to sundown. "I best be gettin' along," he said. "It's gonna be dark pretty soon. Maybe I can get to the creek before it gets too dark to pick up a trail." He nudged Joe with his heels.

"Good huntin'," Luck called after him as he rode away. "And keep a sharp eye. Those two are the devil's disciples, and that's a fact."

"Much obliged," Cole replied without looking back.

Chapter 12

It was already approaching darkness by the time Cole reached the east bank of Chugwater Creek. The dark clouds hovering over the shallow valley appeared swollen and closer to the ground than they had been an hour before, threatening to rupture at any second and cover the prairie with snow.

Cole felt an urgency to cross the creek while there was still a little light to see which way Corbett and Sanchez had fled. It was easy to see where they had entered the water, so he crossed and picked up the tracks on the other side.

Fighting the almost overpowering urge to close his eyes and sleep, Slade suddenly became alert upon hearing the sound of a horse climbing out of the water. In his efforts to keep warm, he had crawled to a gully that was deep enough to get most of his body inside. It had helped a little to withstand the biting cold, and it afforded him protection against anyone searching for him. He was certain that someone would come to finish him, and now they had arrived. The anticipation caused him to forget his pain that had almost crippled him before, as he pushed himself up from the gully far enough to get his head and shoulders above the edge. He waited for his stalker to appear.

In a few minutes, a dark figure appeared in the failing light, walking up from the creek bank, leading his horse. He appeared to have a rifle in one hand, and he was looking at the ground, intent upon the tracks he was following.

A slow, painful smile crept across Slade's face when he realized the man could not see him there in the gully. He rested his gun hand on a sizable stone to steady his aim, although he felt it would be impossible to miss his target as the figure came closer to the gully. In no hurry to take the shot, for it was obvious that his tracker had no idea he was there, he picked his spot to pull the trigger. He thought of Sanchez at that moment, who no doubt thought Slade was dead, and with no idea that in a few moments he would have a horse. The Mexican's days were numbered.

His target was almost to the spot Slade had his .44 trained on, with no indication that he knew of the ambush awaiting him.

Now, Slade told himself, and slowly squeezed the trigger, only to be startled when he heard the metallic click of the hammer falling on an empty chamber. In that horrifying moment, it occurred to him that he had not reloaded his pistol after he shot at Sanchez. In desperation, he frantically squeezed the trigger again, fanned the hammer back, and pulled the trigger again, hoping there might be one bullet left.

* * *

Fully startled, for he thought the creek bank was deserted, Cole reacted as soon as he heard the hammer fall on the empty chamber. Spinning around toward the sound, he fired three shots at the dark object showing above the rim of the gully as fast as he could crank the lever on his rifle. The figure sank down out of sight in the gully.

When there was no return fire, he hesitated for a moment before moving cautiously toward the gully. Seeing the pistol lying in the snow, he knew his shots had hit home, so he moved up to the edge and looked down in the gully to get a closer look. Even in the half-light, he could see that it was Slade Corbett. The black hat with the silver hatband lying close by confirmed it. He took a quick look around him then to make sure Sanchez was not there. Coming back to stare at the body again, he felt a sudden weariness as he looked down at the one man whose name had never left his mind, awake or sleeping. The road had been long and hard before it led him to this creek bank. There was a feeling that his job was done—until he reminded himself that the savage Sanchez was still running free.

One more before I rest, he thought.

With that thought in mind, he decided that he had better look for the tracks of Sanchez's horses before it became too dark to see them. So he hurried back to his horse and continued following the tracks while he could still see. It was important at least to know which direction Sanchez had headed when he left the creek.

After another fifteen minutes or so, it became too difficult to see the tracks anymore, but he had seen enough to know that Sanchez had headed toward a low line of hills to the west of the Chugwater. And if he held to that line, it would most likely lead to a notch he could see in the southern end of the hills. He figured he could pick up the outlaw's tracks in the morning, so he decided to make camp by the creek about thirty-five yards from the gully where Slade Corbett's body lay.

Wood to build a fire was scarce, as was grass for Joe to eat. He fed the horse some grain from a sack he carried for such occasions. The firewood was mostly sticks and small limbs from the many berry bushes on the bank, but it was enough to boil his coffee and cook the deer jerky he had brought with him.

While he turned his jerky over the flame, he thought about how close he had come to being the corpse left lying in a gully. Lady Luck was riding with him, because he had been downright careless. The fact that Gordon had told him that the two outlaws were gone was still no excuse for not exercising more caution. He had to admit that he would be dead right now if Corbett had not tried to shoot him with an empty pistol, for he was at point-blank range and had no notion Slade was even there. When he had checked the outlaw's body, he found that he was wearing a cartridge belt with plenty of cartridges, so it must have been a simple matter of forgetfulness.

How the hell could anybody in that situation forget to load his gun? Cole wondered.

He awoke the next morning to find the creek bank covered with a blanket of freshly fallen snow. He had slept so soundly that he had not even been aware of the gentle shower that covered his slicker and extinguished his fire.

Alarmed that he had overslept, for he was anxious

to go after Sanchez at first light, he roused himself immediately. Coffee would have to wait until he had ridden far enough to have to rest his horse.

He saddled Joe and prepared to leave, but first he went back to the gully where he had left Slade's body. He found the body still there, undisturbed by scavengers. But the smooth white blanket of snow on the bank of the creek made it impossible to see any tracks now. He shook his head in consternation. There was nothing he could do about it. It had been too dark to follow Sanchez the night before. But at least he had an idea of the line Sanchez took when he left the creek, so he stepped up into the saddle and turned Joe toward the notch in the faraway hills to the west. There was still one man to kill before his beloved wife could rest in peace.

There was no improvement in the weather as he continued toward the notch, and by the time he reached it, it had started snowing again. He followed the notch through to the other side of the single line of hills, only to be confronted with endless miles of white prairie.

He reined Joe to a stop while he looked out over the country before him. It was difficult to accept, but he had to admit that he had no clue which way Sanchez might have ridden. There was no road or Indian trail to follow in any direction. Even had there been a game trail, it would have been impossible to see it under the snow. He was going to have to make a decision,

Knowing that he could be no more than half a day's ride from the last of the six men who had destroyed his life, Cole was overcome with frustration. If only he knew which direction to search! Buzzard's Roost came to mind, but Sanchez's trail led far too much toward the west. It stood to reason that he would have run directly north if he was going to Lem Dawson's place in the Laramie Mountains. Maybe he and Corbett had intended to foil the posse by heading west, then changing directions when they got to the Chugwater. But that had not been the case. When Sanchez crossed the Chugwater, he cut back even farther west. Cole was forced to accept the fact that the outlaw had successfully given him the slip.

Suddenly the weariness returned, contributing to a feeling of failure. Slade Corbett was dead, as were all the rest of his gang, save one, and that one's days were numbered, he promised his late wife. Maybe not before spring, maybe not before summer, but Sanchez would pay for his part in the brutal murders of Ann and her sister's family, no matter how long it took. He told himself that his responsibility now was to give his wound time to heal properly and regain his strength so that he would be ready when it was time to begin his search anew.

With that settled, he decided the best place to do that would be Medicine Bear's village where Harley was passing the winter. He turned Joe around to retrace his tracks to Cheyenne, where he had left his buckskin packhorse. He would get the supplies he needed to set out for the Laramie River and the Crow camp there as well.

Mary Lou Cagle brought the coffeepot over to the table where Gordon Luck and Leon Bloodworth were finishing their supper. She filled both cups, then paused to ask if either of them had heard any news of Cole Bonner.

"Matter of fact, he came in the stable this mornin'," Leon said, his arm still in a sling while his shoulder

healed. "Gordon and I were just talkin' about that."
He looked up at Mary Lou and smiled. "I reckon you
won't have to worry about Slade Corbett no more.
He's dead."

That was good news to Mary Lou. "He caught up
with them," she said, thankful that it was over.

"He caught up with Corbett," Luck corrected.
"Sanchez is still on the loose. Bonner said the snow
covered his trail, and he had to give up on him."

Damn! she thought, disappointed to hear that, but
maybe Corbett's death would be enough to satisfy
Cole's desire for vengeance. Then she wondered if he
would stop by the dining room to see her and Maggie, and she realized that she was feeling a little bit
hurt that he had not done so already.

"What?" she asked when she realized that she had
been too deep in her thoughts to hear a comment
Gordon had just made.

"I said there he is now, comin' in the door," Luck
said, then waved his hand and called out to him.
"Bonner! Come on over and join us."

Cole was just about to sit down at a table near the
door when he heard Luck's invitation. Not particularly enthusiastic about having any company while
he ate his supper, he nevertheless decided that it
wouldn't hurt to accept. Watching him carefully,
Mary Lou pulled a chair back from the table, turned
an empty coffee cup right side up, and filled it with
coffee. Then she stepped back to let him pass in front
of her. She had thought not to speak until he did, but
she couldn't resist when he merely nodded.

"Are you all right?" she heard herself ask. "You
don't look like you've been resting that wound."

"I'm fine," Cole answered.

"Are you gonna eat?"

"I figured on it."

"I'll fix you a plate," she said, and turned to go to the kitchen.

Somewhat surprised by Mary Lou's unusual showing of a gentle nature, Gordon Luck grinned, wondering if the independent young woman saw something in the sullen stranger that touched a tender spot in her otherwise bulletproof heart. He wondered if it was something he should be concerned with, for he had more than a casual interest in the young lady. At the moment, however, he was interested in what had happened on the banks of the Chugwater, so he brought his mind back to questioning Cole.

"Leon here tells me you finished the job me and the other boys started," he said. "Where did you catch up with Corbett?"

"Right where you left him," Cole said with a shrug. "He wasn't in much shape to run. He was still there on the bank of that creek."

That was a surprise to Luck, for he had been sure he saw the two outlaws running. "I don't suppose you had any choice but to kill him," Luck said.

"Reckon not," Cole replied, thinking that was his intent regardless and wondering if Luck thought he should have tried to bring him back for trial.

"God's will," Gordon pronounced. "That man was a disciple of Satan himself and brought a lot of pain and sorrow to our community. He left us with graves to dig for some of our most important citizens."

Cole took a long sip of his coffee, already thinking that he had made a mistake in sitting down at their table. He had no desire to talk about what had happened on the banks of the Chugwater. He knew what he had done and that he had done it for himself with no thought of avenging the people of Cheyenne. He was glad to see Mary Lou arrive with a plate piled high with Beulah's popular cowboy stew, which brought a wry comment from Leon Bloodworth.

"Boy, you sure must have a way with Mary Lou. She ain't ever piled one up like that for me."

"You don't need one that big," Mary Lou came back at him. "You're getting too fat as it is." She cast a stern look in Cole's direction and said, "You need to build your strength back up, or that wound in your side won't ever heal up proper." She didn't miss the knowing look Leon flashed to Gordon, and Gordon's frown of concern. She didn't care. They could think what they wanted to. She had decided that this man was someone special, even though his devotion was to a woman now dead. "You two let the poor man eat now while his food's hot."

"Yes, ma'am, Miss Cagle," Leon said with a chuckle.

"You know, I've been sittin' here, thinkin' about something," Gordon said. "We ain't got no sheriff now, and it occurs to me that you'd make a good one. Would you be interested in the job? I ain't talked to the others on the town council, what's left of 'em, but I think they'd most likely agree with me. Whaddaya say?"

Cole was fairly astonished by the suggestion, amazed that Luck could make such an offer. He viewed himself as little more than an assassin and not even approaching a representative for law and order. He finished chewing a large mouthful of beef before replying.

"I figured you to be the best candidate for sheriff," he told Luck. He based his comment on the size of the man and the obvious respect the men in town had for him.

"No, indeed," Luck said. "I've received a higher callin'. I'm pastor of the Baptist church, and when I ain't busy doin' that, I've got a sawmill to run. So the job's open." He studied Cole's face intently, hoping he would at least consider.

"I reckon not," Cole said. "There's still one man I have to find before I'm done, and I ain't got any idea how long it's gonna take to run him to ground. I've got a room in the hotel for tonight, but I'll be leavin' here in the mornin'. I just came back to pick up my packhorse and buy some supplies."

Had he been watching her, he would have seen an immediate look of disappointment on Mary Lou's face. "Where are you going?" she asked. "You said you didn't know which way Sanchez went."

"I'm headin' up to the forks of the Laramie and North Laramie rivers," he said. "There's a Crow village there, and that's where Harley's ridin' out the winter, so that's where I'm goin'."

"I expect they'd rent you a room in the hotel for a pretty good rate," Leon said. "Then you wouldn't need to buy a whole bunch of supplies."

"I won't have to pay any rent in Medicine Bear's village," Cole said. "Harley and I can go huntin' for food in the mountains above the village. There ain't no homesteads to run the game off there."

"Well, I reckon you know what you wanna do," Luck said. "But you might want to think about the job a little more, and if we ain't got nobody come spring, we could talk about it then."

"I 'preciate the offer," Cole said. "But I don't hardly

think I'll change my mind. I might not be back this way in the spring. I don't know where I'll be."

Mary Lou kept an eye on the table, hoping Gordon and Leon would depart for home and leave Cole alone, but they remained at the table, drinking coffee and talking, until Cole had finished and left the dining room.

He woke from a sound sleep, not sure what had wakened him. He had no idea what time it was, but he was sure it was not time to get up. There was no light through the window in his room. Then he heard the sound that had caused him to stir, a gentle tapping on his door.

Who the hell? he thought, expecting to find a drunken railroad man who forgot which room he was in. He didn't bother to pull his pants on, but he took the precaution to grab his Colt revolver when he got up and went to the door.

"You've got the wrong room," he informed his visitor in a loud voice without unlocking the door.

He heard the tapping again, followed by her voice. "Cole, it's me, Mary Lou."

Dumbfounded, he was still too sleepyheaded to think straight. "Mary Lou?" he stammered, but then fumbled with the key to unlock the door. He started to open it but remembered in time to say, "Wait just a minute while I pull my pants on."

She couldn't resist reminding him, "I've seen you with them off before." She waited just the same until he opened the door.

"What is it?" he asked when he let her in. "What's wrong?"

"There's nothing wrong," she said. "I'm sorry for

waking you up, but you said you were leaving in the morning, and I didn't get a chance to talk to you in the dining room."

"What is it that you wanted to talk about?" he asked.

"Cole, why don't you forget about that man Sanchez? I heard you tell Gordon that he was gone and left no trail you could follow. Why don't you let that be the end of it? You can't spend the rest of your life chasing a ghost. If you do, then they will have succeeded in killing you as well as your wife. I'm sure Ann wouldn't want that for you."

He listened to her plea patiently, but it was plain to see that he had charted a course from which there was no turning back. "I appreciate what you're tryin' to tell me, but I've got to see this thing through. I've come too close to quit now."

She exhaled a weary sigh. "I expected you to feel that way," she said. "And I apologize again for disturbing your sleep. But I heard you tell Gordon and Leon that you might not come back this way again. So I wanted to tell you that, if you were undecided about it when spring comes, or whenever, you have people here who care what happens to you. Maggie and I took care of you when you were wounded." She paused for a moment to decide if she should say all that was in her heart. Realizing that this might be the last chance she would have to say what she wanted him to know, she came out with it. "Damn it, Cole, I care about you. I mean, I care about what happens to you. I'm not saying I love you. I'm just saying it matters to me if you're safe or not." She hesitated again, fearing that she had let her runaway mouth go too far. "God," she exclaimed, "you must think I'm crazy. I shouldn't have come up here. I don't know what I was thinking."

Confounded and amazed, he could only gape at her, too surprised to know how to respond to her declaration or confession or whatever it was. So he just continued to stare at her, saying nothing, which didn't help matters as far as the foundering woman was concerned.

In the short time he had known her, she had always been confident and in control of the situation. Never before had he seen her as flustered as she was at this moment. The statements she had just made caught him completely off guard, without time to think about the meaning of them.

When he continued to simply stand there silent and stupefied, she said, "I feel like a damn fool. If you can, try to forget what I just blabbed like an idiot. Go back to bed, and when you wake up in the morning, just know that it was all a bad dream." That said, she spun on her heel to leave.

"Wait!" Cole blurted, finally realizing the significance of Mary Lou's baring of her soul. He caught her arm to stop her before she fled the room. Still not sure what he should say to her, since he had had no warning of the declaration she had just made, he stumbled in his response. "I'd be lyin' if I said I hadn't ever thought about you, but I never let those thoughts go very far before I reminded myself what I have sworn to do. And there wasn't any room for anything else in my brain. It's still that way. I've got to wipe the slate clean before I can even think about what's ahead after I'm done with Sanchez. It means a lot to me, what you came up here to tell me, and I ain't takin' it lightly."

"I still feel like a damn fool," she said. "I didn't

mean to scare you off." Trying to back out of the situation enough to save face, she repeated, "Like I said, I wasn't trying to say I loved you, or anything like that. I just wanted to let you know that I hoped you wouldn't go off and get yourself killed." She stepped out into the hallway then. "Go on back to sleep, and when you get finished with the thing that's driving you, remember you've got a place to come back to, if you need one." She didn't wait for his response but hurried away from his door, thoroughly disgusted with herself for exposing a weakness that she had always hidden from the men of Cheyenne.

"I'm beholden to ya," he called after her, feeling equally the fool.

Sleep did not come easily after Mary Lou knocked on his door and set his mind into a whirlpool of confusion. Having been firm in his belief that there would always be only one woman in his life, he was seriously troubled by the thoughts that kept him from sleeping until the early-morning hours. No one could ever replace Ann in his heart. Of that he was certain. But was there room for another? At the moment, he didn't believe so, and when he finally left his bed at first light, he resolved himself to get his mind back on the business he was committed to. And the best place to heal himself and keep his mind and instincts sharp was with Harley and his Crow friends.

He paid Leon for his stable bill, then saddled Joe and loaded the buckskin with some supplies he had purchased when he returned to Cheyenne the day before. Ready to leave, he hesitated when a notion to visit the hotel dining room came to him. He wondered if Mary Lou saw him this morning, would she tell him to pretend last night had never happened? He decided that he'd better just get on Joe and ride on out of town. Most likely she'd prefer that he did that. He climbed up into the saddle, gave Leon a nod of farewell, and once again rode out the north road, leaving Cheyenne, and all that had happened there, behind him.

Standing at the window near the outside entrance to the hotel dining room, Mary Lou watched the lone rider sitting tall in the saddle as he headed for the north road out of town. She had told herself that if he was seriously interested in her, he would come by the dining room before he left. Since he had not, she assumed that she had made a complete fool of herself in confessing her interest in him.

Well, hell, she thought, *I guess I can't compete with a dead woman. She'll only become more perfect in his memory as each year goes by.*

With a head full of conflicting thoughts, Cole rode back to Medicine Bear's village. He was resigned to heal and regain his strength, for he anticipated a long, hard journey before the cries from the grave could be stilled in his brain. He resolved to discard any random thoughts of Mary Lou Cagle that happened to invade his mind, and prepare himself to complete the vow he had made.

He arrived at the banks of the Laramie River late in the afternoon, crossed over to the other side, riding through the pony herd as he guided Joe toward the Crow village a few hundred yards beyond. Several young boys were watching the herd, and they shouted out greetings to him as he passed, calling him by his Crow name, White Wolf. As he rode into the circle of tipis, he was greeted warmly by each person he passed. It was a peaceful scene, and he could very well understand why it appealed to Harley. It was not hard to imagine that he might be drawn to a similar existence, were it not for the terrible responsibility he was bound by. He could not help comparing this peaceful Indian village with a life of planting crops and raising cattle and hogs, as he had planned when he journeyed west with his new bride. Looking back, he wondered if he would have been contented, even with Ann by his side.

It doesn't make much difference now, he thought, for he was forced to play the hand fate had dealt him.

He found Harley sitting by a small fire outside Yellow Calf's tipi, busy mending a worn bridle. The little man's face lit up at once upon seeing his young friend. "Well, I was wonderin' when you'd show up again, but I didn't expect to see you this soon." He put his bridle aside and got to his feet. "What happened? Did you finally admit your wound ain't healed enough to go chasin' them damn killers in the middle of winter?"

Realizing then that he really did feel weary, Cole dismounted. "I won't have to chase Slade Corbett anymore," he said.

"You got him?" Harley exclaimed, surprised.

"Yeah, I got him," Cole replied calmly.

"Well, glory be," Harley said. "I reckon you can take a little time to heal up now. You got Corbett. He was the big dog. Now you need to work on puttin' it all behind you."

"There's still one more left," Cole said stoically. "That's when I can put it all behind me."

Disappointed to hear that from him, Harley tried

to change his mind, knowing from the start that it was impossible.

"Damn, Cole," Harley said. "You've settled with the main killer. Slade Corbett was the leader of that gang. That Mexican don't amount to much as long as you got Corbett and the rest of 'em. Let it go now. I wouldn't be surprised if he ain't halfway to Texas by now. He won't hardly come back to this territory again." Cole didn't reply, responding only with a weary smile. Harley knew he was wasting words.

"You're right about one thing," Cole admitted. "I'm feelin' plumb wore out. This winter weather makes everything hard work. If Yellow Calf and Medicine Bear don't mind, I figure on stayin' here till I get my strength back. Then I'll feel like I've got half a chance against that savage."

"That's the smartest thing I've ever heard you say," Harley said. "You know you're welcome here."

Having heard Cole ride up outside her tipi, Moon Shadow came out in time to hear Harley's comment. "White Wolf," she said in greeting, "Thunder Mouse right. You welcome here. I make you strong."

Unable to suppress a grin upon hearing Harley referred to by his Crow name, Cole said, "Many thanks, Moon Shadow. I'm obliged, but I plan to earn my keep. I'll supply plenty of meat. I ain't plannin' on lyin' around the fire like ol' Thunder Mouse here."

Despite a hard winter, his welcome in the Crow camp was evidently the correct treatment for Cole Bonner's physical condition, and a partial relief for the more serious mental wounds. As the weeks rolled by, he learned the ways of the Crow hunter and warrior:

where to find the elk and the mule deer when they took shelter from the winter storms, as well as how to find the hiding places of the small critters when larger game was not abundant. It was a learning process that he readily appreciated.

Having thought he was a reasonably accomplished hunter before, he realized that his Crow hosts were far more advanced. Before the first months of early spring, however, he was confident that he was equal to the most skillful of the Indian hunters. This, coupled with his accuracy with his Henry rifle, gained him the admiration of the people of Medicine Bear's village.

No one felt more gratified by the transformation of Cole than his friend Harley Branch. Watching the young man as he recovered from the wound in his side, and the enthusiasm he exhibited when learning the ways of the forest, Harley had hopes that Cole's relentless conscience would release him of the fateful vengeance he had sworn to fulfill. He was encouraged by the fact that Cole seldom mentioned the task that still lay before him, and hoped that maybe his young friend had decided to leave the ugly past behind.

When spring finally arrived, Harley found that an oath once taken by the determined young man was never betrayed. Early on a chilly April morning, Harley woke to find Cole's blankets empty. Figuring he had taken a notion to go hunting, Harley roused himself to see what he had in mind. Then he noticed that Cole's saddlebags were missing as well as his saddle. That told Harley that he was planning to be gone for a while. Outside the tipi, he found the saddle and other gear on the ground and saw Cole coming from the pony herd, riding Joe and leading the buckskin.

"Looks like you're fixin' to be gone for a spell," Harley said. "What's on your mind?"

"I figure it's time I went about tendin' to business," Cole said as he slid off Joe's back and picked up his saddle.

Disappointed to hear it, but wise enough to know there was no use trying to talk him out of it, Harley said, "Hell, was you gonna ride off without tellin' anybody?"

"No, I was gonna wake you up. I told Yellow Calf and Moon Shadow last night after you turned in early. I'm beholden to them for their kindness and I wanted to tell 'em so."

"I reckon your medicine tells you what you gotta do, so there ain't no use in me sayin' nothin'," Harley said. "But you know what I think."

"I reckon."

"I s'pose you know that you're always welcome here," Harley told him. "And if you ask me, this is where you oughta be, or maybe go see them mountains you wanted to see. But you didn't ask me."

"Reckon not."

Chapter 13

As he had done before, Cole rode into Cheyenne to take up his search once again for Jose Sanchez. He had no reason to believe he could pick up Sanchez's trail there, but he figured he had to start somewhere, and it seemed that he was always drawn back to Crow Creek Crossing.

There was another reason he returned to Cheyenne, though, one he was not willing to admit. Nevertheless, it was one he could not truthfully deny. Mary Lou Cagle's last words to him still returned to his thoughts whenever he let his mind wander aimlessly, no matter how much he reminded himself to keep his focus on what he had to do. On this late morning in early spring, however, he found himself at the hitching rail outside the hotel.

It's a good place to seek news about any sighting of the man I'm looking for, he told himself. *Besides, I'm ready for a solid meal for a change.* He decided those thoughts justified dinner in the hotel dining room.

She saw him as soon as he walked through the door. Tall and rugged, he appeared to be fully recovered from the wound in his side. Thinking of the awkward confession she had left him with when he departed, she was hesitant to display the emotion she felt upon seeing him. Admittedly flustered by his unexpected appearance in the dining room, she retreated to the kitchen to corral her nerves and make an effort to regain her more typically callous facade.

Maggie, busy helping Beulah peel some potatoes for the standard stew the dining room was noted for, glanced up at Mary Lou when she came into the kitchen. Struck by the odd look on Mary Lou's face, she took a second look.

"What's the matter with you?" Maggie asked. "You look like you saw a ghost."

"What?" Mary Lou responded, totally lost in her thoughts. Then she said, "No reason." Then she confessed. "Cole Bonner," she declared.

"Cole Bonner?" Maggie asked. "What about him?"

"He just walked into the dining room," Mary Lou replied, trying her best to affect an indifferent expression.

"Ohhh," Maggie responded, dragging it out knowingly, for she knew Mary Lou well enough to be aware of her friend's interest in the sorrowful young man. "Well, we knew he'd show up again, didn't we? I guess you'd better go wait on him. I'll be out in a minute or two to say hello myself."

"Yes, of course," Mary Lou said, still trying to maintain her facade as she left the kitchen.

"Well, hello there, stranger," she greeted him, as casually as she could affect. "Maggie and I were wondering if we'd see you anytime soon. You look a little more fit than the last time I saw you. I guess you healed up pretty well."

"I reckon," Cole said. "You and Doc Marion musta done a pretty good job, 'cause it doesn't bother me a'tall anymore."

She looked a little different to him than the image he had carried in his thoughts over the winter. It seemed her manner had softened and her smile was warmer. He warned himself not to venture any further with those thoughts.

"Is Harley with you?" Mary Lou asked, and glanced toward the door as if expecting the swarthy little man to walk in.

"Nope. I think Harley's gone completely Injun. He's found him a comfortable place in the Crow village, and he's tired of chasin' around after me, I reckon."

Maggie came out then to greet him. Unlike Mary Lou, she gave him a hug. "It's good to see you again," she told him. "We've been hoping you'd show up now that winter's let up a little." Then she asked the question Mary Lou wanted the answer to, but was not willing to ask. "Now that a little time has passed, have you decided to let the past go? Or are you still of a mind to find that fellow, Sanchez?"

"I reckon," Cole said. "Ain't nothin' happened to change that."

"I'll go get you some coffee," Mary Lou said, and turned toward the kitchen, afraid that her disappointment would show in her face.

Damn it, she thought, *I don't know why I waste my time waiting for him to come back from the graveyard.*

"I'll go fix you a plate," Maggie said, and followed Mary Lou.

"'Preciate it," Cole said.

In a few moments, Mary Lou came from the kitchen with his coffee. She was placing it before him when a man walked up behind her. "Mind if I join you?" he asked Cole.

Cole's eyes had been locked on Mary Lou. He looked beyond her then and recognized a familiar face. It came to him at once. "Mr. Manning," he said, remembering the Union Pacific foreman. "Have a seat."

Stephen Manning pulled a chair back and sank down. "I'll have a cup of that," he said to Mary Lou. Turning back to Cole then, he said, "Seems like I keep bumpin' into you."

"Seems that way," Cole said. "I thought your crew was all out of Cheyenne."

"They are," Manning said. "We're workin' over Sherman Hill now. I had to come back to meet some of my bosses from Omaha. They're supposed to get into Cheyenne tonight. I recommended they stay at the hotel here. It's a little too rough at the camp at the end of the line. What I shoulda done is get 'em a room in that little hotel they just put up in Laramie City. That would give 'em a taste of what it's really like at the start of a railroad town." He punctuated his comment with a laugh.

"I never heard of Laramie City," Cole confessed.

"Not many people have," Manning said, then paused to thank Mary Lou when she placed his coffee cup on the table before continuing. "Laramie City's a little town that sprang up overnight when folks found out the railroad was goin' through there. It was mostly tents and shacks at first, but there're already a lot of homesteaders stakin' claims, and some permanent buildings now. I had to go up there with the surveyors, and let me tell you, I thought Cheyenne was wild before I saw Laramie City. But that's the wildest, most lawless town I've ever seen. I was damn glad to get outta there."

Manning paused only when Mary Lou brought two plates of food to the table. "I guess you want to eat," she said to Manning. "You didn't say."

"You guessed right," he told her, then continued his conversation with Cole. The railroad man seemed eager to talk, so Cole was content to let him, even though only mildly interested in the subject. He preferred not to have to hold up his end of the conversation anyway. "The insane part of it," Manning said, "is that the town has a marshal." He gestured toward Cole with his fork to emphasize his next statement. "And the marshal is the biggest crook in town. He wasn't nothin' but a gunman before he made himself the marshal. Big Steve Long is his name. He's got two half brothers named Con and Ace Moyer, and the three of 'em run the whole town. They own a saloon named the Bucket of Blood, and it's a good name for it. The three of 'em have been harassin' some of the settlers around there to turn the deeds to their land over to them. The ones that don't usually wind up in a gunfight with Big Steve Long, and he ain't lost one yet. If a man believes in coincidences, then that's a helluva string of 'em. I'm reportin' to these people from Omaha that they're gonna have to get some government help or something to clean that town up before they think about establishin' a station there. Why, hell, the only people that get along with the marshal are outlaws and gunmen that drift into town."

"Sounds pretty wild," Cole said, not really interested but content to let Manning talk. He seemed to need to tell someone about it.

"You might think I'm exaggeratin' it a little," Manning went on, "but I saw one incident firsthand. I was thirsty one night, so I went into the Bucket of Blood for a drink. There was an argument started at a table in the back, and one of the men got up from the table, pulled out his pistol, and shot the other fellow in the face. And there wasn't nothin' done about it—didn't call for the marshal or nothin'. One of the owners, he was one of the Moyers—Con or Ace, I don't know which—just dragged the dead man out the front door and dumped his body in the street. The fellow that did the shootin'—he looked like he was a Mexican or somethin'—just ordered another drink like it was just all in a day's work."

With his gaze mainly on Mary Lou on the other side of the room, and paying only slight attention to Manning's story of Laramie City, Cole suddenly stiffened upright, an alarm triggered in his mind by the word *Mexican*. "Did you say he was a Mexican?" he interrupted.

"Yeah, a Mexican. At least he looked like a Mexican to me," Manning said.

"Do you know his name?"

"No," Manning replied, astonished by Cole's sudden change of demeanor. "I wouldn't have any idea. I didn't hang around to get acquainted."

Cole's mind was racing. "You think he's still there?"

"Why, I wouldn't have any idea," Manning said.

"How far is Laramie City from here?" Cole pressed. "How can I find it?"

"It's about forty or fifty miles. Best way to find it is

to just follow the railroad right of way. It's right where we'll be crossin' the river. You think you might know that fellow?"

"Much obliged," Cole said, ignoring the question, while rising from his chair. "I'm glad I ran into you, Mr. Manning, but I've got to go now." He hurried to the front of the dining room where Maggie had a little desk by the door, leaving his dinner half-finished. He handed Maggie a dollar. "I've gotta go," he told her when she appeared about to start a conversation. "Just keep the change." She watched him hustle out the door, her eyes and mouth both open in astonishment.

Outside, he wasted no time climbing into the saddle. He turned Joe's head toward the railroad tracks and nudged him firmly with his heels. It was the longest of long shots, but he had no choice other than finding out for himself. He might be simply wasting time, but there existed the possibility, no matter how slim, that the Mexican that Manning had seen was the one he was searching for. It was enough to ignite the burning fire in his breast that had been allowed to smolder when thoughts of Mary Lou had invaded his mind. As he rode out along the newly laid tracks of the Union Pacific, he silently apologized to Ann for having lost his purpose temporarily, and renewed his vow to avenge her death.

Back in the dining room, Mary Lou stopped when she came from the kitchen to see Stephen Manning sitting alone at the table, across from Cole's half-finished dinner. She walked over to the table. "Is Cole coming back?" she asked.

"I don't think so," Manning said. "He said he had to go."

"Did he say where?"

"No, but he asked me how to get to Laramie City," Manning said.

Mary Lou looked over toward the desk where Maggie still sat. Maggie shrugged in response, so Mary Lou walked over to ask, "Cole?"

"Gone," Maggie said. "Something put a burr under his saddle. He took off outta here like something was after him. He even tipped me a quarter."

"Damn!" Mary Lou swore aloud before she caught herself. Then, deciding that Maggie knew of her interest in the obstinate man anyway, blurted, "I'm tired of worrying about that thickheaded imbecile. If he's so set on going after that murderer until he gets himself killed, I'm not wasting any more of my thoughts on him."

"You don't mean that," Maggie said, confident that Mary Lou had finally met a man that had captured her interest. And Maggie knew that there were few men in that category. "He'll never be free of the ghost of his wife until he's finished with what he thinks he has to do to make it right. Once he's free of that obligation, it'll still take a strong woman to make him want to move on from there. You're the kind of woman who might be able to do that, and from what I see in Cole Bonner, he's worth saving. That's just my opinion. I won't have anything more to say on the matter."

Still seething somewhat from what she perceived as a complete disregard for her feelings, Mary Lou muttered, "To hell with him. Let some other woman save him. Damned if I'm going to wait around for him to go chasin' off after somebody." She looked at Maggie, as if expecting her to agree. "He's not the only man in the territory, and damn sure not my only chance for a husband."

"He might be the only one suited to you," Maggie

said, knowing Mary Lou was referring to Gordon Luck, who had been pestering her to marry him for more than six months. "I don't know if you could make it as a preacher's wife."

"At least he'd be home every night," Mary Lou replied, still fuming.

Jose Sanchez lolled leisurely with his back against the flat side of a rock outcropping at the top of a treeless mesa. He had been biding his time there since early morning, watching the little grove of trees bordering a small creek, waiting for someone to show up.

"Well, it's about time," he muttered when a man led a team of plow horses through the trees to water them at the creek. He flipped the stubby butt of a cigar he had been smoking into the gravel below his perch, roused himself up from the rock, and casually climbed into the saddle. He guided the bay gelding down the backside of the mesa and circled around toward the creek at a comfortable lope.

Raymond Anderson was unaware he was about to have a visitor until Sanchez suddenly appeared in the ring of trees surrounding the watering hole. Still holding the traces while his horses drank, Anderson squinted, straining to recognize the rider, but he decided that he was a stranger. Relieved to see that it was not Big Steve Long, or either one of the rogue marshal's brothers making another call to pressure him into selling them his property, Anderson had no reason to be wary. It was not unusual to see the occasional rider passing through his land on his way to Laramie City, two miles away.

"Howdy," he called out cordially as the stranger pulled up at the edge of the creek.

"I think I water my horse," Sanchez stated stoically.

"Help yourself," Anderson replied. Sanchez stepped down while the bay drank from the creek. He watched his horse for a few moments without saying more, until Anderson sought to break the awkward silence. "You lookin' for Laramie City?" he asked.

Sanchez shifted his gaze from his horse to stare at Anderson with eyes seemingly dull and lifeless. Finally he replied, "Nah, I know where Laramie City is. I think maybe you are Anderson."

"That's right," Anderson said. "I'm Raymond Anderson." He was beginning to feel uncomfortable with the way the sullen stranger stared at him. "Is there something you wanted from me?"

"Nah, I don't want nothing from you. Marshal Long send me to give you final offer for your farm."

"I shoulda known," Anderson responded, at once irritated by the marshal's persistence. "I told Long and his brothers that he was wasting his time with his ridiculous offers. They don't want to buy my farm—they wanna steal it. I told him I ain't interested in sellin', so you took a ride out from town for nothin', mister, whatever your offer is."

Sanchez shrugged as if bored. "I bring final offer you gonna take." He suddenly drew the Colt .44 from his holster and leveled it at Anderson's gut, but he hesitated for a brief moment before pulling the trigger, a contemptuous grin on his face. Anderson doubled over when the bullet ripped into him, then made a desperate effort to turn and run. The fatal bullet blasted a hole in the back of his head, and he crumpled to the ground. It brought a smile of satisfaction to Sanchez's face. He replaced the two spent cartridges, holstered the Colt, and drew his skinning knife. "Too bad the Injuns got you," he said to the corpse as he prepared to take his scalp.

When he had finished the grisly business with his knife, he wiped the blade clean on Anderson's shirt. Then for a bit of sport, he dragged the body over to a large tree and propped it up in a sitting position, facing the direction of Anderson's cabin.

"Now you can see them coming," he said.

Expecting to see someone come running when they heard the shots, he pulled his rifle from the saddle scabbard and picked a spot behind another tree to await them. Long had told him that Anderson had two teenage sons, so he prepared to take care of them. He figured it wouldn't be long, because the cabin and barn weren't much more than five hundred yards from where he waited.

He eagerly anticipated the arrival of Anderson's two sons. Killing them would not give him the pleasure he enjoyed with the assassination of their father, but it would still bring him satisfaction. The father's killing was done up close so Sanchez could see the terror in his victim's face when he realized he was about to die. It was much more satisfying than killing at longer range with his rifle. But since there were two targets, he had to make sure he got both of them before they knew what was happening. He had assured Steve Long that he would take care of the whole family, so when the two boys were dead, he would settle with their mother.

He looked toward the cabin, wondering why he saw no sign of the two boys yet.

Maybe they have to get their guns first, he thought.

While he waited, his mind returned to the last time he'd had a hand in murdering a whole family. *That one caused a lot of trouble,* he reminded himself, thinking of Cole Bonner and his dogged pursuit of Slade Corbett's gang.

This time I'll make sure there's no one left. Thinking of Slade Corbett, he wondered if the posse found him there on the bank of Chugwater Creek. Whether they did or not, he figured Slade would die without a horse or any help. The prospect amused him, for Slade always thought he was the prime stud of the herd. One by one, every one of Slade's gang was killed, with only one survivor, and Sanchez knew he would always survive.

His mind was suddenly brought back to the business at hand when he spotted the two boys running across the open plain before the trees bordering the creek—one carrying a rifle, the other a shotgun. Sanchez grinned and unhurriedly raised his carbine to his shoulder, sighting on the larger boy in front. He waited until the boy was in a reasonable range for the rifle, when he was sure he wouldn't miss. Then he held the front sight on the boy's chest and squeezed the trigger. Quickly ejecting the empty shell, he laid the sight on the boy's brother, who had stopped to keep from stumbling over the body. Sanchez hesitated, taking time to enjoy the young man's apparent confusion, not knowing from where the shot had come. Sanchez squeezed the trigger while he had a stationary target.

Seventy-five dollars, he thought, *one more to collect my hundred dollars.* He was working cheap, he knew, but it was the kind of work he enjoyed—and best suited his skills. He felt fortunate to have found someone in Marshal Steve Long who appreciated his talents.

With no need to hurry now, Sanchez walked back to the edge of the creek to look at the late Mr. Anderson's horses. A quick inspection was enough for him to decide they were not suited for much beyond pulling a plow, so he climbed up on his horse and headed toward the cabin to finish the job he was hired for. This would be the part of his business that called for caution. He thought of Skinner Roche, walking into a shotgun blast when he broke down the front door of John Cochran's house.

That dumb gringo, he thought. He wouldn't make the same mistake. *I'm too smart, and that's the reason I'm still here and they're not.*

He kicked the dun into a full gallop as he approached the cabin and started yelling at the top of his voice. "Help! Help! Somebody's been shot! They need help!" He pulled the horse to a sliding stop before the cabin. His performance was successful in fooling Betty Anderson into opening the door. She stepped out on the small stoop, lowering the double-barreled shotgun, frantic in response to his alarm. Too late, she saw the contemptuous sneer on his face and moments later felt the bullet that slammed into her breast. The shotgun dropped to the stoop and tumbled to the ground as she collapsed beside it.

He climbed down, holstered the Colt handgun, and went casually to kneel by her side. She was still alive, but he was sure not for long. He lifted her head to look directly into her eyes. "If you were a little bit younger, I would have let you live a little bit longer," he told her. "You too old and used up. I take the money I get for shooting you and pay a whore for what I need."

For a moment, her eyes appeared to clear, as if staring into the next world. "May God forgive you for what you've done," she managed to whisper.

"Why, thank you, ma'am," he said sarcastically. "I not a bad man. I help you along." He drew his knife and sank it deep in her abdomen, then let her head fall back to the ground. "Maybe, if you hurry, you can go to heaven with the rest of your family."

Finished with his evil business then, he went inside the cabin to see if there were any spoils to add to his payment for making another homestead available for the marshal and his brothers to take possession of. That thought brought to mind the big lawman and the two outlaws he called his half brothers. Sanchez was smart enough to know that when they felt his usefulness was gone, he would have to be wary of a bullet in the back of his head. He was also confident that they would never get the opportunity. He was ready to move on.

It was spring, and for the price of goading a couple of farmers into gunfights, he had been allowed to spend the winter in one of the brothers' confiscated cabins. It was a one-room cabin built by a man named Pickens, who was goaded into picking a gunfight with Big Steve Long. He came in second and Long ended up with the deed to his forty acres.

Sanchez knew that his reputation as a gunman would put pressure on the marshal to arrest him, and the townsfolk would be planning a hanging after they tried him. But Marshal Long wasn't likely to let him live long enough to go to trial. He had too much to lose when Sanchez started talking. Clearly the best thing for him now was to voluntarily remove himself from the scene, but before he left, he was going to get his money for the job he just finished.

Ace Moyer was seated at a back table eating his supper when Sanchez walked into the Bucket of Blood. The swarthy assassin paused just inside the door to look over the room before going farther, a longtime habit. Seeing Ace, he nodded, then went to the bar to order a bottle of whiskey before walking back to join him. Always cautious, he pulled a chair back from the table and turned it so that his back was to the wall. He was met with a scowl from Ace.

"Have a seat," Ace said sarcastically, irritated by the hired gun's assumption that he was welcome to sit down without an invitation.

"You owe me money," said Sanchez, who was aware of Moyer's contempt for him and found it amusing.

"You'll get paid when I know you did the job," Ace said. "Your word ain't enough."

"It's enough for me," Sanchez said. "If I don't do the job, then I don't be sitting here."

"All of 'em?" Ace asked.

Sanchez smirked as he nodded. "Poor folks, they damn unlucky—looked like they got hit by Injuns."

"You didn't set fire to the place, did you? We told you not to burn the damn place down."

Sanchez shrugged. "You said don't burn, so I don't burn."

"I expect you ransacked the house before you were done," Ace said. "Did you find any papers—anything that looked like a deed?" He and his brothers would claim the place at any rate, but it was much better if they had a deed with Anderson's signature forged on it.

"Nah, I don't see no papers," Sanchez replied.

And even if he had, it was unlikely he would have bothered to bring them back with him. He had no interest in papers. His search had been for money, jewelry, weapons, ammunition, and things that bene-fited him personally. He poured himself a drink from the bottle he had gotten at the bar, and offered to pour one for Ace, but Ace declined. After a few min-utes of stony silence, and a couple more drinks of whiskey, Sanchez saw that he was not especially wel-come company.

"All right," he finally said, "I go now. You talk to the marshal, get me my money." He got to his feet, grabbed the bottle of whiskey, and headed for the door. When he passed by the bar, the bartender yelled at him, to remind him that he hadn't paid for the bot-tle. Sanchez made a casual motion toward Ace. "He pay you," he said, and walked out the door.

The bartender started around the end of the bar, but Ace waved him back. He didn't want to lose a bartender. It was plain to see that their hired gun hand might be a little too hard to handle. Ace and his two brothers were trying to keep some appearance of taking care of the fledgling town while making them-selves the principal landowners.

They were certain that Laramie City would grow to be a bustling town with many new businesses attracted by the coming of the Union Pacific Railroad, and they planned to own it. They had already acquired much of the prime pieces of land close in to town. Most of it had come from gunfights between the reluctant owners and Big Steve Long, with Long claiming the victims had drawn first. Raymond Anderson was sitting on a prime parcel just two miles from the path of the railroad, and he refused to budge when approached to sell. Anderson was a religious man who didn't drink, was never in a saloon, and could not be goaded into a gunfight. So it was decided that it was going to take something like an Indian massacre to get their hands on his farm.

And that's when Sanchez happened to hit town. The marshal's first thought was to run him out of town, but then he and the brothers decided that he might be the perfect solution to their problem with Anderson. Now Ace was thinking Sanchez had outlived his usefulness.

Big Steve Long walked from the stables where he had just left his horse, headed for the shack that served as the marshal's office. He was ready to go to the Bucket of Blood where he usually ate his supper, but he wanted to check in at his office first. He noticed the door standing ajar and the first thought that came to mind was that his half brother Con must have been there. For some unexplained and irritating reason, Con never seemed to have learned how to close the door when he entered a room, or when he left one.

Long pushed the door open and called out, "Con?" But the room was dark. He went to the desk and lit the lamp. Once it was going, he turned up the wick, lighting the room, and jumped when he heard the door close behind him. Turning back toward the door, he found himself staring into the barrel of a Colt .44 in the hand of Jose Sanchez.

"Son of a bitch!" Long blurted, caught holding the kerosene lamp in his gun hand.

"I come to get my money," Sanchez said, the sputtering light of the lamp casting shadows across his swarthy face and the ever-present smirk.

Somewhat recovered from his initial fright, since the sneering Mexican had not pulled the trigger, Long railed, "Have you gone loco, pullin' a gun on me like that?"

"You owe me one hundred dollars," Sanchez said. "I think maybe I shoot you if you don't give me my money."

"Hell," Long came back. "You think I keep that kinda money in here when I'm gone? How do I know you did what I said I'd pay you for?"

"I did the job," Sanchez said, and tossed a bundled-up dish towel on the desk. With his free hand, Long pulled the towel open to reveal a stack of hairy objects. It took him a minute to realize they were four scalps. Long could not help grunting in disgust. "That's how you know," Sanchez said. "Now, give me my money."

"All right," Long said, his temper rising. "I'll give you your damn money, and then I want you outta my town, and I mean for good. You understand that?"

"Yeah, I understand," Sanchez snorted contemptuously. "I was leaving anyway."

Sanchez watched as Long pulled a wallet out of his inside coat pocket and counted out one hundred dollars. He placed the bills on the desk and watched while Sanchez picked them up, all the while keeping his eye on the marshal. "All right, our business is done," Sanchez said. "You not gonna see me again."

"If I do," the marshal said, "I'll shoot you on sight." The threat was met with an insolent grin. "I'll give you tonight and tomorrow to get your belongin's outta the Pickens place. After then, it's open season on your ass."

"Why, *gracias*, Marshal. That's mighty kind of you. I'll be sure and be gone by tomorrow night." As cautious as he would be backing away from a rattlesnake, Sanchez moved out the door before holstering his Colt. Wasting as little time as possible, he climbed aboard the dun gelding and loped up the muddy street, fully aware that his former boss was now his enemy.

The marshal stepped outside the door to watch Sanchez depart. He had no intention of letting the sneering gunman ride away with the hundred dollars, and he watched him until he reached the far end of the street, then took the trail that followed the river. Long was satisfied then that Sanchez was heading toward the Pickens place, about a mile and a half from town. He pulled the door to his office closed and headed across the street to the Bucket of Blood, where he found Ace Moyer seated at his usual table.

Ace looked up when he saw his half brother approaching. "Did Sanchez come to see you?" he asked.

"Yeah," Long replied. "That son of a bitch pulled a gun on me."

"You give him his money?"

"Yeah, he got his money, but he damn sure ain't gonna keep it," Long said. "Where's Con?"

"Upstairs with Lulu Belle, where he usually is this time of day," Ace said with a grin when he thought about his brother and his favorite among the whores that worked the saloon.

"Well, let's go get him. Sanchez thinks he's got till tomorrow night to get outta that cabin, and I plan to pay him a little visit tonight."

* * *

As cunning as a fox, Sanchez knew that he must prepare to have visitors sometime during the night. Big Steve Long had too willingly paid him the hundred dollars. He was not likely to let the money go if he thought he might have a chance to trade a bullet in the back for the return of the cash. The simple fact that he gave Sanchez the night and the following day to get out of the cabin told him that they hoped to make him think he had nothing to worry about tonight.

Well, I like to have company, he thought. *I'll have a welcome party for him.*

It would have been a much simpler plan to pack his possibles and keep going while he had a head start. But Sanchez wanted the satisfaction of showing the arrogant marshal what it cost anyone who tried to cheat him.

Darkness had fully set in by the time Sanchez completed the mile-and-a-half ride to the Pickens place. It was helped along by the heavy snow clouds that had settled over the river valley. He peered up at the sky. There looked to be a good possibility that there would be another of the early-spring snow showers that had drifted over the prairie during the past week. He might miss the warm little cabin before the night was over, if those clouds decided to drop their load.

Not worth risking a bullet in the back of the head, he quickly decided.

He left the saddle on his horse and went inside the cabin to roll up a few things in his bedroll. Most of his possessions were already in his saddlebags, so there wasn't much time required to pack up. When that was done, he led his horse down to the lean-to that had served Pickens as a barn and tied the dun behind it.

Back at the cabin, he carried in a couple of armloads of firewood that the late Mr. Pickens had piled near the door. In a few minutes, he had a roaring fire going in the stone fireplace. When he was satisfied that it was stoked to burn for a good while, he left the warm cabin and went back to the lean-to, where his horse was tied, and stacked two hay bales to use as a firing position. With a pitchfork that was kept in the lean-to, he forked off one end of one of the bales and tossed it to his horse to feed on. Satisfied that the horse would be fed and ready to ride in a hurry if need be, he pulled his Spencer carbine, checked the load, and waited. He grinned when he anticipated the reception Steve Long was going to get.

The reception was not to be held for quite some time, at least not as soon as he had expected. Long was evidently waiting to make sure he was asleep. Sanchez had to go back to the cabin twice to keep the fire going in the fireplace. The clouds that had threatened all day finally decided to deliver on their promise, and released a gentle shower of large, soft snowflakes. It was tempting to think of the warm cabin and the hearty fire in the fireplace.

He had almost decided that the marshal was not coming after all when in the early-morning hours, he heard the questioning whinny of a horse. It brought a smile of satisfaction to his face.

He had company.

He rose higher behind his barricade of hay bales and squinted to see in the dark shadows around the cabin. In a few moments, he saw a figure move up beside the single window on the side.

"Buenos días," he whispered softy as he raised his carbine to his shoulder. Squinting to see through the falling snow, he couldn't tell which one of the three brothers it was. A split second before he pulled the trigger, he was startled by the sudden explosion of gunfire as Big Steve kicked the cabin door open, followed by simultaneous shotgun blasts through the single window on each side of the cabin. There were three assassins, just as he had anticipated. They had elected to use shotguns, no doubt thinking to fill the tiny cabin with buckshot. Had he been inside, it was unlikely that he would have escaped injury.

While the man he could see paused to reload his shotgun, Sanchez squeezed the trigger on his carbine. The Spencer bucked and Con Moyer sank to his knees, a bullet in his shoulder. Sanchez tried to quickly fire again, but he missed when the wounded man crawled around the corner of the cabin.

"Damn!" Sanchez swore for missing a kill shot. A few seconds later, he found himself under fire from two shooters at the back corner of the cabin, this time using rifles. They had evidently seen his muzzle flash and were concentrating their fire on his position behind the barn. He returned their fire until his barricade of hay began to come apart from the slugs ripping into it, and he was forced to retreat.

Deciding it in his best interest to run, he rose to fire three shots at the corner of the cabin. He hoped that would force the two men to duck back for cover and give him a few seconds to run to his horse. The distraction almost worked, but he was struck in the back of his thigh just as he jumped up into the saddle. Grimacing in pain, he nevertheless galloped away through the cottonwoods on the riverbank.

Behind him, Big Steve exclaimed, "Get after the son of a bitch!" He and Ace ran back to the front of the cabin where their horses were tied. "How bad are you hurt?" he asked, upon seeing his brother sitting on the ground with his back against the log wall.

"I got hit in the shoulder," Con groaned, "but it ain't too bad, I reckon."

"You stay here," Big Steve said. "Me and Ace will chase the bastard down, and we'll come back to get you." He didn't wait for Con's reply but ran for his horse. In a matter of seconds, he and Ace were charging recklessly through the dark trees guarding the river, unmindful of the danger to their horses.

Already a mile ahead of them, Sanchez veered away from the river and headed out across the dark prairie, reining his horse back to a safer pace, lest he risk breaking a leg on the uneven ground. His intent now was to find a suitable place to set up another ambush for his pursuers, and he had his eye on a low ridge ahead of him that looked as though it would fill the bill. As he neared the ridge, he became more aware of the bullet in his right thigh, cursing his luck when he knew that it had to have been a lucky shot. He would see how bad it was after he found a spot to wait for Big Steve and Ace. At present, it was painful, and there was a growing patch of blood on his trousers, but he didn't feel incapacitated.

When he reached the ridge, he found a deep ravine that led to the top. It looked to be an ideal place to get his horse out of sight and lie in wait for anyone fool enough to ride across the open prairie leading up to the ridge. It would be as easy as the ambush he had set up for the posse that chased him and Slade to the Chugwater. He smiled smugly when he thought about that, in spite of the pain in his leg. Moments before, he was happy to see the snow still falling. Now, thinking about the ambush, he almost wished it would stop, so as not to cover his trail.

There was nothing to do now but wait for them to show up. While he waited, he tried to see how bad his wound looked but found it difficult because it was in the back of his thigh and almost impossible for him to get a close look at it.

"Damn the luck," he cursed, knowing that he was going to need someone to help him, possibly to remove the .44 slug he was now carrying. "Where the hell I gonna find anybody out here?" he asked aloud.

The closest town with a doctor was probably Cheyenne, and he sure as hell couldn't go back there. And the way he was heading now would only lead him farther across the lifeless prairie or into the rugged line of mountains. The only place he could likely get help, he decided, was Lem Dawson's place, Buzzard's Roost. He wasn't sure exactly where he was in respect to the trading post on the North Laramie, but he knew he could find it by going back to strike the Laramie River. If he followed it north, he would eventually come to country he was familiar with.

"First, I'll take care of Big Steve Long and his brothers," he said.

First light found Big Steve and Ace Moyer almost six miles up the Laramie River with still no sign of the man they chased, and no trail in the fresh white snow before them. They had continued following the river because, if Sanchez had turned away from it, there was no way they could tell where he did it. It had been too dark to have seen his tracks leaving the river when they first started after him. And by the time it was light enough to see, the snow had covered any tracks he left.

"It don't make no sense to keep ridin' up this river," Ace finally said. "We lost him and that's all there is to it." Cold and tired, he was thinking of Con, six miles back in that warm cabin.

"One hundred dollars," Big Steve fumed. "The sneaky bastard got away with one hundred dollars of my money."

"Well, I reckon it was worth it. He cleaned out the Anderson place for us."

Chapter 14

Laramie City was a dreary-looking little frontier town on the cold spring morning that Cole Bonner rode up the one short street. The big Morgan gelding plodded along at a slow walk through the mixture of snow and mud that had been churned up to become almost liquid. Stephen Manning had been accurate in his description of the forlorn collection of tents, shacks, and a few permanent buildings. One of these stood out as the center of activity on the street, as evidenced by the half dozen horses tied at the hitching rail out front. It was easy to assume that this was the Bucket of Blood Saloon, and if he was to find the man he searched for, it would most likely be there.

He tied Joe at the end of the hitching rail and paused to take a look around him before stepping up on the short length of boardwalk. He could not afford to be careless, for Jose Sanchez could recognize him, just as he could recognize Sanchez. And the man who came out on top in this lethal game might very well be the man who saw the other one first. Seeing no one else on the street, Cole opened the door and peered into the smoky saloon, waiting for his eyes to adjust to the dim light. The noisy room suddenly became quiet as every eye turned to see who had walked in, but none of the faces looked familiar to him, so he entered. Conversation began to pick up again a few moments later, when no one recognized the stranger, assuming him to be just another drifter who had stumbled upon the town.

Cole walked over to the bar. "What's your pleasure, young feller?" the bartender asked.

"To tell you the truth, it's a little too early for me to want any strong spirits," Cole replied. "I've been ridin' since sunup, and I could really use a cup of hot coffee right now. You wouldn't know where I could get one, would you?"

"Coffee?" the bartender huffed, obviously amused but not unfriendly. "I don't get many requests for coffee, even this early in the mornin'. If you're lookin' for some breakfast, you can find somethin' to eat at the hotel. I ain't recommendin' it, mind you." Cole nodded slowly as if giving it serious thought. The bartender waited for a moment before deciding. "If it's just coffee you want, I've got a pot on the stove I made for myself. I'll give you a cup of that."

"I'd appreciate that," Cole said. "Course I'd pay you for it."

Surprised by the offer, for he assumed Cole was another penniless drifter down on his luck, the bartender said, "Hell, I won't charge you for it. I'll have a cup with you."

"Much obliged," Cole said. He considered himself lucky to find the bartender a friendly sort. It increased his odds of getting the information he needed, instead of a tendency to clam up when strangers asked questions about men on the run.

"Here you go," the bartender said when he set a stained coffee cup, filled to the brim, on the bar before Cole. "What brings you to Laramie? You lookin' to stay for a spell, or just passin' through?"

"Just passin' through," Cole replied.

"Where you headed?"

"Don't know," Cole answered, thinking he needed to be asking the questions. "Are you one of the owners of this place?"

"No, I just tend bar." He paused to introduce himself. "My name's Al. Big Steve Long and the Moyer brothers own the saloon." He paused again, then said, "And just about everythin' else in town."

"Cole Bonner," Cole said. "Pleased to meet you." He took another swallow of the bitter black coffee, trying not to make a face when he did. It had the taste of coffee that had been overboiled a couple of times.

"You say you don't know where you're goin'?" Al asked. "How you gonna know when you get there?" He laughed at his joke.

Cole chuckled to show his appreciation of the joke. "Tell you the truth, I'm lookin' for a fellow, a Mexican named Sanchez."

His comment immediately caused a reaction in Al's eyes, and the jovial expression turned to one of serious concern. "Whaddaya lookin' for him for?"

"He stole a horse from me," Cole told him.

"That bay he was ridin'?"

"That's the one," Cole said, continuing the story he was making up. "That bay was one of my best horses."

"Well, I ain't surprised," Al said. "But I'm afraid

you're too late to catch that feller Sanchez. He hung around here for a while. I don't know why Big Steve put up with him, but he got fed up with him when he shot a feller in here a few nights ago. Steve, he's the marshal, too. He went after Sanchez—him and his brothers. But Sanchez got away."

That was beginning to become a familiar story to Cole. "Which way did he run?" he asked. "Did they say?"

"Well, Ace said he was runnin' right along the river, headin' north, when they finally gave up on him. They mighta kept after him, but Con got shot in the shoulder, so they had to come back to get him. Ace said he was pretty sure he hit Sanchez with one shot, but it didn't slow him down any." Al paused then, noticing Cole's intent expression as he talked. "They mighta been lucky they didn't find him. They mighta had another one of 'em get shot. Sanchez was in here a few times, and I'll tell you there's somethin' downright scary about that man. You might wanna think twice before you head off after him again. It might be best to just figure you lost a good horse and let it go at that."

"Maybe so," Cole said, and forced the last gulp of coffee down. "I expect I'd best be gettin' along now. I thank you again for the coffee."

"Don't mention it," Al said. "You take care of your-self," he called after him as Cole went out the door.

Outside, Cole stood beside his horse for a few min-utes while he thought about what he had just learned. Thanks to Al's friendly reception, he was on San-chez's trail again, even though it was a stone-cold trail, and he could only speculate where he might be heading. But it was better than nothing, he told himself, and tried to speculate on where Sanchez might be heading. Based on what Al had just told him, Sanchez was now hampered by a bullet wound. Surely that would slow him down.

With nothing more to go on, he would have to head up the Laramie River and hope that Sanchez might have to stop somewhere to tend to his wound. Then it occurred to him that Lem Dawson's place was up that way on the North Laramie. Sanchez might be heading there. He had been there before. Committed to that presumption, he climbed up into the saddle and turned Joe's head toward the river. He was not at all disappointed to leave Laramie City without the opportunity to meet Big Steve Long and his half brothers.

He had no way to be sure, but he guessed that it was probably a three-day ride to the North Laramie and Lem Dawson's trading post. When he left Laramie City, he rode until darkness forced him to stop for the night. He was grateful for a letup in the snow clouds and the lack of additional precipitation during the rest of that day as he followed the river on its winding journey into the mountains. Sitting by the fire at the end of the day, he decided that because of the winding course of the river, it was going to take him longer than the time he originally estimated to get to the North Laramie. He was afraid he had made a mistake in leaving his packhorse in Cheyenne. But he had his rifle and plenty of cartridges, so he could hunt when his supplies ran out, and he had seen plenty of signs of game along the river. He could go on indefinitely—and he would, if that's what it took.

On the second day, he came across hoofprints coming from a ravine to intercept the path he was riding.

When he dismounted to study them, he found they were unshod—Indian ponies. They continued along in the same direction he was riding. He was forced to be even more cautious now. Maybe, he thought, if he was lucky, they would turn away from the river somewhere up ahead. But they held to the same course. When he stopped in the middle of the day to rest Joe, he took the opportunity to study the tracks again, this time more closely. Suddenly he realized that one of the prints he found was from a shod horse, and he went back along the trail searching more closely still. There was another shod print, then another. He stood up and stared up the river before him while he considered the possibilities. There were only two: The Indians had one shod horse, or the tracks were not made at the same time, which meant the Indians were following a rider on a shod horse.

It made sense! He constructed the picture in his mind. A party of Indians, four by his estimation, had spotted one lone rider from the hills above the river. They came down the ravine he had passed to get on the rider's trail. How could he explain the fact that there were no tracks of any horses before the ravine? He thought back, trying to remember the scene. There was a small island in the middle of the river just before he reached the ravine—a good place to ford the river. It was Sanchez the Indians were following—he was sure of it—and he had been on the other side of the river to that point. Then he crossed over to this side, and that was why tracks suddenly appeared where there were no tracks before.

What he did not know was how far behind them he trailed. When his horse was rested, he started out again but suddenly heard gunshots some distance up ahead of him. They were rifle shots by the sound of them and there was an initial burst of three shots, followed shortly after by three more. It was hard to say how far ahead. He looked up at the sky. The sun was already settling down upon the mountaintops. It would be dark in a couple of hours. He urged Joe onward at a faster but cautious pace, afraid to push him too hard for the roughness of the trail.

He became more anxious as he continued along the narrow path by the river and the sun dropped lower, casting long shadows across the water from the ridges on the western side. He had to become concerned now about riding into an ambush. There had been no more rifle shots, so there was no way to judge if he was getting closer or not. Suddenly Joe reared as a horse loped down the path toward them. Cole grabbed his rifle from the saddle sling, ready to fire, but discovered the horse was riderless. It was an Indian pony, and it slowed only slightly as it ran on past them. Cole, fully alert now, urged Joe forward again, searching the trail before him. Approaching a sharp bend in the river, he came upon another Indian pony standing a short distance from the trail. It was also without a rider.

Feeling that he must be getting close, he dismounted, realizing he might be an inviting target sitting high in the saddle, even though the light was rapidly fading. Moving cautiously around the bend of the river, he came upon the bodies. Reacting immediately, he dropped to one knee, quickly scanning each bank of the river and the narrow canyon ahead, ready to shoot at the first sign of movement. There was no one in sight other than the dead. Four bodies lay in the snow, and the picture of what had occurred was not difficult to imagine. Sanchez must have been aware that the Indians were stalking him, so he led them into an ambush, and the hunted became the hunter. He led them across a treeless opening, waiting for them in a gully or ravine. When they were halfway across the open space, he laid down a blanket of fire, killing two of them before they knew they were walking into a trap. This seemed likely judging by where two of the bodies lay. The other two Indians looked as if they had been shot as they attempted to run away, for they were some distance from the other warriors, probably shot in the back, Cole surmised. It appeared that the Indians were armed only with bows.

He scanned the walls of the canyon before him in an effort to guess exactly where Sanchez had lain in wait for his latest victims. It was difficult to guess, for there looked to be many suitable places in the high rock walls and narrow gullies. Four more bodies to be attributed to the brutal murderer, Cole thought, and knew that he had to be stopped. Not sure if Sanchez was still watching the clearing, he decided it too dangerous to enter it to pick up the outlaw's trail. So he decided to backtrack a short distance and ride down along the bank of the river where the bushes were thick until he was past the far edge of the clearing.

Coming up on the other side of the killing field, he waited until the last rays of the sun had shrouded the valley in a dusky twilight before climbing up to the path again. There was still enough light to see the single set of tracks, left by a shod horse, and they continued on toward the steep walls of the canyon. Cole paused to look beyond him, his eyes following the trail into the darkness of the canyon where the steep walls blocked out the last fading rays of daylight. He could almost feel the evil butcher's presence permeating the narrow river valley, and he sensed a fatal reckoning after so long a search.

Even in the dying light, the tracks he saw were sharp and perfectly shaped in the snow, telling him that they were recently formed. Sanchez was near. He was sure of it. As he continued to stare at the canyon passage, he had to question the sanity of following the tracks into that dark void. It was a perfect spot for an ambush. But he told himself that it was very unlikely Sanchez had any notion that he was being tracked by anyone after he had dealt with the Indians.

The odds were in his favor, he reasoned, knowing that even if they weren't, he was still going into the canyon. He would not permit Sanchez to get away, now that he was so close to finishing the job he had sworn to do. Although five of the six men who had raped and murdered his wife and her family were dead, the one surviving savage had grown to symbolize the entire evil deed. And the deaths of the five before him would not pay for the tragedy as long as one remained alive. He took Joe's reins in his hand and started walking into the canyon.

Halfway through the dark passage, he realized more than ever that he was at the mercy of anyone waiting to ambush him. But so far, he was still on his feet as the canyon turned abruptly, revealing the end of the narrow gorge. Anxious to escape the confines of the steep walls, he increased his pace to a trot, leading his horse to the open end, where he stopped as soon as he found light enough to examine the tracks again. There were now boot prints along with

the hoofprints. Sanchez had dismounted for some
reason and from that point was evidently leading his
horse. Cole didn't trouble himself with the reason,
but it would seem likely that Sanchez would be making camp sometime soon. Cole looked at the terrain
ahead and guessed that the site he would pick would
be somewhere in the trees that covered the foot of a
slope that led down to the river. Taking up the trail
again, he had started to climb back up into the saddle
when a glimmer of something shiny caught his eye.
He stopped to examine it more closely. It was blood.

Sanchez is still bleeding!

So Ace Moyer *had* wounded him. The discovery
made him hurry even more.

Another one? Sanchez questioned. He was sure there
had been no more than four, but there was now one
lone figure that just emerged from the canyon and
was following his trail.

*Well, we'll give him the same medicine the other four
got,* he thought, and looked around him to pick his
spot.

He had dismounted when his leg felt as if it was
getting numb, thinking that maybe he should try
walking in hopes of keeping it from going stiff on him.
It had only resulted in starting the bleeding again.

Damn the luck, he thought. *I wonder if there's any
more of them behind me.* His only thought now was to
reach Lem Dawson's place. Lem should be able to get
the bullet out of his leg. He wouldn't be the first outlaw Lem had operated on.

The mouth of a ravine just ahead of him looked to
be a handy spot to take care of the Indian still tracking him. He led his horse up the ravine a little way to

get it out of sight. Then he limped back to the lower
end of the ravine and lay down on the snow-covered
lip with his carbine ready to fire. It would be an easy
shot, he thought.

*The damn fool must think it's too dark to see him out in
the open like that.* Waiting for his target to get a little
closer, so that he couldn't miss, he suddenly realized
that it was not an Indian, but a white man. His first
thought was that it was Big Steve Long, still trying to
get his hundred dollars back. The man was hard to
identify, but he was a sizable man like Big Steve. He
couldn't help smiling at that.

*I think I'll let him get a little bit closer so I can see the
look on his face just before I send him to hell.* Thinking to
find a better place, one that would bring his victim
within point-blank range, he picked a spot on the
other lip of the ravine. Then he led his horse farther
up the ravine before coming back to take his position
on the lip. If Big Steve followed the bay's tracks, as
Sanchez figured, he would pass within ten yards of
the ambush waiting down the slope, just over the
ravine's lip.

It was the kind of setup Sanchez enjoyed. He could
witness the stark terror in his victim's face the moment
he realized he was about to die and there was nothing
he could do about it. An evil grin spread across Sanchez's face as his unsuspecting target drew nearer.
Lying in the shadow of a large pine, Sanchez slowly
raised the muzzle of his carbine and set the front sight
on the spot where he planned to pull the trigger. The
man stopped at the foot of the ravine to look up toward
the top. Sanchez jerked his head back in surprise. It was
not Big Steve, but his face was familiar. It struck him
then. The man stalking him now was the vengeful

hunter who had doggedly come after him and the others!

But now he has made his first mistake when he has conveniently walked squarely into my gun sight, Sanchez thought.

This was even better than killing Big Steve Long. Sanchez had an almost overpowering urge to roar out his laughter for the quirk of fate that brought his demon to present himself to be killed. But not wishing to chance a foul-up, he maintained his patience until Cole was directly in front of him at point-blank range.

Now! Sanchez told himself, and rested his finger on the trigger. He started to squeeze it when he was suddenly startled by the low guttural growl of a wolf only a few feet behind him. Without thinking, he automatically spun around to defend himself.

There was no time to think when he heard the growl of the wolf. Cole immediately dropped to one knee and swung his rifle around to bear on the dark form that suddenly separated itself from the shadow of a large pine. Two quick rounds from the Henry rifle found their mark, and the wolf slumped lifeless on the snow-covered slope.

Alarmed now that he had forfeited any advantage of surprise he might have had, he scrambled back to take cover behind a rock at the bottom of the ravine and waited for Sanchez to react. He surely knew he was being stalked now. He watched the dark ravine above him carefully, wondering if Sanchez had already ridden out at the other end, or if he had picked that spot to camp and was now there watching him from farther up the ravine. Maybe he had been too quick and not thinking when he automatically shot the wolf, but it had been too close to wait. Something had attracted it. Possibly it had caught the scent of blood, since Sanchez was leaving a trail of it in the snow.

Time crawled slowly by with still no response of any kind from the upper part of the ravine. Then suddenly a large dark form emerged from the shadows above him, coming down the center of the ravine. Ready to fire, Cole checked himself when he realized that it was a horse, but the saddle was empty. *Some kind of trick?* he wondered, and remained ready to shoot. The horse walked slowly past him. He continued to wait, but there was still no response to his rifle shots. He turned then to stare at the dark lump lying just below the rim of the ravine. Maybe it wasn't the wolf he had shot. Maybe it was something else. No longer concerned with an attack from the upper part of the ravine, for he was suddenly certain, he ran across to the other side.

What had just occurred to him was, in fact, what had actually happened. It was not a wolf. He stood staring down at the body of Jose Sanchez. Two bullet holes were neatly placed, one in the chest, and one in the throat. For a brief moment, the low clouds opened a window for the moon to shine down on the mask of shocked anger frozen on the wanton butcher's face. Cole turned to look at the spot where he had been when he heard the wolf growl. It was no more than thirty feet from where he now stood. Had Sanchez pulled the trigger, he could not have missed. The wolf had saved his life. With that thought, he looked quickly around him, thinking the wolf might still be planning to strike, but there was no sign of the vicious predator. Most likely the rifle shots frightened it away.

Bringing his attention back to the body lying before him, he suddenly felt drained of all his strength, just then actually realizing that his death hunt was over. It brought no feeling of relief. Instead he was struck with a heavy sadness as he thought of his wife, Ann, and he wondered if she would forgive him for taking so long to avenge her. It troubled him that he could not bring her face into sharp focus in his mind. Suddenly exhausted, he sat down a few yards away from the corpse with his back against a tree, his rifle resting across his arms.

It was over. He was done.

When he opened his eyes, it was daylight. Realizing it, he started, suddenly wide-awake. He looked around him frantically, prepared to defend himself, but there was no one. His horse was standing several yards away, still saddled. A few yards beyond the Morgan, Sanchez's bay stood, also saddled. They both appeared to be watching the man sitting against the tree and wondering if he was alive or dead. He looked over at the body, staring up at the morning sky in angry defiance. Even then, Cole had to assure himself that it was actually over. They were all dead and gone to hell, all six of them.

Stiff and cold, he roused himself to get up from his position and move his limbs in an effort to get his blood flowing. He remembered then that he had a little coffee left, so he decided to gather enough wood to build a fire. But before he did, he wanted to look on the slope on the other side of Sanchez's body, curious to see if there had been a pack of wolves that threatened to attack, or if it had been just the one lone wolf. Walking just past the corpse, he stood gazing down the slope covered with a blanket of smooth white snow. He shook his head, perplexed, thinking he must still be groggy with sleep. There were no tracks, nothing to disturb the smooth white slope.

But there had to be tracks, he told himself.

It had not snowed while he was asleep. Even so, he walked down beyond the body and raked the surface of the snow with his boot in an effort to uncover the tracks. This could not be. It was impossible for a wolf to have come so close without leaving one track. And there was a wolf. He was certain of that. He had heard it growl, and Sanchez had heard it growl. If he had not, he wouldn't have spun around to defend himself.

Completely confused now, he decided there must be an explanation for the absence of tracks, but he would have to figure it out later. It occurred to him that this was the second time he had encountered a wolf that left no tracks, recalling the white wolf he had seen near Medicine Bear's village.

I must still be asleep, dreaming, he told himself.

For the first time since the death of his wife, he set out with no promises to keep and no sense of failure. For months, his life had been a hunt for vengeance, and his future had stretched out no further than the next execution. For a change, he was in no hurry to get anywhere. When he left the scene of Sanchez's death, he had to decide where he was heading. His buckskin packhorse was back in Cheyenne in Leon Bloodworth's stable, but he was much closer to the Crow village near the forks of the Laramie and North Laramie rivers, so he decided he would go there.

Maybe it was just his imagination, but the day seemed more springlike on this morning as he continued along the bank of the river. There was even a glimpse of the sun occasionally through the cloudy sky, and the clouds were white and not the dingy dark snow clouds of the past several days. Behind him, he led the bay gelding, saddled and Sanchez's Spencer carbine in the saddle sling. Maybe he could do some trading with Leon Bloodworth to pay for the bill he was going to have when he went to get the buckskin back.

His thoughts returned to the puzzling question about the wolf. He was still certain that he didn't imagine the presence of the wolf.

"I heard the damn thing!" he stated emphatically. "And so did Sanchez." He couldn't help thinking about Walking Owl's interpretation of his dream about the white wolf. "White Wolf," he said, still talking to Joe. "I reckon him and Harley would try to tell me that some ghost wolf or something kept me from gettin' shot by Sanchez. I expect I'll just not tell 'em everything that happened back there in that ravine."

Having said that, he still could not keep himself from wondering about the possibility. Maybe Harley was right. Maybe the Indians knew some things that the white man hadn't learned about the world he lived in.

Chapter 15

"Ah, White Wolf returns," Yellow Calf said when he glanced toward the river and saw the lone rider approaching.

Harley looked up from the length of buffalo sinew he was weaving into a bowstring for a three-foot bow made of ash wood and backed with sinew. He had been a fair hand with a bow in his earlier years with the Crow, so he had decided to try it again, since his supply of cartridges had gotten low over the winter. A wide smile parted the heavy growth of gray whiskers that hid almost all of the elfish face when he recognized his friend.

"It's White Wolf, all right," he said. "Looks like he picked up another horse. That ain't his buckskin he's leadin'."

Harley immediately thought the new horse could be a positive sign, especially since it was carrying a saddle. He chuckled to himself when it struck him that all Cole's packhorses seemed to come with a saddle on them. Instead of a rider, this one had a deer carcass draped across it. He got up from his place by the fire so he could attract Cole's attention.

Cole saw him and guided Joe in his direction. When he pulled up before the fire, he dismounted and dropped the Morgan's reins to the ground. "Welcome back, my friend," Yellow Calf greeted him.

"Thank you, Yellow Calf," Cole returned. "I brought a deer I was lucky enough to get a shot at a couple of miles back. I need to butcher it pretty soon. I thought maybe you folks could help me eat it."

Yellow Calf smiled. "I will call Moon Shadow to butcher the deer," he said, and turned to the tipi to call her.

"White Wolf," Moon Shadow greeted him when she came out of the tipi and saw the deer he had brought. Fresh meat was always welcome. "You bring a nice gift. I will butcher it." She turned to her husband then and said, "Yellow Calf will hang the carcass for me." It wasn't a question.

"I'll help you string him up," Cole said. "It's the least I can do if Moon Shadow is gonna do the butcherin'."

Having always been skilled in his observations of people, Harley stood silent during the casual conversation between them, watching Cole closely. The dark cloud that had always seemed to hover over his young friend was gone.

Finally Harley asked, "You got him, didn't you?"

"I did," Cole answered simply.

"Well, thank the good Lord for that," Harley said, beaming with relief, for he had almost convinced himself that Cole's streak of luck was strained to the limit, and Sanchez might be the one to break it. "Whaddaya aim to do now?"

"I don't know," Cole answered honestly. "I haven't given much thought to what was gonna happen after I settled with all of 'em."

"I reckon there ain't no hurry to decide," Harley said. "We'll have us a feast of that deer to celebrate. Tell you the truth, I was worried about that son of a bitch Sanchez. He was mean clear to the bone. I figured he'd be hard as hell to kill. How'd you track him down?"

"I'll tell you about it sometime," Cole said. "Right now I expect I'd better get these saddles off my horses and turn 'em out with the pony herd." He was still not sure he wanted to tell Harley about the wolf part of the story.

"I reckon you know you can stay here as long as you ain't made up your mind what you're gonna do," Harley said.

"I reckon," Cole allowed. "I've got a good horse down in Cheyenne that I don't plan to lose. So I'd best get down there pretty soon."

Harley nodded thoughtfully. "Yep, there's some folks down there that most likely wanna know if you're all right."

Cole shrugged indifferently. "I don't know about that. All I know is I've got a damn good horse I ain't planning to leave there."

Mary Lou's awkward confession came to mind, as it had more than a few times in the last couple of days. And the more he thought about it, the more it bothered him, because he wasn't sure exactly what he thought about it. He tried to remember her exact words. Was she telling him that she was open to an offer from him? He couldn't help speculating about the possibilities of a union between himself and the strong-willed woman.

Whenever he let his mind ramble unfettered in that direction, he was prone to bring it back abruptly with thoughts of guilt. It was disrespectful to Ann's memory to think of such things. Her death was much too recent to think of moving on. Besides, there was still the craving to see the high mountain country— to ride the Big Horns, the Absarokas, the Bitterroots, and beyond. He had forsaken that dream for the life of a farmer-rancher when he married Ann. He would never regret that decision, but maybe now was the time to revive the dream. He glanced up then to see Harley staring at him, waiting for a response, and he realized his mind had been so deeply absorbed in his thoughts that he had not even heard the question.

"What?" he asked.

"I said, when are you thinkin' about goin' back to Cheyenne?" Harley replied. "Where the hell were you? You looked like you was a thousand miles away."

"I was just thinkin'," Cole said. "I ain't thought about when I'm goin' after my horse—in a day or two, I reckon." Another concern popped into his mind then. "I've got a piece of land I filed on down on the Chugwater. I might wanna do something with that."

"Like what?" Harley asked. "You know anythin' about farmin'?" His expression testified that he already knew the answer to that.

"Can't say as I do," Cole admitted. "But I do know something about raisin' horses and cattle."

Harley was still skeptical. "Is that so? You ain't got much of a start if you're set on raisin' horses—three

horses, and all three of 'em geldin's." He waited for
Cole's answer to that, but Cole declined to reply. So
Harley continued. "I've been ridin' with you long
enough to know you—better'n you know yourself
maybe. You got the wanderin' in your blood, same as
me when I was about your age. You're a hunter.
Walkin' Owl told you that, and you ain't gonna have
no peace till you see the Rockies for yourself. You can
go on back to that place on the Chugwater and set
your mind to raisin' wheat and cattle. And you might
scrape by for a while, but that day will come when the
mountains whisper to you on a fresh spring breeze,
like a beautiful woman callin' you to her bed. And
you'll be standin' there with a hoe or a pitchfork in
your hand instead of a good repeatin' rifle. Then it'll
be fare-thee-well to that miserable plot of land. Hell,
that land around the Chugwater ain't no good for
farmin', anyhow."

Harley's passionate remarks left Cole slightly
astonished, and somewhat amused. He couldn't help
smiling at his gnarly friend. "Damn, Harley, that's
the biggest mouthful I've ever heard you say at one
time." He laughed then, but Harley's words struck a
chord deep inside him. And Cole could not honestly
refute anything he said. "I reckon you're too old to
ride to the high country, if I decided that's where I'm
goin'."

"The hell I am!" Harley protested. "I ain't ready to
squat by the fire just yet."

"Wasn't long ago you told me that the winter was
gettin' in your bones," Cole reminded him. "You
stayed here by the fire when I went back to Cheyenne."

"Ah, hell," Harley said. "I just didn't wanna go

along to see you get killed." He grinned then. "I reckon I didn't know you was the meanest stud horse in the herd. Besides, it's just the damn flat prairie winter that gets into my bones."

He paused to see if Cole would make any commitment to go or stay. Although comfortable in his later years to be with his Crow friends, he had to confess that he would dearly love to see the high mountains once more before meeting his maker. This was especially true if he had a strong partner like Cole to rely on. Finally, with nothing forthcoming from Cole, he pressed. "Are you really thinkin' about headin' up to the high country?"

"I'm thinkin' on it," Cole admitted. "Like I said, I'm goin' down to Cheyenne to pick up the buckskin. Then I reckon I'll decide what I'm gonna do." He didn't tell Harley, but he had already decided to stop by the ruins of John Cochran's homestead on the Chugwater to visit Ann's grave. He would continue on to Cheyenne after he had talked it over with her.

Cole purposely rode wide around Walter Hodge's farm. He had no desire to visit John Cochran's friend, but he was concerned enough to take a long look at Walter's homestead from the top of a mesa about a quarter of a mile away. When he decided that the place looked peaceful, just as it had the last time he visited, he nudged Joe to continue down to John's land.

He felt a cold hand clutching his chest when he topped the rise before the creek to once again see the charred ruins of John Cochran's house. Like a solemn gravestone, it stood dark and silent, the only memorial to the family that had perished there. He found the one large grave to be just as he had left it, with the exception of some weeds that had taken root. But there was no evidence of scavengers, which was a relief to Cole. He pulled the saddle off Joe and built his fire by the side of the grave closest to Ann's body. He wasn't sure what he had expected, or even what he'd hoped for. If it was a message from his dead wife he was looking for, a sign, or a dream, it never came to him.

When finally he drifted off to sleep, he slept soundly, a deep and dreamless sleep, and when he woke the following morning, it was with the feeling that it was time to get on with his life. He said a final farewell to his wife, with the promise that she would always live in his memory.

Then he saddled Joe and turned his head toward Cheyenne.

Crow Creek Crossing, he thought when he rode in from the north end of town once again.

He couldn't help thinking about the first day he had seen the town. Enough had happened since to fill the lifetime of an average man, and most of it not good. On this day, however, the town had a calmer look about it. There were a couple of new buildings under way, and he noticed that the church was finished. Gordon Luck would be preaching fire and brimstone to those in his flock who chose to avoid the sinful path, his long mane of sandy hair lying like a golden shroud upon his massive shoulders. Cole could imagine that the reverend cut quite a figure for the ladies of Cheyenne. He decided that the town had a chance at respectability now that it appeared the riffraff had moved on.

"Howdy, Cole," Leon Bloodworth greeted him when he rode up to the stable. "I was wonderin' when we might see you again."

"Howdy," Cole returned. "You ain't sold my horse, have you?"

Bloodworth laughed. "No, he's still here. I coulda sold him a couple of times, though. But I knew you'd be back for him."

"We'll settle up on what I owe you when I get back from the hotel," Cole said. "I wanna see somebody there first."

"You gonna be stayin' with us awhile this time?" Bloodworth asked.

"Don't know. I'll let you know when I get back."

Maggie Whitehouse glanced out the window as she walked past carrying a stack of freshly washed tablecloths. Something caught her eye, and she took a couple of steps back to make sure it was Cole Bonner she had seen heading toward the dining room. It was him, all right. There was no mistaking the easy long-legged strides as he headed purposefully straight for the door.

Uh-oh, she thought, and turned at once to alert Mary Lou, who was in the kitchen, talking to Beulah.

"You were supposed to leave those in the dining room," Mary Lou complained when Maggie walked in, still carrying the stack of tablecloths.

"I think you've got company," Maggie said, ignoring Mary Lou's tease, as she nodded toward the door.

"Oh?" Mary Lou replied, aware now of Maggie's serious manner. She turned abruptly and walked into the dining room just as Cole came in the outside door.

"Mary Lou," Cole called to her, "I was just comin' to see you."

"Is that right?" she responded, realizing that it was unusual to see a smile on the usually stern facade. She had not expected to see him return to Cheyenne so soon—maybe not at all—and his sudden appearance made for an uncomfortable moment. So she thought the best thing to do was not to beat around the bush.

"Before you say anything, I think I oughta tell you that I said a lot of things that I shouldn't have, things that may have given you the wrong idea about what I was thinking." He started to respond, but she quickly continued before he could speak. "I'm afraid I might even have scared you, and thinking back, I can understand why. Let me set your mind at ease. Gordon Luck has been pestering me to marry him for a long time, and I finally said yes."

She was looking down at her feet when she said it, so she didn't notice the stunned expression on Cole's face. Maggie, who was watching for his expression, did not miss it, however.

Emotionally staggered for a moment, Cole recovered quickly enough to reply. "Well, good for you," he said, trying not to show his disappointment, for he had made up his mind while walking from the stable that he was going to ask her to be his wife. The decision to once again forsake his dream of riding the high mountains had been hard, but he had persuaded himself that it was worth the love of a good woman.

"And good for Gordon," he managed, trying hard to smile.

"I can't picture me as a preacher's wife," she went on in an attempt to keep the conversation light. "I reckon

I'll just be a wife to the part of him that runs the sawmill."

"I reckon," Cole said, and forced a chuckle. "Gordon's a good man. I wish you the best." He glanced at Maggie then, who looked as if she was in pain. "I just dropped by to tell you folks good-bye. Me and Harley are headin' up in the Rockies—don't know when I'll get back this way again. I have to pick up my horse. Then I reckon I'll be on my way." An awkward silence followed that seemed interminable, until Cole finally said, "I wanna thank you both for everything you've done for me." He nodded to each one, then turned and headed for the door.

"I told you so," Mary Lou said to Maggie after he had gone. "He was planning to head up in the mountains with his faithful ol' hound dog, Harley, all along. I made the right decision."

"I guess," Maggie said. It had been torture for her to keep silent during the conversation between the two young people. But she had promised Mary Lou that she had nothing more to say in regard to her love life.

When Mary Lou went to the window to watch Cole walking back to the stable, Maggie stormed into the kitchen, picked up a coffee cup from the table, and threw it as hard as she could.

Bending over the stove, Beulah jumped when the cup smashed against the wall. "Damn!" she exclaimed. "You scared the hell outta me. What did you do that for?"

Maggie turned as if unaware of her presence before.

"Idiots!" she blurted. "Damn fool idiots!"

"Ain't it the truth?" Beulah said.

Read on for a look at
the next thrilling adventure
from Charles G. West,

TRIAL AT FORT KEOGH

Available from Signet in December 2014.

Clint Cooper squatted on his heels and picked up a piece of charred bone, which he used to poke around in the remains of a slaughtered steer. His close inspection wasn't really necessary, because it was obviously not the work of wolves or coyotes. Those predators did not usually build a fire to cook meat. This was the second carcass he had found in the past few days, and the moccasin prints around the kill told him that it was done by a small party of Indians.

The question in his mind was whether it was the same raiding party that had hit a small ranch eight miles east of the Double-V-Bar Ranch two days before. Leonard Sample, his wife, and his two sons were killed in the raid, their mutilated bodies found by their neighbor to the east of them. It was the first attack by an Indian war party in quite some time, at least since the construction of Fort Keogh. Every rancher on the south side of the Yellowstone suffered the loss of a cow now and then from small parties of

Indians around this time of year, when game was difficult to come by. Usually, it was of no real concern as long as it wasn't allowed to get out of control. But the savage attack on the Sample's ranch was enough to cause serious worry throughout the territory.

The signs he was reading now turned up no small footprints, which indicated that the slaughter hadn't been done by a party with women and children, as the first killing had been. This killing was recent—recent enough for him to be able to possibly track down the guilty parties. Clint's boss, Randolph Valentine, was not likely to miss one or two stolen cows from his herd of more than fifteen hundred, so Clint had been inclined to overlook it when the first steer was slaughtered by a party of hungry Indians. But two in a week's time was cause for concern, especially after the murder of the Sample family.

At first, Clint frowned when he thought about tracking down what he had imagined to be a small group of starving Indians who were still resisting the government's orders to return to the reservation. But the winters were hard in Montana Territory. A good many of the trail-hardened longhorns from Texas were lost each year due to natural predators, and it was part of Clint's responsibilities as Randolph Valentine's top hand to see that the number lost was held to a minimum.

Before these two incidents, the raiding of the herds had not really been bad, mostly because the army had built a fort on the south bank of the Yellowstone, at the confluence of that river with the Tongue. Originally known as the Tongue River Barracks, Fort Keogh was only about five miles from the Double-V-Bar. Its purpose was to protect settlers from hostile

Sioux raiding parties, remnants of Sitting Bull's and Crazy Horse's warriors who had escaped after the massacre at Little Big Horn.

The Texas longhorn cattle were a hardy lot and better suited than other breeds to fatten up on Montana grass over the winter before being shipped to the Chicago slaughterhouses in the spring. One thing was for sure: They were a lot easier to kill than the pronghorn antelope native to the area, especially when the hunter had nothing more than a bow.

I reckon I'd go after a cow, too, if the situation was turned around, he thought, *and I was the one needing food.*

He got to his feet when Ben Hawkins and Jody Hale appeared at the top of the ravine and came slowly down to join him.

"Found another'n, didja?" Ben called out.

"Yep," Clint answered. "If I was to guess, I'd say they left here no more'n four or five hours ago, and I don't think this one was killed by the same bunch that killed that last one. Take a look."

Ben dismounted, dropped his reins to the ground, and walked over beside Clint. He squatted on his heels, as Clint had, and stirred the ashes of the small fire. "I expect you're right," he said. "Four or five hours ago, not long after daybreak." He grunted with the effort to stand up again, not being as agile as the younger man. "I reckon you're wantin' to try to track 'em."

"I expect we oughta," Clint replied. "I'm thinkin' this might be that war party that struck the Sample place. Even if they ain't, Mr. Valentine said he didn't intend to feed every starvin' Indian in the territory." He stroked his chin thoughtfully as he turned the matter over in his mind. "I'd kinda hoped when we found that other one a few days ago that they were just gonna kill one and move on through our range. But I reckon this is a different bunch, and they're figurin' on stayin' awhile."

"Looks that way," Ben agreed. He crossed the small stream on the other side of the burned-out fire to take a look at the tracks, stepping from stone to stone to keep his boots dry. After a few moments inspecting the mixture of hoofprints and moccasin tracks, he expressed what Clint had already surmised. "'Pears to me they didn't just go after this one cow. Hell, they cut out half a dozen cows and drove 'em down here to the stream. There're cow tracks and horse tracks, and the horses weren't shod, so they was Injuns, all right."

"And they drove 'em down that side of the stream toward the river," Clint finished for him. "I figure it's that Sioux raidin' party, 'cause I couldn't find any small footprints that would mean there were women and children with 'em. I reckon they butchered this one, then just decided to take a few cattle with 'em for their food supply."

"Looks that way," Ben said again, and took another look around the edge of the water for tracks. He was thinking that if there had been kids, they'd have been playing around the water. "Might be a small bunch passin' through on their way up to Canada to join up with what's left of ol' Sittin' Bull's people."

"How many you think?" Clint asked.

"I figure five, maybe six," Ben replied.

"That's about what I make it," Clint said.

It was not surprising that they agreed, since Ben Hawkins had taught Clint practically everything he knew about reading tracks. Clint had still been in his teens when he'd left Wyoming Territory and made his way down to Texas, looking for work with one of the big ranches. With no ties to any part of the country, he had been prone to wander until he found someplace that suited him. He'd signed on with Will Marston to drive a herd up from Texas to Ogallala. That was where he met Ben Hawkins. Ben had recognized the honest, hardworking decency in the otherwise carefree young man, and had unofficially taken him under his wing.

It had occurred to Ben that young Clint never mentioned family or home, so one day he had asked him about his home and whether there was someone there who might want to hear where he was.

"Nope," Clint answered.

Although it took some digging, Ben was finally able to learn that Clint had no idea what had happened to his mother. His father told him that she had died of pneumonia. He was about two at the time, as far as he could guess. He'd stayed with his father until the older man had an argument over a prostitute in a saloon and it had turned into a gunfight, and Clint was left an orphan. Now, at twenty, the years having softened his memories, he knew that his father's name was Clayton Cooper, and that was all he cared to know about his past. He couldn't recall his mother's name and doubted that he'd ever known it. He also had an odd C-shaped scar on his neck but had no recollection as to how he'd gotten it.

After several years, when a natural partnership developed between them, Clint and Ben had decided to help drive a herd of Texas cattle on up to Montana for Randolph Valentine. Valentine was quick to see the potential in young Clint Cooper and offered him a permanent job. He offered Ben a job, too, but Ben was smart enough to know that it was probably due to the fact that the two were partners, and that Valentine would have to hire both of them to get the one he wanted. As it had turned out, however, Valentine came to appreciate the experience and the work ethic of the older partner as well. He soon realized that he had made a better deal than he had at first thought.

In a couple of years' time, young Clint Cooper proved to be a man capable of running the day-to-day operations of the ranch. And Valentine was aware of the steel-like strength beneath the carefree attitude he most often displayed. At any rate, Clint was physically big enough to handle objections to any orders he might issue to the crew who worked Valentine's ranch. That capability was seldom necessary, though, since Clint's orders always came in the form of suggestions, and he always seemed willing to take his share of the dirty chores. Valentine had never officially announced that Clint was the foreman of his crew, but all the men knew it to be the case. It had not surprised Ben that Valentine had come to look at the young ramrod almost as a son. This was especially true in light of the fact that Randolph and Valerie Valentine had only one offspring, a daughter named Hope, who was a year younger than Clint.

"Well, I reckon we'd best go see if we can recover our stolen cattle," Clint said. He looked up at Jody Hale, who was still seated on his horse. "Jody, ride on back and tell Charley and the rest of the boys to keep moving the cattle back off of that flat. I think it wouldn't be a bad idea to move 'em in closer to the ranch. Me and Ben are gonna go see if we can catch up with these Indians and maybe get our cattle back."

Jody, the fourteen-year-old nephew of Charley Clark, nodded in reply and promptly turned his horse to ride back up the ravine.

Ben looked over his shoulder to watch the boy ride away. "You reckon he'll remember what you told him by the time he gets back to the herd?" he joked.

Clint laughed. "Yeah, Jody's all right. He's just got his mind on other things most of the time—not much different from any of us at fourteen." He stepped up into the saddle then, but paused for a moment. "I didn't ask you if you wanted to stick your neck out to go after a bunch of Indian warriors."

Ben waited to answer until he had crossed back over the stream and stepped up on his horse. "No, you didn't, did you?" he mocked. "But then, you never do. Hell, I gotta go with you anyway to make sure you don't get yourself inta somethin' you can't get out of."

He gave his horse a kick and splashed across the stream to lead out along the opposite bank, leaving his grinning partner with no choice but to follow.

ALSO AVAILABLE FROM

Charles G. West
Wrath of the Savage

Second Lieutenant Bret Hollister is charged with finding two women who were taken hostage and bringing those responsible to justice. But when an unfortunate mishap results in the massacre of almost his entire patrol, he's forced to return to Fort Ellis a failure. Bret resigns from the army in shame. But he hasn't forgotten about the two women whose lives are at stake. He resolves to go after them on his own—no matter who stands in his way.

Available wherever books are sold or at
penguin.com

S0540

Penguin Group (USA) Online

What will you be reading tomorrow?

Tom Clancy, W.E.B. Griffin, Nora Roberts,
Catherine Coulter, Sylvia Day, Ken Follett,
Kathryn Stockett, John Green, Harlan Coben,
Elizabeth Gilbert, J. R. Ward, Nick Hornby,
Khaled Hosseini, Sue Monk Kidd, John Sandford,
Clive Cussler, Laurell K. Hamilton, Maya Banks,
Charlaine Harris, Christine Feehan, James McBride,
Sue Grafton, Liane Moriarty, Jojo Moyes...

You'll find them all at
penguin.com
facebook.com/PenguinGroupUSA
twitter.com/PenguinUSA

Read exce   *hedules*
and rea   *tests.*

Subsc   an
exclusive   nd the
autho   se.

P